Cross Drop

ON THE EDGE
BOOK TWO

ELIZABETH HARTEY

LIMITLESS PUBLISHING, LLC

Cross Drop

First Print Edition: June 2018

Limitless Publishing, LLC

Kailua, HI 96734

www.limitlesspublishing.com

Formatting: Limitless Publishing

ISBN-13: 978-1-64034-379-5

Dedication

For my husband. My very own alpha hero who has loved me unconditionally all these years.

Cross Drop

cross drop
/krôs/ /dräp/
Noun

When a player pushes or drops the puck behind him across the ice and continues skating on without it.

Chapter One

DALT

"I might have to *nut*meg one of those fine young soccer ladies tonight," Wolfe snorts into his beer.

"Keep your eyes off Nikki and your dick off her teammates," I warn my hockey brother.

"Pfft. No worries. Any one of those fine young ladies would kick Wolfe in *his nut*megs if he tried anything," Dak taunts.

"Andersen, my man, you underestimate my talents," Wolfe says smugly and pats Dak on the back.

"Talents?" Batt sprays his mouthful of beer in laughter. "Is that what we're calling your ho-ish charms these days?"

"Who you calling a ho, dick brains?"

"You. You're a fuckin' pig." Batt laughs again.

Wolfe's brow creases in thought before his face relaxes into a wry smile. "I proudly accept your assessment, bro." He raises his glass in a toast and Batt clinks his against it.

"'Accept your assessment.'" Dalt chuckles and shakes his head. "Wolfe, my man, you're an enigma wrapped in a slut."

"An enigmatic slut!" Wolfe shouts. "I thank you for the compliment, oh captain my captain." He bends at the waist, bowing to Dak, and in the process spills half the beer in his glass.

The degenerates—aka, my hockey teammates—and I are having our own party at a separate table from Nikki and her friends, although the party celebrating our win over Brown today is somewhat tamer. My boys are drinking beer instead of shots. They insist on filling a mug for me to toast the winning goal I scored in over-time. But I'm sticking to water and electing myself the designated driver for me and Nik tonight.

"Seriously, though. The soccer ladies are really gettin' their party on tonight." Wolfe flicks his chin toward the table where Nikki and her teammates are celebrating the big win they had over New Hampshire today.

"I know. Nik was on fire. She scored three goals in the first half of their game and one in the second." A contented smile crosses my face at the sight of my beau-tiful girl having such a great time. The way she works her ass off in school and leading her team as captain, she deserves a night out to let loose.

"Yay, Nik!" Batt hollers to her, raising his beer mug in a cheer.

Nikki waves, raises a shot glass, then tips it back, emptying its contents with one swallow. The pyramid of empty shot glasses on the table in front of her and her teammates is evidence of the slightly excessive but well-earned celebration.

The adrenaline rush from the game and the enjoyment of seeing Nikki laugh and have fun is all the festivity I need. Just watching her makes me happy. Her joy for living, even when she hasn't overindulged in too many shots of Red-Headed Sluts, is contagious. If it's possible for someone to seep under your skin and infect you with happiness, Nik has me chronically afflicted.

She glances over every few minutes and waves or blows me kisses. I nod and smile back. No airborne kisses, though. I'm sure as hell not going to let the asshats at my table see me blowing kisses to a girl. Even if she *is* the most incredible girl on the planet.

Don't get me wrong, these guys are my brothers for life and if I needed anything they'd have my back faster than a slapped puck shoots across slick ice. That doesn't mean they're not always on the lookout for ammunition to bust each other's balls.

Like the time Wolfe was sitting next to me in our Public Speaking class. He caught me grinning and staring all dreamy-eyed at Nikki when she was giving a speech. He leaned over and whispered, "Yo, dude. You growin' a vagina over there?"

Imagine what would happen if they caught me catching and blowing kisses across a bar like some lovesick teenager. The never-ending rank-out which would ensue has me cringing just thinking about it. No thanks. I like my balls just the way they are. Besides, Nik knows how I feel about her. I don't need to make a public display or spout romantic sentiments. I *show* her how I feel whenever we're alone. When I'm done showing her, she gets the message loud and clear.

"Holy shit. Looks like Nik's on fire tonight too!" Wolfe yells across the table.

Here's the problem. Well, not exactly a problem, more like a dilemma: an I'm-one-lucky-sonovabitch versus sometimes-I-wish-I-wasn't-quite-so-lucky, dilemma. Nik is every guy's fantasy come to life. She can keep up with the guys at everything. At sports? A champion at everything she tries. Soccer? She moves the ball with such speed and accuracy, she makes any guy playing against her resemble a statue. Talking teams? She can rattle off players and team stats faster than Howard Cosell ever could. She can match any guy beer for beer and then some. But even with all her badassery at keeping up with the boys, she's a goddess of womanhood, with an angel face, and a body built to bring men to their knees. Full tits, round ass, lean muscle, platinum blonde hair down to her waist. Yup. Every man's fantasy, and there isn't one guy in this bar right now whose dick isn't pointing right at her. The fact her exuberance has escalated to a this-may-be-something- she'll-regret-in-the-morning level isn't helping to keep the drooling dirtbags away from her.

She's on top of one of the tables at the Thirsty Whale Pub, dancing and singing "We Could Be Heroes" at the top of her lungs. Which isn't bad—Nik's hot when she sings and dances. Except the way she's obviously feeling the shots has things a little too torrid. Her micro-mini skirt is flashing glimpses of her lacy purple thong and tight, apple bottom cheeks to everyone in the bar as she sways. The only way I'd be enjoying this level of heated happiness is if she were doing it solely for me on top of my table at home.

"Nik's got a fine ass, dude. Now I see why you're so fucked when it comes to this chick." Wolfe continues his astute commentary as he leers at Nikki.

"What the fuck are you doing eyeing my girl's ass, dickhead?"

"It's kinda hard to miss, man. I mean look at her. She's rockin' that thang. Am I right, guys?"

The other guys at the table don't say a word. Instead, they all fidget uncomfortably in their chairs, trying their best to look anywhere but at Nikki. Every guy may want her, but a fellow hockey bro knows better than to ogle another bro's girl. Batt's right about one thing. Wolfe, our goalie, is also our resident pig. No filter. No restraint.

By the sound of the loud whistling in the bar, I think it's time to break up the party before I have to break up some guy's face. I especially don't want to have to break Wolfe's face since he's one of my roommates and also one of my best friends. Besides, he's a good goalie. The team needs him.

Still, that doesn't mean I have to be happy about him ogling Nik. "Look away, asshole, or the only puck you're going to be stopping is the one I shove up your ass."

"Geez." He places his hand over his heart pretending to be wounded. "I was just trying to give you a compliment on your lady's fine—"

I shove him out of the way. Making my way to the

table where Nik is doing her burlesque routine, I reach up to take her hand to help her down.

"Let's go, sweetheart. I think it's time to get you home to bed." She bends over and gives me her pearly white ear to ear smile.

"*Can't hear you, hockey boy,*" she sings to me in the tune of the song, while continuing to sway her hips, "*music's too loud.*" When she leans toward me the whistling in the room gets louder.

I cup the hand not holding hers around one side of my mouth and yell, "I said I think it's time to get you home to bed!"

"*Ooo, yay. Bed! I'm cooomming, oh mighty sex god,*" she continues singing, but adds a prolonged moan to the word "coming." Then she winks and jumps off the table into my arms.

Jesus. Oh mighty sex god?

See what I mean? She has a joyful spontaneity, always the first to take a running jump off the rock diving cliffs of life, or tabletops in bars. Maybe the party should have ended five shots ago.

The room is too crowded to carry her to the door. I have to put her down. She's a little wobbly. I keep my arm around her waist to be on the safe side. As I steer her toward the door, I'm hailed with an outburst of loud boos and hisses from a table full of douchebag football players. When I glance over and answer their jeers with a dagger-dripping looks-might-not-be-able-to-kill-but-I-*can*-glare they get the message and shut the fuck up. Nik, oblivious to my telepathic interaction, dances and sings her way out while the rest of the students in the bar clap and cheer her exiting performance.

Tucking her into the passenger side of my car, I make sure she's all buckled in and secure before I go around and get into the driver's seat. Almost before I'm in the seat Nik is out of her seatbelt, climbing into my lap, one knee on either side of my hips, begging me, "Please, Dalt. Now please. I need you now. *Please*."

See what I mean? Every guy's fantasy.

My life hasn't been perfect, but I have had some great days: the first day I put on a pair of hockey skates, the day I got a full ride to Bernard University to play the greatest sport on the planet. And the best day? The day I laid eyes on Nikki for the first time. Now my girl is straddled across my hips begging me to fuck her. Can life can any better than this?

Her hot girl skirt hiked up on her thighs, she's grinding down on me and kissing me, pleading with me to fuck her. It's blissful torture.

"I want you, Dalt. Right now. Right now, please. I'm so hot for you. I need you inside me."

"Wait, Nik, honey." I chuckle and moan at the same time, trying to keep her overactive fingers from roaming to places which are adamantly protesting the idea of stopping her.

"Nooo. Come on, Dalt. I can't wait."

Damn. She's like a female Bruce Lee, fast hands moving everywhere at once. She fumbles with the button of my jeans.

"Nik, sweetheart," I smile. When my button pops open, I place my hand over hers to stop her from tugging down my zipper. I need to slow her roll for her sake and my cock's. He's pushing with rigid determination against that zipper and in imminent danger of getting snagged.

"Come *on*, hockey boy. Need to nail your big, *hard* love hammer," she purrs into my ear.

"My *love hammer*?" I have to smile. She's so damn cute. But I've never seen her like this. Like I said, she has a pretty high tolerance for alcohol, at least for beer. She may have met her match with the multiple shots of Jäger-meister. I'm sure anyone with a functioning metabolism would have.

"Mmm. He wants me. I can tell," she coos, stroking her hand down my jean-covered shaft, sending my hormones into overdrive.

"Fuck, Nik"

"'Zactly what I had in mind"

Normally, there's no way I'd have sex with a girl who's feeling her alcohol like this. I'm a hockey player, not an asshole. But Nik and I have been together for months and our hot and heavy addiction to each other is nothing new. Needless to say, my *love hammer* is ready to do some nailing of his own to give my eager girl what she needs and no amount of advice from me is going to calm him down. Neither one of us can ever say no to this girl.

When I run my hand under her skirt and feel how wet her sliver of a thong is, I can't get my jeans unzipped fast enough, while taking care not to damage anything. As soon as I do, Nik reaches down between us, wraps her hand around me, and places my hard as fuck cock right where she wants it.

She has me so crazy out of my mind I might come in

her hand. Trust me when I say stamina has never been a problem for me before. Before Nikki, that is. She gets me racing in ways I didn't even know there were roads.

I rip her thong off and she lifts up and drops back down on me with a quick, hard push. Then she lets out a loud groan of pleasure, loud enough it's a good thing there's no one else in the parking lot.

She keeps moaning and pulling up and pushing back down on me. Doesn't say a word; just makes the sexiest *ahhs* and *mmms* I've ever heard. Every tight clench around me when she pushes down sends more blood rushing to my cock, making it demand a release. I focus on holding back, fighting to hold on a little longer, making sure I give her what she needs first. Doesn't take long. Her legs begin to tremble and clamp around my hips. All I can hear as her warm pussy convulses around me and I explode into her is, "Ah, ah, mmm, yes, yes, *yes!*"

Nope. Life definitely doesn't get any better than this. I hate to admit it, but sometimes the idiotic things which come out of Wolfe's mouth are right. I'm totally fucked when it comes to this girl.

To be honest, I've enjoyed more than my fair share of fangirl honeys. It's the same old story of being one of those popular hockey jocks on campus who can pretty much have any girl he wants anytime he wants and has a reputation for taking advantage of the gratuity. I'm not bragging, that's just the way it is for me and my teammates. All good guys, just not relationship material, and none of the guys are shy about letting it be known. They make it clear what's happening before hooking up with a chick. I'll admit I've done my best to enjoy the perks of the long line of enthusiastic puck bunnies who have been on the same page of the 'no monogamy' clause in our policy.

Nik's changed it all for me. It's the craziest damn thing. I wasn't looking for it and never thought I *wanted* to feel any of this for one girl, but I'm not interested in any of the ready and willing fangirls anymore. Nik is the only one I want, every day, every night, all night, to the point of distraction. Like I said, blissful torture.

To add to the fantasy, Nikki brings her spontaneity into bed or...at the moment, car. She approaches fucking with the same gusto she approaches everything in life, with natural enjoyment. She isn't one of those chicks who wants to get down and dirty as much as any guy but thinks she has to pretend to be all timid and standoffish about it. Pretentious bullshit isn't for me. Nik knows what she wants and she's not shy about letting me know. Tonight, though? Tonight, she's even more spontaneous than usual.

We shattered together in mind blowing ecstasy, but she's still clenching around me working my cock, moaning my name. She's got me hard as iron and ready for round two.

"Mmm. Dalt. I want more," she pleads, planting kisses all over my face.

"Nik, honey." I'm smiling so wide my face hurts.

"Hmm?"

"How 'bout we wait 'til we get home? I can give you anything you want on a nice comfortable bed. Doesn't that sound good?"

"*Anything*?"

"Everything."

"'Kay. Let's go." Just like that she plucks herself off me and climbs back into her seat. I tuck my disgruntled cock away and reach over to pull her seatbelt across her, buckling her in once more.

"You good over there?"

"I'd be better over there," she says in a flippant tone. I'm sure she'll be down for the count by the time we get home. Or maybe not.

When I turn the ignition key, the radio blasts Charlie Puth's "Let's Marvin Gaye and Get It On" and Nik joins in with her own level of slightly off key singing. When she flails her arms around as she rocks to the beat, I narrowly miss getting punched in the face.

Oh boy. It's going to be a long night.

NIKKI

"Are we there yet? What's takin' so long."

Geez. Why is he driving so slow?

"Yup. We're here and it only took five minutes. Not too long, right? You okay?"

I don't know why he keeps asking me if I'm okay. I'm fine. Do I look like something's wrong with me?

"A-OK." *Except, I can't move. Why can't I move?* "Get this thing off me."

"Just a sec, Nik. Let me come around to your side to help."

When the car stops moving, Dalt hops out.

"Get this stupid strap off me."

"I got it. Here we go. Come on, sweetheart."

He bends down and swoops me up into his arms.

Wheee. I'm flying.

"Oh hi, hockey boy." I wave at his beautiful face. "Are you gonna carry me?"

Mmmm, he smells good. I'm gonna' keep my nose planted right here in this little space under his chin.

"Yeah, baby. I'm going to carry you. How you doing?"

"I'm doin' great! How you doin'?" Whoa! My voice got real low. Ha! I sound like Rocky. "Yo, Adrian." Amazing! I sound just like him.

Dalt's chest rumbles when he laughs.

"Mmm, you smell good 'nough to eat." I lean my head back to see him. "And you're *beautiful* when you laugh."

He chuckles. "Thanks, babe. You're pretty gorgeous all the time."

He's still smiling. I love when he smiles.

"Listen, Nik. Can you stand right here for just a second while I unlock the door?" He props me up against the wall.

"A'course, I can. Standin's easy. Do it all the time." I wave a hand through the air to accentuate how ridiculous the idea of my not knowing how to stand is.

Whoops.

I can stand, just can't wave my arm around while I'm doing it. I'm melting, shrinking just like the Wicked Witch.

"Whoa. Hold on. I got you. Put your feet under

you." Dalt wraps one arm around my waist while pushing the door open. "There we are. You good?"

If he asks me if I'm okay one more time.... Do I have two heads or something? Wait. It kinda' does feel like I have two heads. Why are my legs bein' so dumb? Dumb legs.

"Yup. Standin' all by myself. Told ya I could do it. If this floor would stop moving it would be way easier though."

Dalt smiles at me. He's so happy tonight.

"You're pretty when you smile, Daltie."

Wait a darn minute.

"This isn't home. Did you get lost, my honey man?"

He lets out another big laugh. We must be having a lot of fun.

"Yes, it is. It's my house. Remember?"

"Oooh. I remember. *Bed!*"

"Yes. Definitely bed." He grins and nods a bunch of times. He thinks I'm super smart for remembering where we were going.

"*See?* There it is. You have such a beautiful smile. You know that?"

"I love that you think so, baby. Can you sit here on this chair for a minute? I'll get us a couple of bottles of water to take upstairs to the bedroom. Okay?"

"Okie dokie. Oh wait. I have to take my clothes off for bed. Why do I still have all these stupid clothes on? I hate clothes. My shirt doesn't want...to...to come off. It's...it's stuck."

"How 'bout we wait 'til we get upstairs before we take your clothes off?"

Aww. There he goes, smilin' his come-n-fuck-me-smile. "Daltie." I waggle my finger at him. I know his tricks. "You wanna help me get my clothes off so we can hide the puck again?"

"Hide the puck?" He snickers. I'm very funny tonight. "First let's have some water. Be right back." He starts walking away from me.

"Wait!"

"What is it, babe? You okay?"

"I wanna show you somethin'. Let me just...uh... push...myself up. There. Watch how easy this skirt is. Boom. See? Just a few little snaps. All gone."

"Jesus, Nik. I think we might have to lay off the Jägermeister forever. It's a little too dangerous."

Mmm. I love the way his eyes crinkle when he smiles.

"Oops. Oh no! What happened to my undies? They 'dispeared. Had 'em a minute ago." I try to bend down to search between my legs. They must be somewhere. Whoa! My head does not like bending over.

"Okay. That's it, you need sleep." Dalt walks across the room and scoops me up in his arms.

"You gonna' carry me again?"

"Yup. I'm gonna' carry you again."

"Okay. I'll be right here. Right here on these muscles." I pat his chest, his beautiful, rock hard chest, to make sure he knows where he can find me. "I'm gonna' put my face right here. 'Kay?" All of a sudden, I'm on my back with my arms wrapped around Dalt's neck.

"Here we go, baby. Doesn't the bed feel comfy? You lay back. I'll get these boots off."

"Wait, Daltie!"

"What is it, baby?"

"I love when you call me baby," I whisper in a tiny little voice right against his beautiful soft lips so he can hear me.

"And I love calling you baby because you *are* my baby. But I want to take your boots off and then get some water for you. Okay?"

"'Kay. Wait!" I pull him back down.

"Ooph. What do you need, sweetheart?"

"My legs are weird."

"Your legs are weird?"

"Uh huh." I nod. I don't feel like talking anymore.

"What do you mean? Nik? Are you still awake? What do you mean your legs are weird?"

"Umm. Sticky...yuk." My eyes won't open but I can hear Dalt talking to me.

"Sticky? Did you say...Oh. Fuck! No condom!"

"Night night, Daltie. Love you."

Chapter Two

NIKKI

Eighteen Months Later

When you're in college things are measured by semesters, not days or months. I fell in love fall semester of my freshman year. I was dumped spring semester of my sophomore year. I received the greatest blessing of my life in the fall of what should have been my junior year. It's how I remember things, how I recall the seasons which changed my life forever. Now I'm back, trying to complete my junior fall semester more than a year later.

I shouldn't be here tonight, though. I swore I was off hockey for the rest of my life. Sort of. Not the Bruins, or the Penguins, or the Stars. Okay, I swore I was off any hockey involving the Bernard University team, and one particular hockey whore.

I'm not a stupid girl. Not usually. I've worked hard

to get to where I am and to keep checking off all the necessary boxes to get where I want to go. Get a scholarship to an Ivy League college. *Check.* Manage to keep my GPA over 3.5 to maintain said scholarship. *Check.* Become captain of the women's soccer team and lead them to a championship win of the America East Conference during my first year as captain. *Check.* I'm not ashamed to admit I was doing pretty well at this thing called life, despite a few colossal obstacles along the way. Until about three years ago, when I checked off a few boxes which should *not* have been checked.

The special brand of stupid I began demonstrating back then and am continuing to exhibit at this very moment is spelled D-a-l-t-o-n W-a-l-k-e-r. When it comes to that irresistible specimen of whoredom, I become a mindless idiot.

I've been trying with every neuron in my body to stay away from Dalt. But I couldn't stay away from the first game of the season, partly because I love hockey almost as much as soccer and partly because Trace and Alex insisted I come with them. If I'm being honest, the main reason I came is because of number 14, the gorgeous, powerful guy moving up and down the ice with the stealth of a panther, dominating the opposing team with the precision of a machine.

Dalt and his three roommates, Dak Andersen, Damon Wolfe, and Dante Battaglia, work together on the ice like four parts of the same brain. No wonder they've been nicknamed the D-structors. It's both a play on all their names beginning with the letter D and the way they operate together to demolish every team they face. Watching them maneuver on the ice like a fine-tuned instrument is the sexiest damn thing I've ever seen.

Dak has the puck and is zigzagging behind the net. I can read it on his face, the way he's sending vibes out to Dalt and Dante—or Batt as we call him—to get in position. The defense on the opposing team is putting on extra pressure because I'm sure they're aware of the reputation these guys have for making magic happen on the ice. It doesn't matter what the opposition does when Dalt, Dak, and Batt are in the zone and working together like they are right now. It's like Dalt and Batt can read Dak's mind as he moves from corner to corner.

He passes down the left side to Dalt, who flicks it over to Batt. Batt passes it back to Dak in the right corner, which gives Dalt just enough time to perform his exquisite bewitchery. I can't take my eyes off him. I sense every stroke of his blades, every flex of his muscles, down to my core. His agile power reminds me of the feeling of his body when he was naked on top of me. The memory causes me to squirm in my arena seat.

Dalt moves to the right and then makes a quick, barely perceptible cut around and spins to the left. I don't even bother watching the puck because I know where it's going to be in about two seconds. I keep my gaze fixed on Dalt which, unfortunately, is right where it wants to be all the time anyway.

His swift maneuver manages to fake out the opposing defenders. They split, leaving him open and ready when Dak shoots him the puck. Dalt blasts the perfect laser shot to the back of the net just as the horn sounds. The goalie doesn't even have a chance to react.

We win the game and everyone in the stands at the Bernard arena goes crazy. I almost feel sorry for the opposing team. I can relate to the shocked and confused expressions on their faces. Dalt and his boys can have that effect on people on, and off, the ice.

When Trace and Alex finally stop jumping up and down in celebration, I lean in and yell to Trace so she can hear me over the crowd. "I'm heading home! See you back at the house later!"

The dorm and my new roommate, with the whips and handcuffs hanging in her closet, had become the seventh circle of Hell. I consider myself fairly open minded when it comes to sex. I'm not one to judge other people's sexual proclivities, but when she started dressing in black capes and fishnet stockings, nothing else, and prancing around our dorm room, end of story. Exit, stage left. When Trace offered me the extra room in the house she's renting, I jumped at the chance.

Except for the uncomfortable location of Trace's house being right next door to Dalt's and the other infamous D-structors', it was a godsend. Trace, Alex, and I have become good friends in a short time. Although since Trace is dating Dak, captain of the team and Dalt's best friend, it makes socializing a bit of a sticky situation.

"What? Why?" Trace cups her hands around her mouth and hollers back. "We're going out to celebrate." She points toward the wall of the arena to demonstrate the direction of out. "Don't you want to come? First game, first win!"

"No. Not tonight. I have some work to get done." I

mimic typing with my fingers. With the level of noise in the arena it's easier to mime than talk.

While Trace is aware of my obvious uneasiness around Dalt, I haven't explained why things are so awkward. I haven't told her, even though he dumped me in the cruelest way and under the worst possible circumstances, that I, as stupid and unbelievable as it is, still want him with every fiber of my being. That's right. I haven't told her or Alex when I get anywhere near the fucker my inner strong, independent, intelligent self plummets down into the space between my thighs and morphs into all things throbbing and wet. Every smart decision vanishes into the orgasmic void.

I proved to myself the first week back I'm not ready to be near him in a social situation. My foolish body lapses into brain-stupefying, vagina-demanding cravings. And I am *never* going to let that happen again.

DALT

Thank fuck I managed to score that goal. Practice sessions and scrimmages for the past few weeks have sucked balls. My passes to Batt are usually dead on. Lately, though, I don't think I could connect with him if I was Kylie Jenner and he was an Instagram account.

I glance up into the stands, searching for the main reason my head is everywhere but on the ice. The only thing that would make this moment more exciting would be if I was sharing it with Nik. I know exactly where she's sitting. Even if it wasn't the same place she sat at every game when we were together, I could still sense her presence. I don't know how.

I read in a book in my first-year philosophy class that people and even some animals have soulmates. There can be an almost physical connection you can sense, tugging at you even when they're not with you.

At the time I sneered at the idea of there being one 'special' person out there. I thought my soulmate was whoever the next puck bunny was to get between my sheets for the night and tug at places *other* than my heart. Until I met Nikki. Now I think if there is such a thing as a soulmate, she may have been mine.

It's the kind of connection I had with her, the kind of connection I still feel for her. It's what I want to share with her once more, what I miss so much it's like a dagger to my heart when I see her and she won't even glance at me.

She's moving down the steps to make her way off the stands. I will her to look at me. As pathetic as it is, just one glance, one smile, would make my night even better than scoring the winning goal. But she doesn't glance at me. The ever-present weight on my chest since she left me presses down, making it difficult to breathe.

I don't know what the hell happened. One minute we couldn't keep our hands off each other, didn't want to be away from each other, spent every free hour we had together, and the next minute she disappears from school for two semesters and wants nothing to do with me. She wouldn't take my calls or answer my texts. Not a word.

I stalked her for a while on social media and even got

Wolfe to hack into the school's computer to get me her home address. Wolfe is a weird dichotomy. One half golden glove hockey slut and the other half computer wizard. Having a wizard in the house helps in times of emergency.

He got me the address to Nikki's farm, which is only a little over an hour away from Bernard. But I've never been one to pursue a girl who's not interested in me. Even though it sucks big time because *I* was beyond interested in this particular girl and I know she *was* interested in me. Like I said, our connection was magical.

We shared everything. She gave herself to me and confided in me in ways I thought meant we were more than fuck buddies. She opened up to me about her family, her shit stepfather, and all the stuff she's had to overcome to be able to work on fulfilling her dream of becoming an illustrator and writer. She's freakin' awesome.

I shared things with her I've never told anyone except the guys I live with. Dak and Batt already knew about my family. Dak and I grew up together and Batt's dad has worked with my dad on several movies.

Things can get weird when people find out who my father is. I don't want them judging me, befriending or rejecting me, based on my family's wealth or status. I didn't go into the exact logistics of my wealth when I told Nik about my family's affluence. None of it was even a blip on her radar. She said she didn't care if I was rich or poor, she only cared about me.

I'd come millimeters away from using the L word and then she was gone.

Making my way off the ice and into the locker room, I'm greeted with pats on my back and high fives jostling me out of my thoughts.

"We're heading to the Thirsty Whale to suck down a few celebratory brews and a few puck bunnies after!" Wolfe yells over to me. "You have to come with, bro. Your current level of hero worship will attract the fangirls." His tone is matter-of-fact, like he's referring to some manual, like *Wolfe's Tips on Hockey Whoredom 101*. Yep. Hockey ho.

I'm not interested in sucking down any puck bunnies, as Wolfe so gallantly put it, but I do need to try to absorb some of the adrenaline and cheer buzzing through the locker room and pull myself out of this funk.

"A cold beer sounds good. I'll let Dak know."

A night out with my boys might help. The pain of missing Nikki is so overwhelming even my hair hurts. It's ridiculous. I can't keep this up. Can't keep moping around like some lovesick puppy.

"Hey man, we're going out for a few brews to celebrate. You comin'?" I holler over to Dak.

"Nah man. Got plans!" he calls back. I've never seen him strip out of his gear this fast. Even though I thought he had something going on with Trace, I saw him with Sabrina after the game. She's a figure skater and one of the fangirls who has made her rounds of the guys but seems to have a special thing for Dak. Given the way he's speed undressing, I'm guessing he's is in a real hurry to get to Sabrina tonight.

I push through the guys and the congratulatory

smacks on my ass to get over to Dak. I don't want to have to yell over the loud decibel of celebrating.

"Oh, yeah. I saw sweet Sabrina hanging all over you."

"No, dude. Not with Bri." He gives me a side glance as he continues to peel his sweat-drenched pads off.

It must be Tracey he's rushing to get to. I know the feeling. I couldn't wait to get back to Nikki whenever we were apart. I didn't care if we were just hanging out watching some chick flick, or studying, or playing a one on one soccer game at the quad, or whatever. I would have been with her 24/7 if it was possible, and look where it got me, pining away for a girl who doesn't want anything to do with me now. I'm happy my man Dak has found someone else. I'm also a little worried. I've seen the way a broken heart crushed him and nearly took him out once before.

"Shit, man. You got it bad for this chick, huh?"

"Nah. We're just friends. Yeah, maybe. I don't know."

"Shit. You're so fucked. I hope you know what you're doing, dude."

I want to be all positive. I should be telling my bro how fucking awesome it is he's found a great girl like Trace. Except Nik is the most incredible woman I've ever known and *she* left me broken and empty.

I don't know what happened but I intend on finding out. I've got to get her back. I'm pretty sure there's only one soulmate to a customer.

Chapter Three

DALT

Seven Months Later

"Why the hell are we doing this? This is fuckin' lame."

I *can not* believe I let Dak talk me into this shit, performing on stage in front of half of the school and most of the team. And the cherry on top of this scoop of humiliation is Nikki will be sitting at the table right in front of the stage. Dak, the charmer, convinced Nikki to bring Trace to the show tonight without letting Trace know what was going down.

"I told you, I'm in love with her. I'll do whatever it takes to get Tracey back." He says it. Right out loud. Dak states his love for Tracey, no hesitation.

I'm a little envious of his ability to express his feelings for Trace without holding back. He doesn't give a crap what the guys on the team think. He loves her and he's not afraid to say it. I wish I had been as upfront with Nikki when I had the chance. Although some of this current public expression of Dak's love is based more on a *need to* rather than a *want to* situation.

It has something to do with a naked Sabrina sprawled out on top of him. Tracey kicked him to the curb after she walked in on them. The guys and I have been suffering through all his sickening, poetry-filled attempts to get her back, but this is the last ridiculous straw. What the hell am I doing performing in a talent show at the Blue Goose? My main talents are on the ice and between the sheets. I *do not* sing and dance.

The Blue Goose is a college town bar with a small concert venue. When bands want to try out new music or just have a smaller, more intimate show, they book the venue and spend a few days enjoying the idyllic coastal environment of Bar Harbor. Tonight is the annual talent show. Anyone with an amateur act and the entrance fee can participate.

Dak decided it would be the perfect opportunity to win Trace back. He enlisted the backup support of Alex, Erik, Batt, and me. He's going to sing a goddamn love song to Tracey in front of the whole world, while we perform the choreographed steps behind him, which Alex taught us. Alex is on the figure skating team and an amazing dancer and choreographer. That doesn't mean his talents are going to transfer to a bunch of hockey slobs.

"Take your places, divas," Alex directs us onto the stage. "And don't forget, it's a grapevine to the left *and* right before you do the body rolls."

26

Christ. Grapevines, body rolls. The only body rolls I want to be doing are the ones I did when I was on top of Nikki, rolling my hips into her so hard I fucked her into oblivion.

I agreed to this nonsense because I'd do anything to help out my man. Dak's been a mess since Trace walked out, something I can relate to, when the woman of your dreams dumps you. If this craziness will help him get her back, I guess I can handle a little humiliation.

The curtains open in a protracted glide, grating across my nerves with every slow inch. The stage lighting is set to a dim, hazy blue with one brighter spotlight on Dak. My gaze is drawn through the glow of the spotlight right to the goddess sitting at the table in front of the stage.

Our eyes lock in a heated glare. My breath catches. She's beyond gorgeous. Her platinum blonde hair is hanging to her waist in loose waves. Even with her long hair, her perfect tits are on full display being pushed up and overflowing from some kind of red laced-up top. One of her toned, never-ending legs is crossed over the other. Her barely there skirt is exhibiting nearly every inch of them. Part of me wants to jump off the stage and cover Nikki with a blanket so no one else can enjoy the vision. Another part of me is hoping she'll spread those long legs and let me get a glimpse of the sliver of lace I'm sure is barely covering her sweet pussy. Fuck. I'm such a perv. I'm getting hard just seeing her and thinking about all the things I'd like to be doing between those legs and tits right now.

I have to do something to distract my single-minded

dick. I'm blasted back to the cold reality of what we're about to do by the raucous cheers coming from the tables adjacent to Nikki's. They're filled with guys from the team. Wolfe is whistling and yelling out catcalls. He refused to join in the Win Trace Back Mission. I believe his exact words to Dak were, "I love ya, man, but no fuckin' way am I getting up there and making a fuckin' fool of myself."

I'm gonna *fuckin* kill him when I get off this stage for being smarter than me.

When the first notes of "I'll Make Love to You" stream from the sound system, we start moving behind Dak and he begins to sing. A brief hush sweeps over the crowd. I assume we're fucked and are going to get booed off the stage. To my shock, every girl and some of the guys in the fully packed theatre begin oooing and ahhing and screaming like it's Drake on stage.

Apparently, Dak is good. I should have known. The fucker is good at everything he does because he refuses to accept the concept he can't do everything like a pro. I decide to take a page from Dak's book of confidence. Tracey is practically drooling as he jumps off the stage and gets down on his knees in front of her to sing. Not Nikki. Nikki's staring at *me* like she's imagining all the ways she can strangle me.

Like I said, I can't sing, but I *do* know how to make a lady drool. I focus on Nik, zoning out every other person in the room. It's the same way I clear the mechanism when I'm playing hockey. Tonight, though, is not about scoring goals on the ice. Tonight I'm going to use every move of this freaking choreography to seduce Nikki right off her chair.

NIKKI

I guess I'm just destined to be at the wrong place at the very wrong time when it comes to Dalt. Why did I agree to this? Simple. Trace is my best friend and roommate. We girls have to have each other's backs when it comes to maneuvering the labyrinth of love. Since she's dating Dalt's best friend, at least she *was,* it's getting more and more difficult to avoid Dalt. I have to find a way to interact with him which doesn't involve our tongues probing each other's mouth or my wanting to cut his dick off and staple it to his forehead. Okay. I may still be a little angry. Anyway, with Dak's persistence and the way I know he and Tracey love each other, it's only a matter of time before they're back together. Like in two minutes when Dak is finished singing a gooey love song to her.

They had a slight misunderstanding a few weeks ago. Trace walked in on a naked Dak with a naked girl on top of him. Apparently it wasn't what it appeared to be, as hard to believe as *that* is. The guys have been helping Dak in his Win Trace Back conquest. I've seen Dak since they broke up. He's a mess and Trace isn't much better. They obviously love each other. I'm willing to give him the benefit of my *very* big doubt.

I agreed to assist in this friendervention to get the two lovebirds back together, because I thought I had gotten to a place where I could handle being this close to Dalt in a social setting. My job was to get Trace to the show. She wasn't aware of the routine Dak and the other guys were going to perform. It was meant to be a surprise.

But fucking hell. Why does Dalt have to be the personification of an orgasm doing the choreographed steps Alex taught him and the other four guys up there?

With Dak singing in front of them, it's like an orgy for the eyes. Seriously. Despite the fact they're hockey players—Alex being the only figure skater—they make one scorching hot pseudo-boy band. The slow, synchronized dance moves the guys are performing are causing waves of seduction to ooze from the stage and saturate the audience *and* my panties.

Just great. One more you-know-you-want-to-fuck-me enticement from these hockey manwhores. And yes. Yes, I do want to fuck one particular hockey whore on the stage right now; the one obliterating my resistance with his scorching gaze.

Dalt is one of those aberrations of humanity. He's flawlessly gorgeous: dark, tousled, slightly wavy hair, classic chiseled jaw, perfect straight nose, soul piercing blue eyes, plump, very gifted lips, if you know what I mean. Everything about him screams sex. His black button-down shirt and dress pants accentuate every muscled line of his perfect Michael Stokes model body.

And he knows just how to use all his perfection to get what he wants. He's not accustomed to hearing the word no, at least not from any oxygen breathing female. He's using his locked and loaded molten gaze at this very moment, turning my bones to Jell-O and annihilating any wise decision-making on my part.

I want him so bad it hurts. It's like staring at the shiny, poison apple, knowing if you taste it you're doomed, but unable to resist its shimmering perfection. There's more than just *my* heart to consider now, though. We have a lifelong connection he's not aware of. Nevertheless, I have to disconnect my feelings for him. The man I fell in love with is not the man he turned out to be. He made his choice. He doesn't get to have his cake and eat it too, even with those gifted lips.

Yet the uncomfortable situation I find myself in right now is my fault. Did I need to dress like last night's hooker while fulfilling my part in the top-secret mission? No. No, I didn't. Another case of my intelligence having left the building.

We're seated at a reserved front row table allowing Dak the opportunity to get down on his knees in front of Trace and sing to her, which is the reason I'm close enough to see the way Dalt is giving me a hungry glare from the stage, the one which says 'all the better to eat you with.' Based upon the level of throbbing going on between my legs, I'd say my V-jay wouldn't mind being his midnight snack.

There's a slight possibility I *may* have dressed for him in a black, figure-hugging, Band-Aid sized skirt and red lace-up bustier I scored at the Old Hollywood Vintage Clothing Shop in Portland. I accept the humiliating culpability I was thinking about Dalt when I bought it. I wanted him to notice me, taunt him with what he threw away. Immature? Possibly. Problematic? Definitely. The little plan backfired because *I* miss *him* so much it feels like my heart is cracking wide open when he stares at me.

There's no denying the way my body craves him. I've never been able to keep my hormones in check or my pussy from turning into an aching, traitorous entity when I'm anywhere near him. He's an addiction I can't shirk.

The good news is, by the way Trace is wrapped up in Dak's arms it's apparent the guys and I succeeded in our mission to get young love back on track and I'm free to make a hasty exit.

It's obvious I have not yet reached the place in my life where I can defy the Dalt Walker force field enveloping me and pulling me in. Time to engage the retro boosters and get the hell out of here. Because the other big problem with being this close to Dalt, beyond my pussy craving him for her next fix, I am totally still in love with the jerk.

God only knows why. I gave him everything I had without making sure he wanted it. He didn't. And it hurt...it hurt so damn much I had to give my heart time away from him to remember how to beat in a normal rhythm. Although after all this time, it still does its ridiculous pitter patter skip a beat thing whenever I'm too close to him.

Given the way Dalt treated me, or should I say dumped me, one glance from his dreamy silver blue eyes shouldn't have my heart doing the hot dog drive-in commercial routine, flipping around threatening to jump out of my body. It shouldn't make me feel like I'm ready to spontaneously combust from the heat he's throwing my way. After all this time, the loss of his kisses and memory of his lies shouldn't be causing massive-coronary-level pain when I breathe.

"Hate to break you two lovebirds up, but I'm heading out. Are you going in Dak's car? Want me to drive your car back to the house?"

"You're going home? You okay?" Trace's brow pinches in concern. Guess I'm not as good as I thought at keeping my broken heart off my sleeve.

"I'm good. Happy you guys worked it out." Dak is still showering kisses all over Trace's face and neck, oblivious to our conversation or the audience's continued applause and loud whistles.

"It appears Alex has his ride home for the night too." I tip my chin toward the stage where Alex and Erik are face-fucking so hard they may swallow each other.

I'm happy for Alex and Tracey. But the truth is, seeing my friends euphoric and in love makes me just a touch jealous and causes me to miss Dalt even more.

"Are you okay to drive?' Trace asks, untangling herself from Dak and digging her keys out of her purse for me.

"I'm fine. See you back at the house later. Oh, one thing, hockey god." I address Dak to force his attention on my statement. "If you break her heart again, you'll be singing soprano in the future." I give him the scariest glare I have in my arsenal.

"No worries, Nik." Dak laughs and holds his hands up in surrender. Guess my scary doesn't intimidate him. "I'm going to spend every day trying to prove to this girl right here how much I love her."

Wow. I wonder what it feels like to have a guy vow to love you unconditionally forever? Another tinge of pain zaps through my heart. I shake it off and try to focus on how happy I am for my best friend.

"Good. 'Cause I wouldn't want to have to kick your ass." I give them both a quick hug before making my way through the crowd to the exit, although I'm completely serious about the ass kicking if he hurts Trace again. I've had just about enough of the heart demolishing shenanigans of these hockey sluts. I may love hockey but I fucking *hate* hockey players.

Trace's Jeep is parked around back in the rear parking lot of the Blue Goose. It was the only available space by the time we got here. It's not hard to locate. Not only because the lot has already started to empty, but the lizard green color of the car practically glows in the dark under the lights.

I shiver and pull my black leather jacket tighter around me and make my way toward the car. It's not unusual for it to be this cold in Maine in April. But it isn't just the cool ocean breeze making me shiver, it's the thought of Dalt. How whenever I see him I want to wrap myself around him like a monkey and never let him go.

How am I going to see Chloe's beautiful face every day for the rest of my life and not miss him?

When I press the remote key, two large hands grab me around the waist. I recognize the cologne instantly—the musky scent of leather, lemon, and man. The faint aroma has me swooning even before I gaze into the liquid-silver blue bedroom eyes.

"Don't leave, Nik," Dalt whispers, his lips grazing my cheek.

"You...you shouldn't sneak up on a woman like that if you value those crown jewels of yours." I have to force myself not to lean my head back onto his hard chest and dissolve into his arms.

"Don't leave, please. I miss you so much," he says, kissing the spot on my neck just under my ear, the trigger point which shoots fireworks through my veins.

I turn slowly in his arms to face him. Big mistake. When I look at him I pant. Actually, freaking *pant*! I can't be this close to him without having trouble breathing.

"I...I have to get Tracey's car back to the house." I brace my hands on the car to assist my legs in their inability to support me, or it could be the way Dalt is gripping my waist keeping me up. Either way, it's like the temperature just shot up twenty degrees and I'm melting at his feet.

I can't let him break down my defenses; can't allow him to use me whenever he pleases. I'm an expert on how men use women. The year my mom and I spent with my douchebag stepfather in our house when I was only thirteen was filled with sickening lessons I never want to learn again.

"Damn, Nik. You smell so good I want to eat you," he says in a hungry growl.

Here he goes with his leg-spreading words of seduction.

I put my hands on Dalt's chest and give him a little push. My breath catches when I touch him. God. I love the feel of his chest. I'm on a first *hand* basis with his pecs, familiar with every cut line of muscle under the thin fabric. I'd love to be trailing my lips down them.

Snap out of it.

I have to remember what's best for Chloe and me.

"Let me go, please." I shove the wall of muscle, but he doesn't budge. "By the way, you guys were great tonight. Perfect routine for a bunch of manwhores. I didn't know you had those kinds of moves in you." I hope my harsh tone will get him to back away from me. There's no oxygen when he's this close.

"Could you please not stand in my breathing circumference?" I demand.

He ignores my request and puts his hands on either side of me, caging me in and using his palms to brace himself on the hood of the car. He leans into me, one leg stretched behind him, using the other to nudge my legs apart. His face is level with mine.

"Maybe you've forgotten how good *we* move together." Dalt sweeps his lips across mine and then grinds his hips into me. His hard shaft presses against my thigh through the fabric of his pants.

Nope. I haven't forgotten.

My eyes flutter closed and I can't hold back the uninvited whimper escaping onto his lips.

"Fuck. Nikki, I want you, bad." His voice is raspy with need as he continues to grind his massive erection on me. My short skirt is hiked up even higher on my thighs and this time when he presses into me it's right where I want it. I think I just heard my pussy scream, "Oh God. I want you too!"

When he crashes his mouth onto mine it's not a gentle request. It's a hard, urgent need. My lips part in a gasp. He takes full advantage, tangling his tongue with mine. The heat moves like a fireball from my toes to between my thighs. All reason flies out of my head, leaving only the craziness of desire. Common sense and self-respect be damned.

Wrapping my arms around his neck, I pull him closer and rock my hips on his thick erection. Raw need and desire overwhelms me. I want to fuck him right here, right now, in the middle of this public parking lot. When I open my eyes, the intensity in the heavy-lidded gaze staring back at me jolts me out of my heated haze. Suddenly I see it. I see the reflection of my little girl in those eyes and I remember everything he's done to me. To us.

Who does he think he is? Does he think he can— what was the warning Sister Edith gave the girls in my Catholic school sixth grade class? *"Boys will use you like a dirty dish rag and throw you away."* That's it. Does he think he can throw me away like a dirty dish rag and then come back like nothing ever happened? He must be mistaking me for one of his groupies. I can play the field as well as any guy and I'm not about to let someone treat me like dirt.

"I have to go." I drop my arms and spin around, pulling the car door open. When I do, my head doesn't quite stop spinning and I stumble back. Dalt grabs me around the waist to keep me from falling. I'm not sure if it's the intoxicating sensations of his touch pulsing through my body or it's the too many drinks I slurped down during the show causing the car in front of me to swirl in a hazy green blur.

"You're not driving. Give me the keys." His words are a raspy snarl as he pulls me away from the door and sticks his hand out, demanding the keys.

"I'm fine. I can..." When I try to push past him, he slams the car door closed and keeps a firm grip around my arm.

"You're not driving, Nik. I saw you sucking down the Long Island iced teas. I haven't had anything to drink. I'll drive you home." He blows out a big exhalation and runs his fingers through his long, dark, tousled hair. "I need a ride anyway. I came with Dak and he's going to be a little busy for the rest of the night."

"Yup. Guess your tramp dance worked in getting Dak and Trace back together." I smirk. I hate this. I hate what he's reduced me to. I hate the bitchy things I have to say to him to protect my heart. This isn't me. People can be cruel, but I've never been cruel in return. I'm not a pushover, yet, I try my best to show kindness whenever I can. I figure the world would be a better place if we could all be just a fraction nicer to each other. All those fractions put together would add up to something significant.

It's different with Dalt. I can't be nice. I made the mistake of being *way* too nice in the past, letting him get too close. He cut me deep in the most brutal way and I was hurt...*am* hurt. And angry. This is self-defense.

He exhales another huge breath and walks me around to the passenger side. "Keys." He holds out his hand one more time. I drop the keys into his palm with a reluctant shrug, even though I know he's right. I shouldn't drive after the amount of alcohol I've consumed.

Dalt yanks open the passenger door. "Get in."

I guess I've succeeded in showing him where I stand. He can't play me like a hockey puck; toss me away and come back whenever he gets the urge, crisscrossing in and out of my life and dropping me whenever he feels like it. If it's possible to die of a broken heart, I won't survive being dropped out of his life one more time because I barely managed to glue my decimated heart back together the last time. Who would have thought Sister Edith may have been right? The nasty old prude would be proud of me. I'm using my brain, making a long-awaited intelligent choice to stay strong and defy his charms. A good thing. Right? So why do I feel hollow and completely lost?

Chapter Four

DALT

My boys and I live right next door to Nikki and Tracey. The geographic location of our houses presents no problem for the two of us to drive home together. What *is* a problem? Her heat-inducing body being right next to me in the car and how long it's been since I've been able to touch her. Everything about her gets me hard, even her snarky little remarks.

When I start up the engine, Bazzi's "Why" pumps from the speakers of the top of the line Alpine sound system in Trace's Jeep. Every bass note driving the lyrics strikes a chord in my heart, like it was written and playing just for me and Nikki.

Nikki's obviously not feeling it. Or maybe she is. It could be the reason she reaches over and flips off the radio as I back out of the parking space. She turns her face toward the window, pressing her body against the door like she can't get far enough away from me.

"We need to talk, Nik."

"What could we possibly have to talk about?" Her flippant tone is an attempt to make it sound like I'm an insignificant nothing to her. But I've caught her giving me familiar wistful glimpses when she's not throwing icy glares of hatred, and I heard her gasps and whimpers when she was in my arms tonight.

I give her a sideways glance. "The first thing we need to talk about is why you're trying so hard to pretend you hate me."

Her short skirt is showing way too much of her toned soccer legs...the legs she used to wrap around me to pull me closer. I notice a tattoo high up on her thigh which wasn't there before. It's a heart with a big C in the middle of it. Fuck. Has she fallen for some guy with the initial C? I want to reach over and run my hand up that leg and under her skirt to confirm how wet I know she is for me right now, help her remember the way I can make her feel and forget any other guy out there.

When I glance at her she brushes her bangs out of her eyes. My mind drifts back to the times we were curled together in bed and she would tell me things about her past. Her disheveled platinum hair, royal blue bangs, and the sad expression on her face gave her the appearance of a frightened little girl when she was sharing those stories. Don't get me wrong. Nikki is a strong woman, she knows how to take care of herself, but there were times she needed someone to lean on if only to vent about the things she'd had to endure. I used to be her someone.

"I'm not *pretending* anything." She huffs an indignant snicker and gives me a quick glance before refocusing her gaze out the window.

"Come on Nik. What's up? Why'd you leave me?" I pull into her driveway. Technically it's *our* driveway since the gravel making up both driveways is separated by only a thin strip of grass.

"Why'd you leave school without a word and block my calls and texts? And in the months you've been back at school you've been avoiding me. No, worse. You've been *ignoring* me." I turn off the car and hope she doesn't bolt out the door before answering me.

She doesn't. She sits there for a minute, her stare now riveted straight ahead through the windshield. She finally turns to me. Nik has these amazing Abyssinian eyes, just like the cat. When they're gazing at you filled with longing, they can melt your heart and fry all rational thought right out of your brain. But when they're glaring at you like they are at me now, let's just say even in the dim driveway light I would swear if she had super powers she'd be using her sapphire blue eyes to pulverize me with laser beams.

"Stop it! Why are you doing this, Dalt? It's not funny. It's cruel! Haven't you hurt me enough? I don't want to play this game anymore. You have to leave me alone. Find someone else to be your subfuck until you get back to California."

The anger in her eyes is washed away by glistening tears. If her words weren't shock enough, the welling of tears in her eyes is. Nik hates to cry. She says it's a weak, crybaby thing to do or some such crap.

"Nik, what are—"

"Don't." She holds up her hand like she wants to push me off the face of the Earth. "Why did *I* leave *you*? Your memory is as full of shit as your promises."

She pulls the keys from the ignition before I can ask her what the hell she's talking about. The speed she's developed from her years as a soccer player has the door of her house slamming closed before I even realize she's out of the car.

Her words are like a punch straight to the gut followed by a left hook to the jaw. I want to go beat down her door and ask her about a million questions. What game? How did I hurt her? What the hell is a subfuck? But with the amount of alcohol she drank tonight, it's probably not the best time to have a meaningful conversation. Still, what does she mean my promises were full of shit? I didn't break any promises to her. Dammit. *She* left *me*. What the hell is she talking about? What the fuck happened?

Chapter Five

NIKKI

"They organized a touch football game at the quad and I told the guys I'd cook tonight after it," Tracey practically chirps. I haven't seen her this happy in weeks. She's bouncing around the house like a kid on Christmas morning.

In fact, ever since the night of the talent show she's been floating on air. From the sounds of orgasmic bliss coming from her room at night, I'd say Dak is definitely the reason for her exuberance. And he's just as bouncy, walking around with an extra spring in his step. It's kind of cute how in love they are, even though I can't help but ache for Dalt when I hear them. The walls in this house are thin and the two of them have no problem being *very* expressive when in the throes of young love's passion.

"I want to have a dinner together with everyone before we leave for spring break. You have to play football and stay home for the dinner, Nik. Since you won't come with all of us to Malibu over the break, you have to party with us before we leave."

"I already told you why I couldn't go away over break. I want to stay here to spend time wi...uh...to help my mom on the farm and work on my book."

I hate lying to Trace, but I can't tell her about Chloe. I can't tell anyone.

Dalt's father is the monster villain in my fairytale noir. I can't risk his trying to take Chloe away from me if he finds out about her. He has the money, power, and malevolence to do it. Even though he made it perfectly clear two years ago neither he nor Dalt want any part of me in their family's future.

"Are you sure that's why you're not coming?" Trace's voice snaps me out of my nightmarish memory. "'Cause if it's because of Dalt, he's not coming with us. You won't have to see—"

"Dalt's not going? Why not?"

"I don't know. He says he has things to take care of here. You sure you two aren't planning some kind of romantic vacay all by yourselves?" Trace arches a brow.

A tiny spark flickers in me at the thought of spending a romantic spring break alone with Dalt. Ugh. Did I mention I fucking *hate* player, whore, hockey players? Add my traitorous heart to the list of top ten things I hate.

I'm such a fool. I stupidly almost gave in to Dalt's soft words and kisses the other night in the parking lot. Why do I still love him like this when I know he doesn't feel the same, when I know he's on the verge of marrying his Malibu Barbie?

There was no need for his father to emphasize the difference in our lifestyles the night he came to my dorm. I know I have absolutely nothing in common with the rich elitist people making up the majority of the student body at Bernard. I'm painfully aware Dalt and I come from different backgrounds. That's the understatement of the millennia. Dalt is a rich, privileged Beverly Hills boy and I'm a small-town farm girl with nothing but our animals.

After listening to his father's disgusting words in a transfixed stupor, I ran out of the student lounge and left him standing there, pen to checkbook. I barely made it outside. I waited until I got out the door to throw up instead of doing it on his thousand-dollar shoes. I should have done it on the shoes.

He made it excruciatingly clear to me. Dalt and I could never be together and we haven't been ever since. Well, except for one more blissful night of every kind of mind altering sex

The night of the first keg party of the semester was the last time I relapsed into a fix of the tall, dark, and handsome crack. Dalt and his housemates throw a party every Friday night when they don't have a game.

I saw Dalt at the Thirsty Whale Pub earlier the same night. It was also the first time we had seen each other in eighteen months. He hadn't changed. He was his usual ovary-exploding, mouthwatering self when he walked up to the table I was sharing with Trace and Alex. He was polite, inviting us all to the party at his house later.

The whole time he was talking to Trace and Alex he never took his eyes off me. I tried to remain oblivious to the way those bedroom eyes have the ability to undress me, fuck me, and make me come in my pants without one touch of his hands. In other words, to resist his charms, I was rude and bitchy and basically told him to fuck off. The Walker father and son team have been excellent mentors in the art of cruelty.

Still, I appeared to lose my newfound skills in vindictiveness later in the evening at Dalt's house. I had agreed to meet Trace and Alex there. It was the first time I was going to be in the hockey bordello since coming back to school.

Panic prickled through me at the thought of going to the party, but I wanted to prove to myself I could do it. I could be there, in Dalt's house, and not feel a quiver of desire anywhere in my needy body. To fortify my misplaced determination, I indulged in a one on one get-together with my good friend Jim Beam before walking over to the party.

When I finally made my way into the den of iniquity, my eyes were immediately drawn to Dalt's like pings to a cell tower. The vibes I sent across the crowded room were anything but cruel. Cue the playback. I could swear violin music soared, choirs sang, and the music swelled like a scene in a Hallmark movie. There may even have been hearts and cupids floating in circles around his unkempt hair.

I was coherent enough to recognize Dalt's disheveled appearance and glazed eyes suggesting he had been overindulging in some sort of alcoholic tête-à-tête of his own. I didn't care. My body moved toward his in an involuntary tug, the same kind of gravitational force which pulls me toward him every time he's nearby. Once I was in the grips of his magnetic influence and he was as fuzzy-brained as I was, any form of restraint disappeared as fast as my bottle of Jim Beam had earlier. I had one objective: take what I needed from him. It was just sex. All I wanted from him was sex. At least it's what I kept telling myself.

We spent the rest of the night in his bedroom doing every kind of dirty, filthy, wonderful thing we could think of, craving every inch of each other's body like a thirsty man craves water.

Dalt's body is an oasis of miraculous places to explore and his bedroom skills are magical. He used every position and technique in his well-rehearsed bag of tricks to keep me coming all night. He performed like he couldn't get enough of me; would *never* get enough of me.

With every kiss, every touch, the cunning effects of hormones mixed with the stupefying properties of Mr. Beam had me on the verge of whispering words of love. I managed to block them by whispering Dalt's name over and over in awed pleasure, while Dalt whispered mine in reverential groans.

When the next morning's clarifying rays of sunshine streamed through his bedroom window, I wasn't feeling blissful. It was just another stupid Dalt-inspired mistake on my part. I slipped out of his house before he or anyone else woke up to avoid my monumental walk of shame. I swore I would never leave myself open to his charms again *and* I would also suspend my friendship with Mr. Beam, along with any other form of alcoholic fuck-me-over acquaintance.

I can't blame it entirely on the alcohol though. I knew I was incapable of denying Dalt or my own need for him.

Dammit. Why isn't he going to Malibu?

I can't be alone with him.

Wait. Everything's copacetic. He doesn't have the address to the farm. There's no chance of my seeing him.

What did Trace ask me? Oh right.

"I've told you a gazillion times there's nothing going on with Dalt and me. I have no idea why he's staying at school over the break. But I'll be busy moving some of my things into Alex's house and then I won't be here the rest of the time. I won't be seeing him."

"Are you sure you want to move? I told you you don't have to just because Dak is moving in here after graduation. We have the extra bedroom and we both want you to stay," Trace says, unaware of the skirmish going on inside my head.

"Thanks. I know I can stay, but Alex's isn't far and I think it's best to give you lovebirds some space."

"Are we still that loud at night? I've been trying to quiet it down." Trace's face flames to pink.

"No. I don't want you to quiet anything down. When two people are as in love as you guys are, you should be able to let your orgasm flags fly. That's not why I'm leaving. Since Alex has room in his house now, he's been bugging me to move in with him for a few months before he goes on the figure skating tours."

Alex and Tracey are on the figure skating team. The three of us have gotten close this past year. But after graduation Alex is going to be leaving to join a company which does skating shows on cruise ships. He says he wants to "travel the glorious world" before he settles down and starts coaching, which only leaves me a few more months to spend with Alex and the main reason we want to live together now.

Because I left school two semesters, and Tracey's in grad school, with Dak taking both undergrad and grad classes, the three of us will be here another year. Somewhere along the way Dalt decided he was staying to get his MBA. I'm not sure when he made the decision to stay since, according to his monster father, he's supposed to be rushing home to marry his childhood sweetheart and begin working for the Walker Production Company.

*Fuck him, his father, **and** Barbie.*

Or whatever her name is.

"Okay, fine. I'll let Alex have you for a little while. But you have to party with us today," Trace insists.

This is one of those times I'm going to have to try to reign in all Dalt-related anxieties to be able to hang out with our mutual friends.

"Sure, I'll get in on the touch football game today and help you make dinner."

Would it be okay if I lace Dalt's with an added touch of spicy arsenic?

Chapter Six

DALT

"I'm already on Dak's team," Nikki informs me when we're choosing teams. Dak gives me a one-shoulder shrug. He knows as well as I do he hadn't picked her yet for his touch football team, but she's determined to stay away from me so neither of us says anything.

Our teams are an interesting combination of hockey, soccer, football players, and a few figure skaters. Once we have the teams even, with both male and female participants, we decide my team will be the no-shirts, except for the girls, or none of these guys would be interested in playing football. Therefore, in the interest of healthy, outdoor, activity, which doesn't involve distracting bare tits and uncomfortable hard-ons, the girls are going with sports tops. Dak's team has on red pinnies we borrowed from the athletic department.

My first handoff is to Murphy, our football team's

star halfback, and he easily outmaneuvers everyone to run it in for a touchdown. Dak throws a long pass to Sanders, one of the football team's wide receivers, and he takes it in to even up the score. It pretty much keeps going back and forth like this: some touchdowns, some fumbled passes, some interceptions.

When Dak fumbles the ball and one of the soccer girls on my team recovers it, I tease him. "Yo, Anderson. What's up, dude? A little too much nookie fogging up your brain?"

Laughter, cheers, and wolf whistles ripple through the crowd. Dak runs across the field, dips Trace over his arm, and plants a big kiss on her lips. When he lets her up, they high-five each other. Those two never have any problem with their PDA. In fact, they're totally proud of it. The thought plays over in my head that if I had been more open with Nikki, I wouldn't have lost her. If she ever gives me another chance, I'm going to tell her a thousand times a day how much I love her and shower her with touching and kissing everywhere we go.

Dak laughs and taunts me right back. "Don't hate me 'cause you ain't me, dude."

Everyone's laughing and having a great time, until Dak throws a pass to Nikki and some dirtbag football player on my team tackles her. They're lying on the ground, Nik's underneath him, and he's fucking whispering in her ear.

"Stop it, Cliff. Get off me." Nik giggles and gives him a little push. By the time I get over to them her slight push has become more like her hands running up and down his bare chest. "No. Not now." She continues to giggle, while he's still busy at her ear.

"It's *touch* football asshole. Get the fuck off her!" I yell.

"Exactly what I'm doing, man." The douchebag grins and runs one hand underneath Nik's pinny. That's it. I put my hand on his shoulder and yank him off her.

"What's your problem, dickhead?" The guy jumps to his feet, plants his hands on my chest, and shoves me. I take a step backward, then I'm right back in his face. I'm going to break every bone in this asshole's body!

"*You're* my problem, shithead." Before I know it, my fist is connecting with his jaw and he's sprawled out on the ground, this time flat on his back.

"Dalt! What the hell are you doing, bro? He's on your team!" Dak runs over and holds me back away from the asshat on the ground.

"I don't give a fuck whose team he's on. He shouldn't be touching Nikki!" I want to add *she's mine* but I don't. When I look down, Nik is cradling the asshole's head in her lap.

"Are you okay, Cliff?" she asks in this syrupy sweet concerned voice and my insides clench along with my fists. Then it occurs to me. *His name is Cliff.*

"This is the prick's initial you have tattooed on your thigh?" I growl at her while trying to push out of Dak's hold.

Nik looks up at me with fear in her eyes. "No, Dalt. It's not...it's..." she sputters.

Christ. Is she *afraid* of me now too, along with

hating me? I wish I could climb inside her beautiful fucked up head to see what the hell's going on.

"Fuck it. Let's call it a day. I've had enough *touch* football with fucking soccer *and* football players." I walk to the sidelines, pick my t-shirt up from the ground, and head to my car. Drained of all ability to hold myself up, I collapse behind the steering wheel and drop my head back onto the leather headrest of the brand-new Levante my dad had delivered to me a few months ago. A ridiculous car for a college student but nothing unusual for my calculating father.

What the actual fuck?

I mean, except for my conniving bastard father, I have a fairly good life. I had a decent childhood, at least while my mom was still around. After she died, my brother Garrett and I tried to make up for the loss of her love by always being there for each other. Material crap became the compensation for a father who gave zero fucks about his family. Still, I got into one of the best universities in the country where I was given the privilege of playing the best sport in the world. I'm healthy, wealthy, and by the response of the ladies to my dick, things in that department are pretty fucking awesome. So why am I keenly aware of the shrapnel-like pain stabbing inside my chest confirming there is indeed such a thing as a broken heart?

What am I going to do? I don't just want Nikki, I *need* her like sunshine and air. Without her my so-called good life is desolate, uninhabitable.

I can't even think about her with someone else, especially not some dickhole football player. I've been trying to ignore any signs of her being with other guys.

Fuckfuckfuck.

I just remembered I'm supposed to have dinner at Nik and Trace's tonight. If she's there with that dirtbag, I'm going to lose my shit.

Chapter Seven

NIKKI

"I can help with dinner. What are we making?" Dak offers when we get back to our house.

The walk back from the quad was so quiet I could almost hear the spring flowers pushing out of the ground. Thankfully Dalt had his car and didn't walk with us. I doubt he would have walked with *me* anyway.

The hurt that swept across his face when he asked about my tattoo was evident. I freaked when he mentioned seeing it. I should be happy he thought the *C* stood for Cliff. Still, I can't get the vision of the pain in his eyes out of my head.

The truth is, I haven't been a nun since Dalt punched a fist-size hole in my heart. Hardly. I've been with a few guys...um, a few more than a few. I've been working my way through some of the other athletes. Why athletes? Because of their reputations for stamina, a lot of experience using their tongues, fingers, and massive dicks. One time I indulged in a fling with an engineering geek. I figured it couldn't hurt to try a variety of options to see if I could find someone to measure up to Dalt's skills and scrub him out of my soul.

Shallow? Perhaps. I make no apologies. I'm not interested in love. That bridge was crossed and burned. I might rebuild it someday, but for now I'm only interested in someone to help heal the wounds left by Dalt and wash away his memory.

Cliff was one of them. I hooked up with him a couple of times. He's a nice guy. Almost as much of an Adonis as Dalt with ridiculous sculpted muscles, suntanned chiseled face, dreamy chocolate brown eyes, huge...uh...biceps. Bit of a player, but still always shows a determined interest in getting me to go out with him. I guess he's not a total hit and run slut. Problem is, he's not Dalt.

I don't turn into a mushy mess of feelings and sensations when I'm within twenty feet of him. When he gazes into my eyes or gives me the slightest touch, my throat doesn't go dry, I don't lose all capacity to think or speak, and my pussy doesn't throb at a level ten on the Richter scale. Nope. Only goddamn pain in my ass Dalton Walker does that. So I keep things light and friendly but stick to a no dating rule. I don't need any messy complications. I have other important responsibilities right now to consider.

I know Dalt *must* know I haven't been a saint for the past two years. I haven't kept it a secret. Truth? I'm a little ashamed to admit some of my whoring around may have been with the devious thought to make him jealous.

Yet my chest hitched at the agony in his eyes when he saw me with Cliff.

Dammit.

I don't know why he would care if I'm with the whole football team or have every one of their initials tattooed on my ass. He didn't want my ass or any part of me anymore.

"Uh, no we're good. Nik and I can handle it," Trace says and takes my mind off feeling sorry for Dalt, the man who had his dad offer me money to get out of his life. I'm such a pathetic mess.

Trace flicks her chin in the direction of the stairs. She's either trying to tell Dak she wants to have her way with him upstairs right this second or she wants him to leave the room to give her time to interrogate me.

"Oh. Right. Okay. I'm going to take a shower, then. The uh...water will be running...I won't be able to hear anything going on in the house." Dak makes his smooth I-have-no-idea-what's-going-on comment and heads upstairs.

Interrogation it is.

Trace chews on her bottom lip while she waits for him to get out of sight. "Okay, Nik, I think you better tell me what's going on between you and Dalton. He's usually so laid back. I've never seen him angry. Not to mention he looked like someone ran over his puppy when he thought you were with Cliff. What's going on?"

"Nothing's going—"

"Don't even." Trace holds up a hand and stops me. "Don't try denying this thing between you and Dalt. We all see the way you look at each other and you could cut the tension with a knife when you're both in a room together. Dak told me you guys were inseparable a couple of years ago and it looks as if you're both still crazy in love with each other."

"Dalt's not in love with me." I flop onto the crazy ass sofa Tracey's mom bought for her. Too bad its wild, over the top colored flowers can't spew sunshine and happiness up my ass to alleviate the level of depression spreading over me.

"But you're in love with him." Trace states the answer like it's obvious. "When I was going through everything with Dak, you were there for me every step of the way. Hell, you even threatened to kick Dak's ass. Remember?" Trace smiles and sits next to me. "Talk to me, Nik. Let me help you like you helped me. If it hadn't been for you, Dak and I may never have gotten back together."

"You guys would have gotten together no matter what. You both are too much in love not to be together." I drop my head back onto the sofa cushion and stare up at the ceiling. I thought I had that with Dalt. How could I have been so wrong?

"I think you're wrong about Dalt not loving you." I would think the little smarty could read minds if I didn't know how long it took her to read Dak's love-crazed thoughts for *her*.

"Did you see the way he reacted when he saw Cliff put his hands on you?"

Irrelevant.

I won't be deluded any longer into thinking Dalt's capable of real love.

"That's because he's used to getting what he wants when he wants it. It has nothing to do with love. It's just no one ever says no to the great Dalton Walker and his horrible father," I sneer and run a finger under my eye to swipe away a tear. I refuse to shed one more tear over the thought of the nauseating *Harrison* Walker.

"What are you talking about?" Trace's sweet naiveté shines in her wide-eyed, shocked disbelief. "I've never thought of Dalt as that type of guy. He strikes me as...I don't know...someone who is sensible and comforting and...and dependable. He's always there for Dak when he needs him. I've never seen the demanding selfish side of him you're talking about. And what does his father have to do with it?"

"That's because you've never seen the side of Dalt I have." I exhale a huge breath.

Except for my mom, I've never shared the truth about what happened between Dalt and me with anyone. I've kept the pain and anguish inside me for two years until the ache has grown to the point where it's gnawing at my insides like some parasitic alien devouring whatever's left of my heart.

Maybe opening up to a friend about the repugnant story of my love life wouldn't be such a bad idea. It might help alleviate some of the suffocating ache.

"It's true, Dalt and I were together for a while. It was...well...magical. I *was* crazy in love with him. I almost didn't believe it was possible to love someone so much. It was like we were the only two people in the world, like we didn't need anyone else and we could do anything together. I believed those ridiculous platitudes. *He's my other half. He completes me."*

I sneer at how naive I was to believe all the romantic fictional slop about relationships. But Trace is nodding like those insipid clichés make perfect sense to her. I almost feel guilty telling her the tale which will suck all her restored belief in true love's kiss right out of her sails.

"So, what *happened*?" She pushes. "I think I still see some of the magic stardust swirling around you two." She uses a finger to make an imaginary circle around me.

"Hmph. That's not stardust, that's fallout. I *thought* he felt the same way until his father showed up at my dorm one night when Dalt was away at a game." I swallow the huge lump in my throat and fight back the stupid tears welling in my eyes.

"His father came to your dorm without him?" Trace furrows her brow.

"Yup. He came to do the dirty work to save his precious son from this evil, gold-digging vixen."

"Get the fuck out." Trace's voice raises two octaves.

"When I came down to the student lounge, he introduced himself and started right in on what I assume was a well-rehearsed, recurring speech on Dalt's behalf. I can still hear his voice like it was yesterday." The noise of his words repeats inside my head like the sound of a dental drill.

I drop my voice to a deep, pretentious tone. *"'It's just like Dalton to get himself into this kind of situation with a woman.'* A situation. I had become a *situation* to Dalt. *'It's the reason I agreed to come here and tell you myself, since he couldn't bring himself to do it.'* And then he laid it on me, the truth about *comforting,* dependable Dalt."

"What truth?"

"You're going to love this. It went something like, *'Dalton is engaged to a young woman from a very fine family at home in California. They grew up together and they plan on marrying as soon as they graduate from college.'"*

"Get. The. Fuck. Out." Trace's mouth drops open in shock.

"No shit." I'd make the Girl Scout's scouts honor gesture to demonstrate my veracity but I was never a Girl Scout and don't know it. Therefore, she'll have to settle for the universal clout of the 'no shit' declaration. "But he wasn't finished. He said, *'They've been planning it for some time now. I'm sure this must come as a shock to you.'"*

A shock? More like an electrocution. Dalt was *engaged*? The illogical, heart-shielding thought skittered through my mind he was talking about some other Dalton Walker. But as he continued to educate me on how different my lifestyle was from Dalt's the realization he was talking about *my* Dalton Walker, the guy who had become my universe, dropped me like an Acme piano to my head.

"No. I don't believe it. No way is Dalt engaged to someone. Dak would know it if he was."

"His father made it very clear my lifestyle was much different than Dalt's, while his *fiancé's* was everything he wanted and needed."

"Ridiculous. What do your different lifestyles have to do with being in love?"

"Apparently *everything* to the Walkers. He was willing to be very generous to get me out of Dalt's life."

"Generous how?"

"Generous to the tune of fifty thousand dollars."

"What...what do you mean?"

"I *mean*, Mr. Loathsome Walker said, '*You must realize your lifestyle is much different than what Dalton is accustomed to. That is why I'm prepared to write a check for any sum within reason which will assist you in getting on with your life after college. You won't need Dalton for that.*' I won't need Dalton for that! What the hell was that supposed to mean? I gave no fucks how much money Dalt had. I never did. But the elder Thing One and his offspring Thing Two must have thought I was all about the money. He made me an offer he *thought* I couldn't refuse. He said, '*Dalton suggested I agree upon an amount with you and take care of it right now. I think fifty thousand dollars would be quite generous. Don't you?*'"

"What? No way!" Trace shrieks.

"Hold on to your lug nuts. You haven't even heard the worst of it. After making me the offer he upped the ante. '*Although I can see the reason for Dalton's infatuation with you. You're quite a lovely little thing. Perhaps you would consider having dinner with me?*' And then he ran the back of his hand down my cheek."

"Mofo scumbag! He's completely creepy." Trace shudders like she's trying to rid herself of the disgusting sensations of Harrison Walker. She won't succeed. I haven't been able to accomplish it in two years.

"You have no idea. If every muscle in my body hadn't

been immobilized by what he was saying and doing, I would have punched his lights out for touching me."

"You totally should have."

"I was numb. I think I stopped breathing for a full minute and then I just ran out of the building without saying a word. I left him standing there holding his repulsive designer checkbook in his disgusting hands. A few days later I left school and finished the rest of my course work for the term online. I took a couple semesters off. The university agreed to hold my soccer scholarship for me or I would never have been able to afford to come back."

"Pervy. Son. Of. A. Bitch. What did Dalt say when you told him about the creepy slime ball coming to your dorm?"

"I never told him. Why did I need to tell him? He's the one who sent his father to deliver his sweet message. I never wanted to see him or talk to him again. I couldn't believe how heartless and cruel he was. Not just the lies but letting me fall insanely in love with him when he was engaged to someone else and then not even having the decency or courage to tell me himself. I thought if I went home for a while it would all just...I don't know...go away."

I don't tell her the main reason I left school was to give birth to Chloe without anyone knowing it. If it hadn't been for my mom's unwavering support, I would never have been able to pull myself together and come back to Bernard to pursue my degree while she helped me raise my precious baby girl.

"Wait. You've never talked to Dalt about this?" Trace

spreads her hands out in front of her like she needs the world to stop spinning for a minute to think about what I told her. And then she starts shaking her head. "Nik, you know I've got your back, always, and I would never want to make you feel worse than you already do. But… are you crazy!" She looks at me like I just told her the Earth is flat.

It's a definite possibility. The crazy part, not the flat Earth part. "Yes. I am totally crazy for falling for a hockey slut like Dalt Walker. I knew better. I knew those hockey boys were trouble and I walked right into the deep end."

Trace stares at me for a second, chewing on her bottom lip. Her eyes glaze over. Only then do I realize what I said.

"Oh. No. Not Dak. Dak's different. He's a sweetheart and I know he loves you."

Trace breathes a huge sigh of relief. It's not like I have a crystal ball. If I did I would never have glanced into the dangerous blue depths of Dalt's eyes to begin with. But Dak appears to be a good guy. I have to hold onto a thread of faith in mankind, even if he *is* a hockey player.

"I guess in Dalt's case the rotten apple doesn't fall far from the dreadful tree." The brimming tears I've been holding back let loose and stream down my face.

Dammit.

I hate crying, and even if I didn't, Dalt doesn't deserve any more of my tears.

Just then Dak comes back down the stairs. He stops midstride at the bottom of the steps. "Oh…uh…sorry. Should I go back up?" He points up the stairs like we don't know where 'back up' is. "I thought it was getting close to the time for everyone to be here."

"Oh shit. Dinner!" Trace jumps up from the sofa. "It's okay. I prepped everything before we left for the game. I just have to put it in the oven and throw the salad together. You can help me in the kitchen, Dak. Why don't you go up and take a shower, Nik? You'll feel better. But we are *so* not done talking about this and what you need to do."

Trace stomps off to the kitchen and I walk past poor Dak. He's standing there running his hand back through his surfer-blonde hair trying to think of some way to handle the fate-worse-than-death situation of having to speak to the crying mess of female he's been left alone with.

"Relax, hockey god. I'll be fine. Go help Trace. I'll be down in a minute." As I sniff my way up the stairs, I'm trying to think of a way I can escape down the shower drain with the water.

Chapter Eight

DALT

"If the dickhead's here I'm not coming in," I inform Dak when he opens the door.

"Which dickhead would you be referring to?"

"The fucking football player who was feeling Nikki up on the field, that's which one."

"He's not here. Get in here. I'll get you a cold one. You look like you need it. We're just about to sit down and eat." Dak puts his arm around my neck and pulls me in the house. "Why don't you just talk to the girl and tell her you can't live without her precious kisses and end this torture, man?" He chuckles and pats me on the chest.

Even though I'm a few months older than Dak, he's the captain of our hockey team and like the big brother watching out for everyone. He's always there to offer help and advice when needed, just like he has been throughout our lives growing up together.

"I tried, dude. She doesn't want anything to do with

me. It's like she hates me. She says I broke my promises to her or some shit."

"Well *did* you?"

"Nah, man. I was in lo—I mean I really liked Nikki. I still do. Sure, I've hooked up with a few of the puck bunnies since her, trying to forget about her. But it's not...they're not..."

"I know. Been there done that. That shit never works when you lo—uh, like someone."

"*Right?* And it's like the meaner she is to me the more I want her."

"Exactly, dude! It's the human comedy. Welcome to God's little joke." He laughs and circles the arm around my neck tighter, like a loose headlock. If he tries giving me a noogie, he's getting an elbow to the gut.

"But wait." Dak gets serious and lets go of my neck. "That's not the *only* reason you want her, right? Because she treats you like shit?"

"No, dude. Of course not." I run my hand through my hair to push it back into place. "She's the only one I've wanted since the day I met her. She's all I see. All I want to see."

"Welcome to the dark side, bro! You're a man in love." He laughs and drapes an arm around my shoulders. Seems to me the ass is enjoying himself a little too much at my expense.

"Listen, how 'bout we bust out the old sheets and you can write poetic messages across them for her? We'll hang them across the porch like I did to get Trace to talk to me. Of course, then we might have to get the guys back together to do a sexy Magic Mike routine one more time to completely melt her heart...and other areas."

"Hard. No. Nikki's not into sappy poetry and I won't sing or do dancing routines *ever* again." I cringe and yank his arm off my shoulders. Dak throws his head back and laughs.

"You know, you're kind of an ass. I'm not exactly sure how you got an amazing chick like Tracey to fall in love with you." I laugh and give him a shove. Sometimes he *can* be an immature man child, but at least he has me laughing at my dilemma instead of brooding. I guess the way he knows what to say to make people feel better is one reason he's such a good friend and captain.

"No shit, me either." Dak gets this faraway, wistful gaze. The dude's so in love it probably won't be long before we're throwing rice.

"Okay, Shakespeare. How about the cold beer?" I've stalled long enough. Time to face Nikki and make another attempt to get her to talk to me.

"Yo, Walker, about time. Where ya been, man? We're about three beers ahead of you." Batt's stretched out on the sofa, his gigantic feet up on Trace's hideous black and white checked coffee table. His arm is draped over one of the figure skaters who played on our team today. She's whispering something in his ear, which has him licking his lips.

Batt's our right winger and one of the main reasons we completed our season as Frozen Four champions. I tip my chin in greeting, my eyes searching the room for the only person I want to see. That is, if I see her *without* the roaming hands scumbag. She's not in the living room. I head into the kitchen and my eyes are rewarded when they catch sight of the back of the blonde who, although she's petite and lean, is solid muscle. More rewarding is the fact there isn't a dirtbag in sight.

Nikki has on a black tank top and cutoff black shorts, tiny enough to show off all her toned attributes. Her long white-blonde ponytail is sweeping across the top of her ass as she sings and sways in time to the music streaming from Trace's stereo.

Christ.

As she circles her hips, while singing "Havana, Oo Na Na," I want to reach out and pull her to me. I remember how her full, round ass feels pushed back on me and how—No. I have to stop that train of thought before it exits the station or I'm going to have to exit the room to hide the effects.

"Hey, Dalt!" Trace looks up from the food she's placing on the table and does a quick sideways glance toward Nikki, who almost chokes on the abrupt termination of *na na nas*. The sweet sway of her hips comes to a halt and her back stiffens. She slowly turns around, away from the salad she's tossing in a bowl on the counter.

"Hey, Trace. Nik." I try to keep my eyes from lingering on Nikki too long. I force my greedy eyes away from the Rocky and Bullwinkle characters stretched across her perfect tits.

What can I say? I'm a tits man. What guy isn't? Flash us a pair of boobs and all our brain cells shoot straight to our cocks. I've never been particular about the size or shape, as long as they're attached to a willing female.

The truth is, despite the fact that Nikki's tits transcend the world of round globes of soft perfection and are on a whole other plane of exquisite existence, it's not just her perky boobs I love. It's everything about her. It's the reason these unfamiliar emotions, which surpass anything physical, have always scared me.

Unfortunately, it's a problem to hide the way my emotions affect my cock from yearning for the physical. Another dilemma afflicting almost every guy on the planet.

"Smells good. What are you ladies cooking up?" My attempt at small talk to relieve the tension in the room and in my pants.

"Uh...it's *lasagna*." Nikki points to the table where several pans of lasagna are lined up. Her unspoken words and tone say, "*It's right in front of you, dumb ass.*"

"It's *spinach* lasagna, actually," Trace counters in an attempt to make me appear not quite as brain cell deprived. "I'll be right back. I have to get more paper plates from the pantry."

"But there are plenty..." Nikki calls after her, pointing out a stack of about five hundred paper plates on one side of the table already. Her effort to keep Trace from leaving us alone in the kitchen is too late.

"Sorry about what happened on the field today. I shouldn't have reacted that way." I take a couple of steps toward her and she backs up a step.

"No, you shouldn't have."

"I just couldn't take seeing that guy put his hands all over you. It makes me crazy," I say in a softer voice and take another step toward her.

She doesn't step back this time but her words are no

warmer. "I can't see how it's any of your business who has their hands on me." Her hand shoots to her hip to emphasize the defiant statement.

"Of course it's my business, baby. I...you're..." I close the gap between us and reach out to her but she slaps my hand away.

"Don't call me baby," she snaps. "That's only something you can call me when you *mean* it. I'm your *nothing*. You made it crystal clear two years ago." She moves around to the other side of the table, putting it between us.

"Nik, I swear to Christ I don't know what you're talking about. And by the way, I take it back. I'm *not* sorry about what I did to the asshole today. He deserved it. I should have broken his fingers for touching you!" I call after her as she runs out of the room.

Trace comes back in the kitchen just as Nikki runs past her. "Did she tell you?" Trace asks after doing a double take at Nikki's escape.

"Tell me what? That for some reason she thinks I told her I wanted nothing to do with her? Where did she ever get such an idea? She was like my oxygen when we were together. She was everything. I wanted to attach her to me somehow so I never had to be away from her."

Okay. Getting a little too female here.

"Wow, Dalt. That's beautiful. I'm totally impressed. She needs to hear you say all those things. She thinks you're—" Dak walks in the room and interrupts our conversation.

"Hey, bro. You still don't have a beer." He pulls a

cold beer from the fridge, twists it open, and hands it to me. "Here you go."

"She thinks I'm what?" I ask Trace, absently taking the beer from Dak without looking at him.

"Um...she thinks...I mean, you didn't do anything *really* stupid a couple of years ago, did you?"

"Of course he did," Dak chimes in. "He's a guy, for chrissakes. Stupid comes free with the penis."

"No. I mean really *bad*, stupid," Trace persists, ignoring Dak.

I don't know. Did I? What would a chick consider really **bad** stupid?

"I don't think so. I did nothing but lo—but try to show Nikki how much she meant to me."

I'm not ashamed to say the word love, it's just that I want to tell *Nikki* I love her before I tell everyone else. If she would fucking *let* me!

"I think you need to talk to her ASAP, Dalt. It's important. You guys should get together over spring break while everyone's gone. You definitely need to hear her side of the story and explain to her what happened."

"I don't know how I'm supposed to explain to her what happened if I have no fucking idea what happened." I gulp down half of the bottle of beer getting warm in my hand.

"Just talk to her over break. It'll be nice and quiet and ro-man-tic." Trace grins. "I'm sure if you just talk to her you can work it out."

"Okay, Dear Abby. I think that's enough advice for one night. Can we eat before everyone dies of hunger?" Dak kisses Trace on the cheek. She turns her face to him

73

and they're at it again, sucking face like they haven't seen each other in a year.

I clear my throat to remind them I'm standing here before they start tearing each other's clothes off. "You need me to set up the folding table?" I ask to pull them back down from the clouds.

"Already got it, bro," Dak answers. "I put the pink tablecloth on it. Is that okay, babe?" he asks Trace.

Damn. My man is for sure in love if he's putting pink cloth on tables for dinner with a bunch of hockey slobs. But I have to admit I'd like to be doing something just as ridiculous for Nikki right now.

Chapter Nine

NIKKI

"These are so good, NikkiDix. I didn't realize I had such a talented friend," Trace says when she walks in my room and finds me working on some of the illustrations for the children's book I've been writing for my creative writing class. Doing my own illustrations is taking care of two birds with several colored pencils, so to speak, since I'm using the drawings for my art illustration class. The drawings are spread out around me on my bed.

"Uh, thanks? But what's with the NikkiDix?"

"Tryin' somethin' new. The guys have nicknames for each other. I thought why can't we? Since your last name is Dixon and Nik kind of rhymes with Dix, well, you know, NikkiDix. What do ya think?"

I squint and purse my lips in one of those 'I think I smell shit but can't find it,' expressions.

"No good?"

"Girl, good shouldn't be within a hundred-mile radius of that nickname." I laugh.

"I can't very well call you Dix. I couldn't deal with the deluge of required explanation." She moves some of my drawings and plops down on the edge of the bed.

"How about you just stick to Nik or Nikki? I'm good with that." I continue drawing my latest illustration of the flying girl for my book.

"Ugh. You're so boring. I'm pretty sure Alex will agree with me on this," she protests while rifling through my drawings.

"Pretty sure he won't. And if he does, it will be very sad to have to do away with my two best friends at one time."

"What-*ever*. It's hard to believe someone with so little imagination can be so creative." Trace rolls her eyes and laughs. "These drawings are beautiful." She thumbs through a few more of my drawings.

"Thanks. This stuff is my form of meditation. Takes my mind off all things shitty. You know what I mean?"

"I'm hoping by the time we get back from spring break everything in your life will be rainbows and sunshine. All things shitty will be talked about and vanquished. *You* know what *I* mean?"

"Don't get your hopes up because it's never going to happen."

"Dinner was pretty civil last night...considering. I know as soon as you and Dalt talk things over you're going to find out it's just one big misunderstanding. Dalt loves your sweet ass. I'm certain of it. There's no way he would've had any part of this fifty thousand dollar payoff scheme. It's too ridiculous." She flicks her hand through the air. "Like something out of a cheap, sleazy novel."

"It is. *Right*?"

"Right. Your boobs alone are worth that much. He should have offered you *five-hundred* thousand. At least." She keeps a straight face until she sees my shocked expression and then bends over into a big laugh. I'm expecting her to begin rolling around on the floor in glee.

"Thanks, bitch." I can't keep from smiling.

"Sorry. Only kidding. I don't mean to joke about your problems, Nik. It's just the whole thing is absurd. *Talk* to Dalt. Find out what's going on. There's no way he'd have any part in his father's scuminess. It just doesn't sound like him." She picks up one of my drawings and inspects it a little closer. "This little girl is gorgeous and there's something so familiar about her. Is she someone you know?"

Damn.

Of course, Trace would see someone she recognizes in Chloe's beautiful face. She's the spitting image of Dalt, the same stunning silver blue eyes and almost black hair. Not to mention Trace is a *very* observant, super smart, and at the moment, extremely fucking annoying friend.

"Uh...yeah. She's a little girl I know from back home. I based the character in my book on her." It's not a total lie, just not the complete truth.

"It's weird. I could swear I've seen her somewhere." Trace pulls the drawing closer to her eyes. I'm holding my breath waiting for the other hundred-pound shoe to drop, waiting for her analytical, memory efficient brain to make the connection between Chloe and Dalt. When she doesn't, I inhale for air like a chain-smoker who's been standing behind a pesticide sprayer. Thank goodness she's too preoccupied with the drawing to pick up on my oxygen deprived gasp.

Gathering my drawings together, I stack them into a neat pile, using it as an excuse to extend my hand for the one Trace is still holding. She returns it to me without hesitation. I don't know what I'm worried about. There's no way she would ever suspect I had Dalt's baby. Why would she? I never told anyone or brought Chloe to school and no one has ever been to our farm.

"Don't you guys have to leave for the airport soon?" I ask.

"Now, actually. I still wish you were coming with us though. I hate leaving you here by yourself. You sure you won't change your mind? We can check to see if there's any seats left on our flight."

"No. I wish I could, but I have a lot of work to finish for final projects in these classes." It's definitely not a lie. I do have to get my writing and illustrations done before the end of the semester. I want to take a day or two getting them done before I head home and spend the break with my mom and Chloe.

We have a small working alpaca farm, enough to make a bit of a profit. I try to get back there whenever I can, not only to see Chloe, but to help on the farm. Even though it's small, it can be a lot of work for one woman.

It's one of the reasons why when my dad passed away, after only a few months my mom jumped head first into a relationship with my scumbag stepfather. Thankfully now *ex*-scumbag stepfather. At first I was angry she moved on from my dad so soon after his death. Then I realized Bert helped to diminish some of the grief and loneliness I saw in my mom's eyes after the loss of my dad. And when he helped out on the farm, my mom didn't appear as depleted and rundown. Anything to ease her weariness made me happy for her. Until the night I woke up to find him standing next to my bed. It shattered my trust in humans forever and broke my mom's heart all over again.

"You won't be alone anyway because you're getting together with Dalt to have an enlightening convo. Right?" Trace's words remind me of my own heartbreak in the here and now.

"Um. I'll think about it." Not happening. I totally misjudged Dalt. I didn't realize how important his wealth and status were to him. I've been a casualty of enough deceitful dirt bag men to last a lifetime.

Trace's belief in the ravishing heroes providing the happily ever afters in her shelf full of romance novels is clouding her usually perceptive abilities. She won't accept the fact Dalt's future bride is a well-to-do California winery heiress, not a fledgling children's book author slash illustrator who's going to inherit a struggling alpaca farm.

"Don't think about it, Nik. Just do it. You and Dalt belong together. I'm never wrong about these things."

"You sure about that?" I tease, because it wasn't too long-ago Trace was a mess, thinking she could only be attracted to the wrong guy.

"Well, *almost* never." She bends to give me a quick hug goodbye. "Have to go. When we get back the four of us will go out on a double date," she states and walks out my bedroom door.

"Yeah. Okay, *Pollyanna*," I call after her.

"Nice one, but too long and a little old-fashioned. You should totally sign those drawings 'NikkiDix,' though!" she yells back.

Chapter Ten

DALT

I'm going over. Everyone's gone for the break and Nik's home alone. I've got her favorite pizza. She won't be able to resist it, even if she can resist me.

When I knock on her door I hear the muffled steps of her coming down the stairs, but she doesn't open it. I'm sure she peered through the peephole and is standing on the other side trying to decide whether or not she should ignore me. I hammer on the door. I refuse to be ignored any longer. I have to get her back. I'm nothing without her.

The lock on the door clicks and it swings open a crack. "What?" she says as she peers out from the barely opened door.

Nice greeting.

"I..., uh, I ordered pizza," I stutter out like a kid asking a girl out on a first date.

She doesn't say anything or move to open the door.

"I thought you might be hungry. I got your favorite." I hold out the boxes to let her get a good whiff of the deliciousness. One sure thing about the girls living in this little blue house, they *love* their food. Whoever came up with the saying about food being the quickest way to a *man's* heart never met these girls.

"Uh, that's a hard no." She tries to close the door in my face, but I push the pizza toward her, using it to hold the door open.

"It's Capriciossa. Olives, artichokes, the whole deal. Your favorite."

She hesitates a second then says, "I was going for a run." At the same time she opens the door wider and takes a big sniff.

I'm struck even more dumb by her beauty. Her long hair is wrapped up on her head in a messy bun, loose strands and shaggy blue bangs framing her sexy angel face. Her cut off Popeye tank top is exposing a hint of her toned ab muscles. The inked soccer ball on her right upper arm is taunting me, reminding me of the times I traced it with my tongue. I'd like to be kissing a path down her arm right now, but she barely wants to talk to me, let alone let me touch her.

She opens the door all the way and steps back to let me in. I finally get my Nikki-intoxicated brain to connect with my mouth.

"There's a Stanley Cup match on. Bruins and Senators. You want to watch it?"

She glares at me through narrowed eyes before

breaking her silence with an exasperated shrug. "What do you want, Dalt?"

"Um…I have pizza and there's a Bruin's game on?"

Didn't I just say that?

But Nikki's not dumb. We were together long enough and watched enough television while eating pizza for her to know it usually ended with my licking the sauce from her lips and the sweetness of her strawberry scent from her pussy.

"Whatever. Put it on. I'll get some plates."

As she walks toward the kitchen, her tiny gym shorts accentuate the view of her perfect round ass. Man, what I'd like to do to that ass. My cock twitches in remembrance. It's going to be hard to keep my hands off her. *Hard* being the obvious word here.

She stops on her way to the kitchen and turns back toward me. "I'm not fucking you just because you brought me pizza," she states and continues out of the room.

"Jesus, Nik." I'm somewhat shocked, but more amused.

Of course I don't expect her to fuck me because I brought her pizza. But it would be okay with me if she wants to fuck my brains out because she's totally in love with me and can't keep her hands off me.

"I would hope not!" I call out to her. "At least hold out for filet mignon," I mumble under my breath. I don't think she'd appreciate the joke, even though playful sarcasm was our thing when we were together. My smile caused by her current sass quickly drops when I remember the crushing fact that I'm not the one she's teasing and fucking anymore.

I have to get a grip. First thing's first. Keep my mind off all things involving a naked Nikki. I don't want to ruin this. She's at least agreed to have pizza and watch a game with me. It's closer than I've gotten in a long time.

Trace suggested I talk to her and I'll be able to fix everything between us. Yet Nikki made it clear she's not interested in talking to me about our past. I won't press her tonight for any answers as to why she ran from me, even though I think I deserve an explanation. I'll just take it one step at a time, let her get comfortable with the idea of us hanging out together before getting into a serious conversation.

She comes back in the room with plates and two Dogfish Head beers, the Romantic Chemistry for her and the IPA for me. It's the same beer we drank when we were together. Hmm, *very* interesting she still keeps *my* favorite in her fridge since I know neither Dak nor Trace like it, unless, of course, dickhead Cliff drinks it. If so, I'm switching to a different beer. She places the beer and plates on the coffee table and flops down next to me with a big exhale.

"Any score?" She's the only girl I've ever been with who enjoys watching sports on television. I mean actually likes it, not just pretends she likes it to spend time with me. I'm not interested in spending casual time watching television with any girl but Nikki.

Other girls have been...well...I've enjoyed other kinds of leisure time with other chicks. Not quite as many as the other guys in the house, Wolfe holds the record there. I found out two years ago there's only one girl for me. The few fan-girls I've been with since Nik left me have only been a poor attempt to fuck her out of my mind. It hasn't worked. She's embedded in my soul. The one in my thoughts when I fall asleep, the one I dream about, the one I wake up thinking about, the one I fantasize about to the point of extreme genital discomfort and self-fulfilling release. She's my Stanley Cup. She's everything I want.

"Earth to Dalt. You in there?" She shoves my shoulder and snaps me out of my thoughts. Just in time before I do something stupid like climb on top of her and beg her for what's mine, or at least what used to be mine.

No dammit. It's still mine; she's still mine.

I just have to make her remember, and when she does she'll be screaming my name so loud she'll never remember any other guy's name.

"Huh? Oh yeah. One-minute left in the first period. Bruins up by one."

We eat our pizza and watch the game in silence for a few minutes. I can't even get excited when Krug digs the puck out of the corner passes it off to Backes, who takes the perfect shot on goal and scores. The only thing I can think about is the girl sitting next to me with her toned legs stretched out across the corner of the coffee table.

Fuck.

I want to run my hands up those legs. Better yet, get down on my knees between them. I remember how it drove her crazy when my scruff would brush along the silky skin on the inside of her thighs.

"This game is so inept." Nikki interrupts my fantasies once more.

"What? What do you mean?"

"*In-ept*. You know, tactless. No finesse, like soccer has."

"What're you talking about? It's the *Bruins*," I remind her in disbelief at her absurd statement. How could the Bruins ever be tactless?

"No, I don't mean just this game, I mean hockey in general. There's no finesse," she states matter-of-factly, like it's an obvious point.

I choke on the swallow of beer making its way down my throat. "Are you fucking kidding me?"

"Nope. In soccer there's all this control and artistry. We maneuver the ball down the field with skill. But in hockey the puck's just all over the place. Like I said, no finesse."

"Bull. Shit. Might I remind you we're gliding on razor edges on slick, hard-as-fuck ice, while maneuvering a small rubber disc with a six-foot long stick? Meanwhile, *you're* running on flat feet on soft grass, kicking around a huge leather ball. *And* we still manage to control the shit out of the puck with just as much *finesse* as a soccer player does a ball!"

"While slamming each other into the boards," she adds in between swallows of beer.

"Oh right. And unlike soccer players, we don't lay down on the ice and whine and cry when someone trips us or runs into us."

"Geez. Defensive much? I'm not interested in arguing with you. I was just stating the facts." She presses her lips onto the lip of her beer bottle like she's trying to hold back a grin. Of course. I'm such a fool. It's exactly what she's trying to do, start an argument and chase me away. Not so fast.

"As I recall, *soccer* girl, you use to love hockey almost more than me. Never missed a Bruins game, watched every playoff game, threw things at the screen when the Bruins got sloppy. Never missed one of our home games. Hollered out some pretty creative profanities when we made what you thought were mistakes *and* cheered and whistled louder than anyone else in the stands when we scored."

"Whatever. A girl can have an opinion." She shrugs one smooth bare shoulder. The one I want to bite right now and mark as mine for the whole world to see.

"And a guy can call bullshit." I chuckle and suck down the last of my beer. I don't tell her Coach De Luca agreed with her about a few of those mistakes we made during some of our games.

"You want another beer?"

This is good. At least we're talking...well, bantering. But she hasn't thrown me out yet and she even offered me another beer.

"Sure," I say, "if you have another IPA. You know they're my favorite."

"Um, ya think? It's the reas...I mean, how could I forget, dipshit? You had cases of it at your house and it's what you drank whenever we were out."

I love the way she says whatever's on her mind. No

games. Straightforward. Always upfront, even if she won't admit she's kept my favorite beer stocked for *me*.

Her frankness is another one of about a million reasons why I fell in love with her. I'm in love with Nikki. Turns out it's not so difficult to explain what I'm feeling for her, after all. Now I just have to tell *Nikki* and remind her she's in love with me too. Maybe not today, but soon. I'll find a way to get her back, soon.

NIKKI

Dalt stops on his way out the door. "I'm going for a run around nine in the morning tomorrow. You want to come with?"

He didn't touch me once the whole time we watched the game and polished off two pizzas.

Even though I told him not to, should I be happy about that? No. Of course not. I want him to miss me as much as I miss him. I want him to forget how to breathe when he's near me. I want him to love me as much as I frickin' love him. I want to tell him about Chloe and see his eyes fill with tears of joy, tell me how all he wants in the world is for us to be a happy little family. I want a lot of things. All fucked up fantasies, because what *he* wants from *me* is a pizza sharing running buddy. The wife and family *he* wants is back home in California with a rich girl.

Despite knowing all that, I miss his friendship and companionship as much as his hot as fuck body. How can I be so stupid? Let me count the ways. What Dalt did is not the act of a lover *or* a friend. And he did it when I was four months pregnant, the most fucked up thing of all. Although he didn't know I was pregnant at the time.

I *was* planning on telling him, I just hadn't found the right time. I wanted the mood to be perfect, possibly when we were on the camping trip after he got back from Boston. We planned to camp on one of the islands out past the harbor for the weekend, just the two of us. Our version of *Naked and Afraid,* or not afraid, in our case, because we *loved* naked. Correction. *I* loved naked with *him. He,* apparently, played, cheated, and fucked it over, with *me.*

After his dad paid me the unexpected visit and told me Dalt was engaged to someone else, a romantic trip to an island was further away from my mind than the newly discovered Crater 2 galaxy. I ran out of the student lounge, puked on the grass, and kept apologizing to the tiny human inside of me for having been so careless with his or her future. The panicked thought occurred to me if Dalt found out I was pregnant, he might try to make me get rid of the baby or even worse, my greatest fear, try to take the baby away from me. My stomach convulsed into dry heaving. I decided then and there I could never tell him about the baby.

"It's not a trick question, Nik. Since you missed your run tonight, you want to go with me in the morning?"

He's leaning against the doorframe, his arms crossed over his chest waiting for my answer. The position accentuates his muscled arms and the intricate tattoo he has running down one of them. It depicts crossed hockey sticks inside flames with a puck between them. A recurring thought pops into my head, *if he loves hockey enough to have it branded on his body, why isn't he pursuing it professionally instead of going to work for his father in some high-profile movie studio job.*

I glance up from his arms and one glimpse of those eyes, the ones which would make Vestal virgins spread their legs, makes me want to grab onto those biceps and climb him like a tree.

Damn. I think I just licked my lips.

Yup. By the way he's giving me his *let's fuck* grin, I'm pretty sure I did, and he noticed.

"Unless there's something else you'd like to do for exercise?" He sucks in his plump bottom lip like he's trying to hold back a smile. Can *I* suck on that lip...right before I punch it?

"No, I have to run earlier. I have a lot of work to get done before heading home for the break."

"Okay. We can go at eight then."

"I don't think it's a good idea," I have to avert my ravenous eyes from his when I turn him down or else my determined vagina's answer might be, *Skip the run, just carry me upstairs and fuck me into unconsciousness.*

"Sure it is. Not only is it good for the cardiovascular system, it helps build endurance and makes you a better more *artistic* soccer player." He chuckles.

"Huh?"

"*Run-ning,*" he emphasizes like he can read my heated thoughts. "You said it wasn't a good idea. I was just explaining why it's a great idea."

"Oh. Right. Running. Yeah, *that's* a good idea but—"

"Great. I'll be over at eight. I'll even spring for breakfast after at the little hole in the wall you like so much with the gigantic blueberry pancakes."

"Dalt, I need to tel—"

"Tomorrow, soccer girl. I had a good time tonight. Thanks. I've missed our nights together." He steps closer to me and I'm sure he's going to kiss me.

Please kiss me. I mean, no, don't kiss me.

Dammit. I want him as much as I ever have but I can't let him use me as a cum bucket until he's back with his Malibu Barbie fiancé.

No worries. Instead of kissing me he kisses his own fingers and places them on my cheek with a soft touch. The corners of his mouth tip up in a leg-trembling smile before he turns and walks away. I have to hold myself back from running after him and throwing myself into his arms.

What the hell is wrong with me? I had this guy's baby, ran away without telling him, and have kept her a secret for two years because his father offered me money to get out of his life. And now I want to beg him to fuck me? I. Am. Pathetic. Am I really such a shallow floozy that a pair of thick arms, a porno-size cock, and a pizza—two pizzas *with* artichokes—cause me to throw away all self-respect? Yes. Apparently, I am. It's a good thing he didn't bring me brownies too or I would have spread my legs before the Bruins scored their first goal. Ugh. Stupid, shallow, *floozy*.

Why did I even agree to go running with him tomorrow? Wait. I didn't agree. He made the decision for me, controlling the conversation just like he controlled our relationship. He decided when it started, when it ended, and now when *he thinks* it should start all over. Not this time. It's my turn. I'll go running with him tomorrow and then I'm going to lay the biggest surprise on him he's ever had in his life.

Chapter Eleven

DALT

Nikki opens the door while I'm still struggling to strap on the nylon belt which holds my water bottle.

"Come in for a minute. I have to get my running shoes. There's fresh coffee in the kitchen. Help yourself." She exhales a long breath. Her apparent exasperation doesn't escape me.

Ahh. The smell of fresh brewed coffee is a welcome distraction. I've been living off instant since Batt left. Even though we all try to help out, he's kind of the master chef. I guess having an Italian mom who believed it was her duty to feed as many people on the planet as possible at their kitchen table helped him hone his skills.

"All set?" Nikki walks in the kitchen as I take a gulp of the delicious brew. "Or you want to just stay here and have a relationship with that coffee you're moaning into?"

Little smartass.

"No thanks. I'm good. Been missing the taste of fresh brewed. I'm all set."

"Okay, Juan Valdez. Let's go. I want to get this over with. I've got a shit ton of stuff to do today," she says and walks out.

Nice. Can't get over how thrilled she is to be spending time with me.

I finish my coffee with one more savoring swallow and hurry after her. When I get outside I make a piss poor attempt at stretching and warming up my muscles. I'm a little preoccupied. I can't take my eyes off Nikki as *she* stretches. She's got on her usual spandex running shorts and a Ninja Turtle tank top. As she bends and touches the ground with her hands and then stretches each leg in front of her the spandex clings to every curve of her body. I'm pretty sure *take me I'm yours* just flashed across her ass. No. It may have been my mind the words were flashing across.

I don't want to go running with her. I want to carry her back inside, lay her across her bed, and use our 98.6º furnaces to warm each other up. But she almost didn't agree to go running with me, so I'm fairly certain she'd say 'fuck off' to sex.

We head toward the combination bike and running trail around the harbor. Our feet point us in the direction without our brains giving it a thought. It's the same place we ran almost every day when we were together.

The weather is perfect. The sky is such a clear, vivid blue with the bright sun climbing the horizon, it's the perfect panorama for a picture postcard. A slight ocean breeze is blowing in from the dark blue water of the harbor and a matrix of swaying, anchored sailboats complete the picture. The seagulls squawk over our heads in easy conversation. Makes me wish humans could converse as easily; tell each other exactly what's on our minds without hesitation.

It *was* that easy between Nik and me. In the past, we completed each other's sentences. Now there's this brick wall of uneasiness separating us. I don't know how it got there, or where it came from, but I plan on demolishing it today over breakfast. It's not the ideal place to have the conversation, but I figure if we're in public she won't be able to kick me in the balls for trying to have a serious talk with her.

Will she?

"Having a hard time keeping up, hockey boy?"

I jump out of my thoughts to see Nikki running backward several strides ahead of me. "Ready for those pancakes?" I ask, picking up my pace to catch up to her.

"Fine by me if that's as far as you can go. Like I said, I have a lot of work to do today." She stops running. She's not even breathing hard. And while my t-shirt is drenched, she hasn't even broken a sweat. Guess my dripping shirt is the reason she thinks I'm done. Although, we were together long enough for her to remember how I sweat during *vigorous* exercise and how long I can go, double entendres intended. She's just trying to get under my skin with her taunting.

I don't protest her comment insinuating I'm too

tired to go on. I don't tell her I could go another ten miles if she wants, because *I* don't want. What I want is to get her back into my life as more than a running companion.

"Yeah. That's it for me today." I stop next to her and pull my wet shirt over my head, using it to wipe my face and chest. I don't miss the way Nikki's eyes follow my shirt as it moves over my pecs. It's the perfect opportunity to play with her a little. I drag it in a slow, suggestive circle down my abs to the edge of my running shorts. Her I'm-going-to-eat-you look, which drives me wild, flushes her face.

"I'm *so* hungry." My honeyed tone emphasizes my actions. "Looking forward to those pancakes." Her ogling gaze jerks back up to my face. "Batt wasn't here to make our usual Saturday morning breakfast and I'm starving." I lick my lips to add an extra tease and she closes her eyes for a second. I could swear I hear her whimper. This is good. The brick wall has an apparent fissure. She doesn't completely dislike me.

"Fine." She huffs out a long, frustrated breath. "Let's run back to our houses and take showers before going to breakfast. You look like you need one."

She runs ahead of me toward the house. Yes. After the way I just teased her, *I* need a shower. A very *cold* shower.

"Fuck." When I reach into the nylon belt which holds my water bottle and cell phone and is *supposed* to hold my door key it occurs to me, in my hurry to get to Nik's this morning, I forgot to take my keys. I cup my hands around my eyes and peer through the window on the side of the front door. There they are, minding their own business, hanging from their hook, just where they shouldn't be right now.

I head back over to Nik's, but when I knock a couple of times there's no answer. I send her a text.

> Locked out of my house.

After a few seconds a message flashes across my screen.

NIK

> So what do you want me to do about it?

> I'm at your front door.

> I'm in the shower.

I stand there staring at the screen like a mesmerized idiot. Like she's going to send me some kind of visual confirmation.

> Just a minute.

I can almost hear the annoyed tone in her text. Two minutes later the door opens and she's standing there wrapped in a white towel, all five feet five inches of dripping wet gorgeousness. I will my eyes to stay focused on her face and my dick to calm down. I can't allow myself to linger on the thought of what's underneath the towel. I'm already pushing the limits of restraint here when it comes to being this close to Nikki.

"Can't you just climb in a window or something?" There's the I'm-so-happy-to-see-you tone she loves to greet me with.

"They're all locked and I don't want to break one. The landlord will lose his shit."

She shrugs and steps back, opening the door wider to let me pass. "You can take a shower in Tracey's and Dak's bathroom. I'm sure Dak has something that will fit you. You guys are about the same size," she says and gives me another hungry once over.

"Uh, thanks. I'll figure out how to get in my house after breakfast."

I follow behind her up the stairs.

When she gets a couple of steps ahead of me her short little towel is leaving nothing to my already overactive imagination.

Fucking hell.

"I have to finish washing my hair." She turns and comes to an abrupt stop when we get to the top of the steps. I wasn't expecting her to stop and I plow into her. My hands automatically reach out to grab her arms to keep her from falling. The sweet weight of her towel-covered breasts is pressed against my bare chest. Christ. She smells so fucking good, like fragrant strawberries on a warm summer day. She's trembling and there's no way to will my cock to calm down now. He's totally not interested in calming down. All he wants, what we *both* want, is to be back home inside this woman.

"I...I'll be out in a minute," she whispers, glancing up at me. I think it's the first breath either one of us has taken.

When she walks away I'm still not sure *I* can remember how to breathe.

Chapter Twelve

NIKKI

What the ever-loving hell?

My heart is a fool. I suppose its inability to keep itself from reacting to his fantasy body, head turning face, soul penetrating eyes, and Gigantor cock is understandable. No mere mortal heart can keep itself from beating like hummingbird wings when confronting a combo like that.

I'm not unaware of the inordinate number of women who have fallen victim to Dalt's god-like physical attributes. But you would think after the way he drop kicked my stupid heart, I would be able to see beyond his fool's paradise exterior beauty.

When I fell in love with Dalt, I thought he was beautiful inside and out. He impressed me as being warm and caring, and even loving. Then I witnessed the cruelty lurking underneath the stunning exterior. In Dalt's case, beauty *is* evidently only skin deep. Good, common survival sense should tell me to back away and *stay* far away from him.

Pacing the floor in my bedroom, still wrapped in my towel, the ever-present ache for him thrums through me, pummeling my common sense into submission. The devil and angel sides of my subconscious clash. The devil's tempting need swirls and whispers to me, *You can't go on like this, especially not now when he's ten feet away from you and naked in the shower.* The angel argues, *There's so much more you want from Dalt than the incredible multi-orgasmic sex.* She's a very liberated angel. The devil snaps back, *You can't have it. He's already promised those things to someone else.*

Argh. I can't deal with this inner conflict any longer. It's making me crazy.

Take what you can get, the devil taunts. *Use him to fulfill your need just as he used you and then move on.* I don't give Miss Goody Two Shoes time to respond. I jump in Mr. Id's corner and decide I can play pump and dump just as well as Dalt can. *Jesus.* I may have taken one too many psychology classes for my own good. Whatever. I can do this, use him and toss him away. This time I'm going to be the one in control. I'm going to fuck him right out of my universe and walk away.

I don't bother to knock. When I walk in he's standing in the middle of the bedroom, also wrapped in a towel, his back to the door. The towel is hanging low on his hips and one glimpse of those broad shoulders and the outline of his tight, round ass, has my heart beating like it's trying to get out of my chest. The sight of his massive body and drool worthy muscles standing in Trace's flowery pink and white bedroom would almost be comical if I wasn't as turned on as a nuclear power plant. I think I just ovulated.

When he turns around, the way his surprised expression quickly morphs into a half-lidded gaze filled with oceans of simmering lust would dissolve my panties—if I were wearing panties. The teasing rivulets of water slide down the hills and valleys of his supernatural eight-pack, disappearing under his towel. My gaze follows their journey. In my mind the droplets look a lot like my fingers. I force myself to remember what I'm doing here, remember I'm the one in control.

"We need to talk." I step further into the room.

"*Talk*?" The word catches in Dalt's throat and comes out in a constricted squeak. I can't miss the gigantic pole tenting his towel. Well, that was quick.

"After." I drop my towel and plant a defiant hand on my hip. Dalt takes a long gaze up and down my naked body.

"Holy fuck, Nik. You're my perfect Strawberry Bud."

Where does he get the unmitigated nerve to call me that bullshit nickname? Wait 'til Tracey hears *that* one.

He crosses the room and is standing in front of me before I can blink. "God. I've missed you, baby."

I smack his hand away when he reaches out for me. "I told you not to call me baby."

"Ookay." Dalt runs his fingers back through his wet hair like he's unsure what to do next. The move only succeeds in making his thick black hair more disheveled and his appearance more fuckably hot.

I remind myself how perfect this is. I'm succeeding in making the normally adept sex-god feel a little unsure of himself. I'm the alpha male in this hookup today....I mean alpha woman. Alpha person? Whatever. I'm controlling this little get together today.

Use him and toss him away, my devilish mantra.

I slip two fingers into the waist of his towel and pull it off. His long, thick, porno-size cock springs out in front of me. Christ. His body parts are too good to be true. They belong on a Tumblr page for Hot Men We'd Like To Fuck. I hold back the groan working its way up my throat.

He gives me a cocky half-smile like he knows exactly what I'm thinking. When he leans in to kiss me, I turn my head away. His long, hard shaft grazes my stomach. Sliding my hand down between us, I wrap my fingers around his thick cock—almost, because my fingers can't reach all the way around Gigantor. With as firm a grip as possible, I pull him closer to me.

"Fuck. Take it easy ba...uh...Nik or I'm going to come before we even get started."

"Losing your stamina, *baby*?"

"No. I can go all day and night with you, hon...Nik," he smiles.

Smiles.

Why isn't he as strung out as I am? He tries to kiss me again and I turn my head once more. If I let him kiss me, I'll be unable to keep this up. I'll melt into his arms and overwhelming willpower.

"Is everything okay, Nik?" He leans back and gazes down at me from under his impossibly long black lashes. My eyes linger on his for just a moment but it's long enough for a tremble of anticipation to move through my body. I ward off the sensation and force myself to appear indifferent to his sexy bewitchery.

"Everything's fine," I say curtly, bringing one hand up to his shoulder. "I want you to go down on me." Using the hand still clenched around his cock and the one on his shoulder I push him down to the floor. Unfortunately, as he drops to the floor Gigantor pops out of my grip, because not even *he* is long enough to cover that distance.

"Are you kidding me?" He leers up at me from his kneeling position between my legs and chuckles.

"Don't you want to?" I spread my legs a little wider right in front of his mouth. God. I don't know how much longer I can keep this Fifty Shades of control thing up. I can already feel the imminent orgasm clutching at my insides as he glares up at me through eyes filled with liquid desire and he hasn't even touched me yet.

"Want to? The only thing I want more than eating you is to be balls deep inside you. But you seem a little...I don't know...angry?"

"Oh for fuck's sake. Forget it. I'm not going to beg you to—" I don't get a chance to finish my sentence. Dalt scoops me up and throws me over his shoulder.

"What the hell are you doing?" I punch his back and kick my feet in protest as he walks toward the bed. The thought occurs to me to pinch his perfect, lickable bubble butt in retaliation. Um, no...bite it.

Mmm. Yeah. Bite it.

If I could reach it.

He flips me onto the bed and all thoughts of what I want to do to his delicious ass fly out of my dirty little mind.

"What do you think you're doing?" I snap at him.

"Same thing I was going to ask you," he gibes right back. "What the hell are *you* doing, Nik?" He grabs my ankles, pulls my ass to the edge of the bed, and bends my legs.

"Stop it, Dalt." I try to drop my legs but he's still got my ankles in a firm grip and won't let me move them.

"Oh. Now you want me to stop?" He drops to his knees in front of me. "Isn't this what you want?" He takes one long stroke at my center with his tongue and I'm on fire with the heat of a million stars.

"Ooo. Mmmm. Yeess. I mean no."

"No? How about this?" He uses his thumb to rub slow, teasing circles over my clit.

"Oh God. Yes. Dalt." I push my hips forward. I need more. It's been so long. I need him *now.*

"I want that too, baby," he whispers and stops touching me.

Why is he stopping? Don't stop!

When I open my eyes, he's standing between my still bent legs. Gigantor is throbbing, apparently angry and straining to explode.

"Dalt. Please." I reach out for him, all remnants of me being the one in control gone. I don't care which one of us is the alpha person, I just want him inside me. I want the overwhelming sensation of the way only he can fill all the emptiness I've felt since he left me. And yes. I do mean literally *and* metaphorically.

He climbs over me, placing his knees on either side of me, and wraps his hands around my waist, sliding me up the bed, then gently pushes a pillow under my head. Stretching out over me, he pushes himself up on his forearms, one on either side of my face. I can still feel his cock throbbing with angry, unfulfilled pulsations on my stomach.

Every part of my body is lit up with the electricity generated by Dalt. "I want you," I whimper and wriggle underneath him in an attempt to position him where I need him. But his powerful body is pressed so firmly on top of mine I can't move.

"I want you too, Nik. More than I've ever wanted anything in my life. But this isn't happening until you tell me what's going on, and why you're so angry with me."

Seriously? At a time like this he wants a dissertation on the *Most Disgusting Way To Dump Your Fuck Buddy —Or How to Get Your Douchebag Father To Do It For You?*

"Is it really necessary for me to have to explain why I'm angry?" The bitter memory of his past actions floods my thoughts, extinguishing the raging fire between my legs. "Did you think what you did wasn't going to destroy me and make me hate you? I'm not like you, I'm not made of stone. I'm just mortal flesh and blood." I punch him in the shoulder in an attempt to make him move. "Get off me."

Another colossal mistake. What was I thinking? Being here like this isn't going to erase Dalt from my life, it's only going to make the remaining roots of my love for him wrap around my heart like tentacles and obliterate what little fragments he's left of it.

He doesn't budge when I punch his shoulder. He just keeps piercing me with those limpid blue eyes.

"What did I *do*, for chrissakes?" he persists.

This is ridiculous. He's pressed between my legs, his hard cock throbbing and he wants to have a conversation about the horrific way he treated me.

"Just because you sent Darth Vader to do the horrible deed, doesn't mean I'm going to forgive you." I pummel my fists on his chest. "Get off!"

This time he grabs both of my wrists with one hand and holds my arms over my head. "What. The. Hell. Are. You. Talking. About. Nik?"

"Your *father*? Remember him?"

"My *father*? What the fuck? You never even met my father."

"No? How about the time you were in Boston for an away game and I stayed here to prepare for our camping trip when you got back? Remember the romantic little trip to the island we had planned?"

"How could I forget? It's all I thought about the whole time I was away. I almost blew the game thinking about it. I couldn't wait to get back and have you all to myself for the whole weekend. But when I got here you were gone and you wouldn't answer my phone calls. What the hell does that have to do with my father?" All signs of longing are gone from his eyes, replaced by darkened storm-filled fury.

"Are you actually getting angry with *me*?" He's good.

Somehow, he's going to twist this to make it my fault he's the offspring of Satan. "Did you think you could send Sat...your father to buy me out of your life and I would just take the fifty thousand dollars and think fondly of you? I'm not a whore, Dalt. If you were engaged to someone else, you should've been honest with me."

I can't bring myself to tell him his repulsive father threw in an inappropriate stroke of my face with no added compensation other than offering to take me to dinner. Discussing this much of the sordid interaction while lying naked under him is outrageous and sickening enough.

"You didn't need to pretend you wanted to be with me and then pay me to leave you alone. It was—ugh. Just get off me...please." I drop my head to one side because even though he still has me pinned under him, I refuse to let him see the stupid tears welling in my eyes.

He loosens his grasp on my wrists and sits back onto his legs. Correction. Since I'm still underneath him, he's sitting on my legs. I glance sideways to note Gigantor appears somewhat defeated.

Dalt places a finger under my chin and turns my head to him. "Nik, are you telling me my father came here while I was away and...and offered you money to...to stay away from me?" His voice trembles when he speaks.

"He told me you sent him because you didn't have the courage to do it yourself. He made it sound like you'd done the same thing lots of times before to other girls."

God. I don't want to talk about this anymore. I can't listen to any more of his lies. I should've gone home yesterday.

Dalt doesn't say anything for a moment. He drops his chin to his chest. "And you took the money and left," he whispers.

"What!" I pull my legs out from under him, use my foot to shove him away from me, and sit up leaning on the headboard. "I didn't want your fucking money! I didn't need your financing. I wanted you. I needed you. I was in love with you. But that was before I found out you were engaged to someone else and just using me as a seminal receptacle until you could get back to her." I pull my knees to my chest and drop my face onto them. I just want to curl up in a ball and disappear, make him disappear, make the last two years disappear. Everything except Chloe.

"You...you were in love with me and yet you believed I would do that to you? That I could *ever* do that to you? Is that the kind of man you think I am?" His words are so hushed now they're almost inaudible. I feel the rustle of the bedcover and glance up to see Dalt pulling it across his lap.

This is the first time in our relationship Dalt has been uncomfortable being naked in front of me.

The disconnected thought crosses my mind.

When I raise my head Dalt is staring at me. His demeanor is...what? Devastated? Disappointed?

"Your father...he...he said—"

"I've never been engaged to anyone, Nik. My father has a business partner with a daughter. They've been trying to push us together for years, but neither of us is interested. We grew up together. We're friends, just friends. My father probably found out about you and decided he needed to put a stop to our relationship."

"He *found out* about me? Was I a secret you were keeping from him?"

"No, you weren't a secret. I just wanted to wait to tell him until after our weekend together. But Garrett called before I left for the game and I was so excited I couldn't wait. I told him." He swipes the back of his hand under his eyes.

Is he...crying?

I can't hold back the bitchy words from pouring out of my mouth. "Told him what? You had some poor stupid farm girl wrapped around your little finger?" I can't stop myself, even though one tiny part of my already fragmented heart is breaking again when I see the anguish in his eyes. I don't understand why *he's* anguished. *He's* the one who demolished us.

Dalt shakes his head. A crease forms between his brows like he's trying to figure out what language I'm speaking.

"No, Nik. I told him you were wrapped around my *heart*. I told him I was in love with you and I was going to tell you when we went camping. He must've told my father. They work together. They're close. Closer than I've ever been with my dad." He scrubs his hands over his face.

"You...you were in love with me?" I whisper because I'm sure this is another one of the million dreams I've had of Dalt, my Prince Charming, pleading with me to come back to him, telling me how he loves me and needs me more than Malibu Cinderella and I don't want to wake myself up from this one until I hear him say it.

His shoulders begin to shudder and for one horrible second, I think he's crying but then a throaty chuckle pushes through the fingers still covering his face. He's *laughing*? I don't know what's worse, his crying or laughing after what I just told him.

"That's it?" he sniggers.

"*It*?"

He drops his hands from his face but he's not smiling now. "You stayed away from me and hated me all this time because you believed him?"

"I..."

"Fuck! Nik!" Dalt runs both hands through his hair and tugs at the strands wrapped around his fingers. "Why didn't you just ask me? How could you believe him?"

What is he saying? I can't...

"Did I ever give you the slightest indication I wanted you out of my life? Think about it." His hands are resting on his thighs now "And if I *did* want us to break up, I would've said so and walked away. Why the hell would I need to pay you? Why didn't you trust me enough to ask me?" Well, his words and his eyes are pleading with me but *they're* not the words Prince Charming is supposed to say.

Oh God. What have I done?

The ramifications of what he's saying are slowly creeping through the caverns of my brain. Torrents of emotions surge through me, one rolling over the other: confusion, guilt, shame, shock, hurt, anger.

*Why **didn't** I trust him?*

Why didn't I know he was a much better man than the one in his father's cruel scenario?

Even though the current anger I'm feeling is for my own accountability in destroying our relationship, I hang onto a thread of self-protection. I direct the anger at Dalt and roll with it, like any self-respecting woman who has just been informed she's royally fucked up her own life would do.

"Trust you? Why would I? How could I know what your father said wasn't true? You talked about working with Garrett at your father's company all the time. I thought you were close to your father. As far as I knew you were willing to give up hockey, the one thing I knew for sure you *did* love, to go work with him. I thought if you were willing to give up the thing you loved most in the world to work with him, throwing me away would be insignificant. I assumed you would be more than willing..."

"Nikki." He reaches out for me. "I never wanted to throw you away. You...you were my world."

I...what? There he is. Charming is finally delivering his lines.

For the first time I notice another tattoo on the underside of his forearm; one that wasn't there the last time we slept together. It's an infinity sign. Around the curve of one side is printed the word love and around the curve of the other is printed...

Oh my God! It says Nikki.

He had my name branded on his arm, giving me ownership to all his Grade A perfection.

"When...when did you get this?" I whisper, tracing the symbol with my fingertips.

"The day after the keg party, the last time we hooked up." Dalt watches my fingers tracing the tattoo. "I thought we were going to be okay, that you had finally come back to me. When I woke up the next morning and you were gone, I just figured you had something to do and I went out and got this." He places his hand atop mine to stop my fingers from stroking his arm. "I planned on showing you that night, but when I tried calling and texting you...well, you know what happened. Fuck. What a gi-fucking-gantic fucked up mess. I know I never said the words 'I love you,' but Christ, Nik, how could you believe the things my father said?"

I don't know what to say. I'm drained in the same overwhelming way I was the day his father offered me the money to get out of Dalt's life.

"I...I don't know Dalt. How could I *not* believe him?" I shrug.

How am I going to explain something I don't even understand myself? He's staring at me like he's waiting for the rainbows of oh-that-makes-sense words to pour from my mouth.

"It was...awful. I was so in love with you. You were my...my everything...my hero...my...don't laugh...knight in shining armor." He doesn't even grin. "Someone I didn't think even existed outside of novels, and even if he did, I would never be the one to have him. I didn't need a hero, anyway. At least, that's what I told myself. But then, there you were. You did exist. You were real. My feelings for you were real. And I needed you, after all.

Then when your father...I don't know...knocked you off your white horse and blackened your armor, I was blind with anger for letting myself become weak enough to believe in the fairytale. I couldn't think straight."

"Life isn't a fairytale, Nik," he whispers.

"But it *was*. You were my fairytale come to life. You filled my world with every fantasy I had ever been afraid to let myself dream possible when it came to love. All I wanted was you. I wanted to call you or drive to Boston and confront you and curl up in your arms when you told me it wasn't true. But it was so...so painful. The things your father said crushed me. I didn't know what to do. I went home to try to figure things out." I sweep my thumb under his eye to sweep away the lone tear clinging to his cheek.

He grabs my hand, squeezes it, and holds it still. "For two years, Nik? All that time, when you finally came back to school, you couldn't just ask me?" He's still squeezing my hand and shredding me with the devastation filling his eyes.

"It was...complicated by the time I got back. Are...are you saying your father...he...he lied about—"

"Everything." He drops my hand and I shudder at the loss of his touch like a silly girl swooning in a silly fairytale.

"Complicated? 'Do. You. Love. Me?' Four words. How complicated is that?" He doesn't wait for me to come up with an answer to his challenge. I don't have one to give him anyway.

"My father's a very powerful man. He's used to getting his way, especially when he believes his way is what's best for Garrett and me, or at least is the best way to control us. He wanted us to work for his production company when we got out of school. So that's what Garrett did and what I'm supposed to do after I graduate. He wants us to marry wealthy girls from the types of families he perceives to be the *right* kind of people. I guess when Garrett told him I was in love with you it had him worried. I've never gotten serious about a girl before. He figured he could buy you off and get you out of my life. Fucking hell. It would be comical if it wasn't as fucked up as a Shakespearean tragedy. He probably got a good laugh. He managed to split us up and it didn't cost him a dime. He must have been pretty pleased with himself over that deal. He likes to win." Dalt blows out what sounds like every bit of air in his lungs. He sits there, shoulders slumped. I don't know what to do, what to say.

Yeah. A comedy of errors. Did I say something about not being a stupid girl? Turns out I'm an incredibly stupid girl after all. I should have known, should have realized the guy I knew, the man I fell in love with, would never have been part of his father's sleazy scheme.

Tracey was right. In the short time she's known Dalt, she understood him better than I ever did. Dalt's not cruel. He's never been cruel. He's thoughtful, honest, and kind. All the reasons I put him up on a white horse and fell in love with him. In fact, the first time I ever saw him lose his temper was at the quad the other day when he went after Cliff. But that's exactly what a hero protecting his woman would do. Right?

I've wasted two years of our lives. Spent two years

missing him, wanting him, hating him, *loving him*, without being able to tell him. I want to wrap my arms around him. Hold him, tell him everything is fine, we're fine. But this is a fuck up of epic proportions on my part. Star Crossed Lovers, a Shakespearean fuck up. He loves me, I hate him. I love him, he hates me. How can he ever forgive the way I mistrusted him; the horrible things I believed about him? And God! Chloe! How do I tell him about Chloe?

Chapter Thirteen

DALT

"I'm sorry, Dalt. You're right. I should've trusted you. But when your father made it clear to me the kind of life you have in California, the way you grew up, the future you had waiting for you, I believed him when he said we weren't right for each other, and that it would never work out."

"Oh, I get it. You're like a reverse snob. You think people with money can't relate to down home people like you and your family. We're not regular enough *folks* for you."

I can't stop myself from spitting out the angry words. I'm pissed off, and at the same time wounded by the way she mistrusted me, by how little she thought of my integrity. What the actual hell? How can she say she loved me and have thought so little of me?

"No...I..." she sounds exhausted, searching for the words to explain why she thought I could be capable of being the same kind of heartless prick as my father. "I told you what it was like after my dad died. We literally had nothing but our farm animals. There were times if we wanted to eat, we had to eat what we grew ourselves. You probably wore Armani hockey pads when you were growing up. I wore dollar store two for one specials. Not hockey pads, but you know what I mean." She sucks her bottom lip between her teeth, waiting for me to say something. I don't.

She lets out a long breath and continues, "You drive a Maserati. I have a rusted 1982 Ford pick-up which sometimes doubles as a manure hauler."

She gives me a little smile, but I don't say a word. I let her keep talking to explain how we got here to this screwed up place in our relationship. I mean, here I am sitting stark naked with the woman of my dreams, the woman I've been losing my mind over for two years, and we're discussing how my fucking father managed to ruin yet another important part of my life.

"You told me how your mom would take you and Garrett to the theater to see plays when you were younger."

Her words remind me of the other woman in my life my father fucked over. I try to focus on what Nikki's saying, instead of thinking about all the other fucked up things the bastard has done.

"We had one staticky channel on an old television set, sometimes two if the antenna on the roof was having a good day; my fancy form of entertainment. And then, if my mom hadn't thrown his sorry ass out, you know what almost happened with Bert. I don't want sympathy. I'm just trying to explain where I was coming from. My life wasn't even in the same stratosphere as yours. But I didn't spend time boo-hooing over the differences of my life and yours because someone like you wasn't even on my radar. I had never considered the possibility of a guy like you in my life. But then, somehow, you were." She stops and takes a deep breath.

Maybe I'm slow on the uptake but I still don't get why she believed my father.

"It didn't take much to convince me my life was too screwed up to drag you into it, to convince me I wasn't good enough for you. I didn't think beyond any of the different life experiences nonsense much anyway because I was wrecked thinking about the other things your father told me. Thinking about you marrying someone else? It hurt. Really hurt. The pain was physical. I thought I was having a heart attack. I couldn't even breathe, let alone think straight."

She places her hand on mine and it occurs to me how petite and fragile her hand is on mine.

"After I got past the initial pain, I tried to convince myself the wealthy California girl was better for you, the kind of girl who fit into your lifestyle and could make you happy...until I saw you and the hurt floodgates reopened, followed by a volcano of anger." She hesitates. "I thought about scratching her eyes out. But, well, I don't like to fly."

One corner of her mouth quirks up and she shrugs. I know what she's doing. She's trying to make a joke out of this fucked up situation. It's the same thing we always used to do: joke around about everything, keep everything light. But I don't smile or return the sarcasm like I would have done in the past. I'm trying to process what she's telling me. I can't find a reason to smile about any of this.

Nikki slides off the bed and walks over to the towel she had dropped on the floor. I can't take my eyes off her as she bends to pick it up and then holds it in front of her body.

She's an artist's dream of God's flawless female form: perfect curves, perfect tits—which look as if they're slightly larger than I remember—long blonde hair, creamy skin, full pouty lips, soul-penetrating eyes. Christ. Not just an artist's dream, she's *every* man's wet dream come to life. But the first time I saw her she wasn't beautiful. I mean, she *was,* I just couldn't tell.

It was at a soccer game. The girls' team was having a stellar season and we'd heard about the new freshman who was breaking records all over the field. Some of the other guys and I went to a home game to check out the new soccer star.

We had practice and got there late. The game was into the second quarter. We knew immediately the girl with blue bangs and long blonde ponytail swaying from side to side as she out-maneuvered her opponents was the new hotshot on the team. She was lightning fast, dribbling the ball down field, cutting in one direction with the ball while glaring right into her opponent's eyes and then making a quick cut in the other direction to fake out the opposing player. Then setting up the perfect pass strategy, she placed herself in the right place to rocket launch the ball into the net.

The guys were blown away. Her skills were off the charts. But as for her physical appearance, she was covered in mud and sweat; no indication of the goddess under all the grime.

I knew I had to find out who number five on the soccer team was. Something pulled at me, told me I had to meet her and find out more about her. I told the guys I'd meet them back at the house. They didn't pay attention to me when I took off and chased after her like a puppy chasing a ball as she was leaving the field. She was gathering her things from the team bench and stuffing them into a gym bag.

"Hey." The intelligent greeting the only thing I could think of to say.

When she looked up and hit me with those baby blues, I had to remind myself to breathe.

"Hey." One word. That was it and she started walking off the field toward the field house. I stood baffled for a moment. I'd never had a problem talking to a girl before and they usually didn't walk away from me when I did. I ran to catch up to her.

"Great game. You were amazing out there."

"Yeah, thanks." She just kept walking, even picked up the pace like she was trying to get away from me.

"I'm...I'm Dalt by the way." Like an idiot I stuck my hand out to shake hers. She stopped and stared at my outstretched hand but didn't make a move because her hands were full with her bag and some of the equipment.

"I know who you are, hockey boy." The words 'hockey

boy' came out like they tasted sour on her tongue. And she started walking away from me again. I couldn't believe it. When I caught up to her, she stopped and turned to me.

"What do you want, hockey boy?" She threw me off my game so bad, I think I stuttered.

"I...um...your name would be nice for starters."

"For starters?" She quirked a brow.

"Then I thought you might like to get a beer or a burger or something at the Thirsty Whale." She scanned my body from head to toe and back up. Then the damnedest thing happened.

"No thanks. I don't do dates. Not looking for a boyfriend. I just like to, you know, keep my options open." Say what, now! Had she just turned me down for a date? Not that a burger and beer was really a date but I had never even offered that much to a girl I didn't know. I didn't want them getting the wrong idea, thinking I was asking them on a date.

I was dumbfounded. It took me a minute to regain my equilibrium and glance up to see her twenty feet ahead of me. And you guessed it. I chased her just like a fucking puck bunny.

"That's good because I don't do dates either. I'm not boyfriend material, if you know what I mean. Just sort of play the field." Christ. I babbled like a nervous virgin, grinned like an ass, and flicked my thumb over my shoulder in the direction of the field. She gave me a side-ways glance like I was some kind of lunatic and kept walking.

"Just figured it was dinner time and you were probably

heading to eat anyway. I thought I'd offer. Have you ever been there?"

She stopped, shrugged and let out a sigh. "Where?"

"The...the Thirsty Whale."

"No. Not yet."

"Awesome. Then let me take you. My treat." Her eyes narrowed and I thought she was getting ready to walk away once more.

"Not a date, just a celebratory dinner for the great game you played. You know, one athlete to another." I remember wondering what the ever-loving hell I was talking about.

She pursed her lips and sighed again. "Okay. I have to shower. Wait for me outside the locker room," I shit you not, I had to stop myself from clapping and jumping up and down like a kid on Christmas morning.

"Hey, soccer girl?" I called to her as she pushed the door open to the field house.

"Yeah?"

"What's your name?"

"Nikki." The corners of her mouth tipped up in a coy smile and ladies and gentlemen, game over. I was already totally fucked.

Twenty minutes later when she walked out of the locker room, her hair in braids, wearing a red wool knitted hat, Mickey Mouse leggings, a thick black wool army sweater that appeared to be three sizes too big for her, and black Dr. Marten boots, I think my heart stopped beating for a few seconds. She was the most beautiful girl I'd ever seen.

End of story. We were together from then on. Once I got to know her, I found out there was way more to Nikki than physical beauty.

Even though she had some rough patches in her life, like losing her dad when she was only twelve and then having to deal with a scumbag stepfather, those things never defined her. She held onto her love for life, her optimism, and her determination to make her way.

Sure, her experiences may have caused her to adapt by taking on a bit more of a tough warrior exterior off the soccer field as well as on, but I saw the vulnerability, the touches of insecurity which revealed a glimpse of her need for someone to have her back. I wanted that someone to be me. I even made up a silly nickname for her, my Strawberry Bud. Like one of those candies, hard on the outside but gooey, sweet warmth on the inside.

What a joke. I was supposed to have her back. Instead, because she hooked up with me, she crossed paths with my father. Not even Nikki is strong enough to fight a seasoned monster like him. He ripped her heart out and kicked her when she was down.

Still, her lack of faith in me breaks my heart. We were good together, until she bought the whole bullshit story the bastard sold her, never once giving me the benefit of the doubt.

"I'm sorry, Dalt." Her hushed words remind me she's standing there watching me, no doubt waiting for me to say something. When I don't, she says, "I believed every-thing your father said because...I don' know...maybe you're right, maybe I am some kind of reverse snob. I was persuaded into thinking our lives were too different for you to ever pick me over Malib...over the girl in California. I guess...I guess I didn't think I deserved you. Guess that's why it was easy for him to convince me of all the lies."

Her voice is quiet, defeated. She turns toward the door. I don't tell her she's wrong or move to stop her. I can't. My brain is still doing battle with my heart.

For two years she's avoided me, hated me, put us both through hell, all because she didn't believe in me enough to know I would never do something like the disgusting thing my father pulled.

She believed I was capable of that kind of cruelty.

The thought keeps hammering in my head.

The door slamming closed jerks me out of my thoughts. I sit frozen in place, unable to wrap my head around everything that's happened between us. Although my brain may be trying to hold me captive, spouting all the clichés about love and trust, my heart wins the battle and wills me to move.

"Wait! Nikki!" I jump off the bed. I'm still naked, but I can't take time to find clothes. I can't lose her, can't let her walk out of my life again. I'm so fucking in love with her. I can't think about the shit that pulled us apart. I just need to figure out a way to put us back together.

When I step into the hallway, she's standing outside the door sobbing. Sobbing! My Nik, who hates to cry. I put myself in her place, think about what she must have felt the night my father ambushed her with lies, what she must have been going through all these months. My father is a malevolent force too great for any sweet, unsuspecting girl to overcome. Hell. He even had *me* convinced I needed to follow the path he chose for me. Not anymore. Never again.

I reach out for her hand and thread my fingers through hers. "You said you were in love with me, Nik, as in *were* in love in the past tense or are you *still* in love with me?" She's clutching the towel in front of her and has her head down, eyes fixed on the floor as she gasps for air in between sobs.

I place my hand under her chin and tilt her head up to look into her eyes. The joy has been replaced by shimmering sapphire pools of sadness. Fuck. What have I done to her? My father and I did a great job of draining the happiness and warmth from those beautiful blue eyes.

"It's not a trick question, Bud. Are you still in love with me or not?"

If she says no, I'll die for the second time today.

I move closer. We're still holding hands and her other arm is between us grasping her towel. Bowing my head and placing my forehead on hers, I take a minute to breathe in her sweet strawberry scent, another reason for her nickname.

God. I've missed her scent filling my senses, infusing my sheets.

"Because I'm still so in love with you, I want to swallow you and then I'll never have to let you go. I can just keep you inside of me forever," I say in a soft voice. I want to give her a minute to let my words permeate her heart and mind. "Please tell me I haven't lost you. Please tell me you still love me."

I should have told her how much I love her a long

time ago. If she knew, she would never have believed my manipulative father. She still hasn't said a word. She gazes at me, her beautiful eyes glistening. The sadness has been replaced by questioning uncertainty.

"Say something, baby. You're driving me crazy here."

"I've been such a fool, Dalt. How can you still love me?" she whispers.

"I'm not going to argue with you, soccer girl. You've been seriously foolish not to see how much I love you." I place a kiss on the tip of her nose. "But I was an even bigger fool not to say the words out loud, tell you how much you mean to me. How about we make a deal?"

She scowls. "I think I've had just about enough *deals* from you Walkers."

"Not that kind of fuck wad deal." I feather kisses over the tears on her cheek. "I mean a deal to start over."

I want to crash my mouth to hers. Let my lips show her what I'm feeling. But she's been living in an even worse kind of hell than I have these past months, hearing my father's sick lies play on repeat inside her head. I have to let her make the decision where she wants to go from here. Wherever it is, I fucking hope it includes me.

"A deal to erase the past two years." Moving further down her face, I place another kiss on the side of her lips. They taste salty sweet. "A deal to forget all the past crap and just remember how much we love each other." I touch another gentle kiss to the other side of her lips. "What do ya say? Can you do that for me?"

"I love you so much, Dalt." She throws her arms around my neck and her towel falls to the floor. We're skin to skin. Her body pressed onto mine. My cock is already straining to be welcomed home.

She showers my face with kisses and after a moment we're both giggling. Her laughter is the most beautiful sound I've ever heard. I let out the huge breath I didn't even know I was holding. I can breathe freely for the first time in a long time. My world is back on its correct orbital path. I'm centered, not spinning out of control. I know where I'm going, what I need to do. I have my girl back in my arms where she belongs. It's just the beginning of the way I'm going to make her eyes twinkle with happiness like they did before.

"You want to swallow me to keep me inside of you all the time? That's kind of weirdo creepy, hockey boy," she teases. "By the way, you do realize those Strawberry Bud candies are gross, right?"

There's my little smartass bringing me back to reality. No poetic mush for her.

I lift her off her feet and spin her around before walking her back to the bed to finish what we started. The need for her raging through my body is overpowering.

"I don't know about the candy, but my girl is so fucking sweet I'm going to begin the swallowing right this very second." I lay her across the bed.

Her face is flushed red from crying and her eyes are swollen. Droplets of tears cling to her long golden lashes. She's the most gorgeous thing I've ever seen. And the way those eyes are beaming up at me, filled with tenderness fueled by wanton need, has my heart racing fast enough to crack a rib.

I crawl over her. I can sense the tension of her arousal. Fire races from my body to hers. Placing my hands on either side of her face, I lean in and gaze directly into her smoldering liquid eyes. I trace the seam of her lips with my tongue.

She opens with a hungry invitation and I'm right there with her, starving for what I've been missing all these months. Our tongues swirl and curl together. We feed off each other with ravenous urgency, making up for the time we've lost.

I'm going to kill my fucking father for causing us to lose that time.

The angry thought flashes across my mind, but I push it away. I can't think about him now. I have Nikki, *my* Nikki, here writhing under me. She's the only person I want to think about. My world is right when I'm with her.

"Nik," I moan against her lips. "There's about a million things I want to do to you, and I promise I'm going to do every one of them...but...right now I need to fuck you so hard and deep...."

"Do it. Do it, Dalt. Hard," she demands, and wraps her legs around my waist, pressing her heels into my back.

I close my eyes and with one quick thrust I ram myself home. Christ. She's so wet and tight. Even though it's not our first time, every time I fuck her it feels like it is.

My need for her is primitive. I keep pumping into her with relentless thrusts, harder and faster, like I'm trying to punish her. Punish her for not believing in me enough, punish her for keeping us apart for all these months, punish her for making me love her so much there's no air in my world if she's not in it. There's nothing soft or gentle about it. This is months of wanting her, needing her, and not being able to have her.

My cock is ruthless, plowing into her. With each deep, hard thrust she clenches me, grips me tighter, and moans my name, like she's begging me to relieve her own frustrated need. I'm hanging on to my control by a thread. The inferno of pleasure keeps building like a ticking bomb ready to detonate as we keep kissing, touching, groaning, and I keep pounding into her.

"*Fuck*, Nik. It's so good. I can't hold back. I'm gonna come."

"Dalt! Oh God. Yes!" She screams as she ignites in forceful spasms around me. With one more deep thrust I explode into her. Her soft, warm pussy keeps milking my cock with tight clenches, while I fill her with what seems like never ending pulses of heated release.

When I collapse on top of her we're both gasping for air. Fucking Nikki is beyond any physical or emotional experience I've ever had. With her I'm completely out of control, unguarded, defenseless. It's almost like a supernatural out of body experience.

Pushing myself up on my elbows, I place a soft kiss on her lips.

She puts her hand on the nape of my neck to pull me in closer. "Wow that...that was..."

"Yeah. It was." I never want to pull out. I could stay like this forever. Only then, when I finally slide out of her do I remember. "Oh fuck."

"I know. I don't want to move either. I just want you inside me all the time." She sighs.

"No...I mean yes, babe. I wish I could stay inside you forever but...shit...no condom. Sorry. Second time you've made me this crazy I forgot what I was doing."

Her relaxed muscles stiffen underneath me when I mention the lack of a condom.

"It's...it's okay. I'm on the pill this time."

This time.

We got lucky the last time, the only other time in my life I was senseless out of my mind with hunger for her and forgot to saddle up. Nikki has that effect on me. It was the night we had been out celebrating after our winning games. When Nikki climbed on my lap in the car and begged me to fuck her, chasing her Jägermeister fueled desire, I was triggered to a DEFCON 1 and couldn't get inside her fast enough.

I don't ask why she's been taking the pill, since *we* haven't been together. I know she's been with other guys in the months we've been apart and it kills me, but I haven't exactly been a saint. I assume her tense reaction to my lack of protection is because she's worried about where *my* dick has been. I continue trailing kisses down her neck.

"You don't have to worry, babe. I haven't been with anyone since the last time we were together." I gave up trying to forget Nikki by fucking my way through the puck bunnies after the night of the keg party. I knew there was no way I could ever forget her by using meaningless one-night stands.

"You haven't?" she laces her fingers into my hair and uses it to tug my head up to look into my eyes.

"Oww-wah?"

"But it was months ago. Like the beginning of the semester at the—"

"At the first keg party we had at our house. Yeah. I remember. Like I said, the next morning I rushed out and got this tattoo like some lovesick co-ed. That night, it's all I've been living on...thinking about for all these months."

"You were pretty drunk. I wasn't sure you even remembered, let alone *this*." She lets go of my hair and trails her fingers over the infinity tattoo.

"Not remember? Are you kidding me, Bud? I remember every single thing about you from every time we've ever been together. The way you purse your lips to one side when I say something that annoys you, the way your eyes get all liquidy when I say something romantic, or the way they get all fiery when I say something dirty, the way you taste, your scent, how your fingers feel touching me, how your lips feel wrapped around me, how it feels to be inside you, how your nipples respond to my touch." I run my fingertips across one of her breasts with a light touch and her nipple puckers in response just like it always does. Also something I remember: she loves a little sweet dirty talk. If I have to, I'll keep whispering in her ear 24/7 to keep her wet just for me.

"Dalt? Mmmm."

Fuuuck. She's moaning and arching into me and my dick is as hard as granite. She, on the other hand, is soft and warm from the flush of our lovemaking and she smells like heaven.

"Yeah? What is it babe?"

"Thank you for telling me that. I love you," she whispers and then begins nibbling and sucking a path down my neck.

Now I understand how the Grinch's heart grew ten sizes inside his chest, because it's exactly what mine just did.

"I love you too, Nik." I press a hard kiss onto her lips and rock my hips into her to show her what she does to me. I'm rigid with need, straining to push into her once more.

"Mmm. As much as I want to flip you over and ride you like a surfboard, I'm starving." Her words touch my lips.

Say what?

I lift my head to look at her just to make sure I heard her right. Her beautiful face is still flushed but now languid with contentment. "Did...did you just say you want to ride me like a surfboard, Beyoncé?" I chuckle, remembering how Nik always used these inventive terms to describe my cock or how she was going to ride it: 'ride the bull', 'nail your love hammer', 'hide the puck', a few examples of her creativity. They would have been ridiculous if they hadn't come from Nikki's prolific imagination. Slipping out of her delectable lips, the peculiar metaphors succeeded in sending surges of warm blood down to said 'love hammer.' Surfboard is a new one, but the idea is having the same, even more enlarging, effect.

"What? Dak's been teaching Trace the positions and

dynamics for surfing and she's been explaining them to me. We both decided surfing is like sex. You have to get up on the board, wait for the climax of the wave, grip the board with everything you have, and then ride the wave to blissful completion. Trace and I said it's like fucking and Dalt said, '*Well, yeah, almost as good.*' Sooo, I'm going to ride you like a surfboard." She tilts her head and gives me a cute little grin and then taps the tip of my nose. Like I said, every man's wet dream.

"The thought of you riding me any way you want is fine by me, but please stop talking about Dak and *his* surfboard while you're talking about riding mine." She giggles under me and the sensation penetrates my soul. "Tell you what, if you promise to give me a *surfing* lesson afterwards I'll treat you to those blueberry pancakes now."

"Oh, you're definitely treating me to those pancakes, hockey boy. You already promised those if I went running with you." She pushes me off her and scoots off the bed.

"No surfing lessons?" I pout and give her my best puppy dog eyes.

"You are totally getting those surfing lessons. But for *that* I expect dinner." She winks and walks out of the room with a little sway to her hips. My dick twitches in hopeful anticipation. Sorry, dude. Hang onto the thought, though.

Chapter Fourteen

NIKKI

Oh my God. What just happened?

*Dalt loves me, is **in** love with me!*

Maybe I *am* dreaming. If I am, I never want to wake up.

I close my bedroom door behind me and do the most joy filled happy dance I've ever done in my life. I even do the one thing I'm always telling Chloe not to do; I climb on the bed and start jumping up and down, screeching and giggling while swinging my towel over my head.

"Hey, you okay in there, soccer girl?" Dalt calls from down the hall. I can hear the smile in his words. He knows exactly what's going on in here and that I'm more than okay.

"I'm just fine, hockey boy. I'll be right out. Don't think you're getting out of buying me breakfast that easily." I jump off the bed and head back into the shower.

I can't believe this whole thing has been a gargantuan

misunderstanding initiated by his awful father and bought hook, line, and sinker by gullible me. As I lather my strawberry body wash over me, my skin warms at the thought of Dalt's words and how incredible it was to make love to him after all this time.

I never thought he would remember the last time we were together at the party. My mind drifts back to that night as I towel off and blow-dry my hair.

I didn't want to delude myself into thinking the night was about anything more than the hottest sex ever. I knew, or at least I *thought* I knew, Dalt didn't have any feelings for me. It didn't matter. I couldn't give up the chance to be with him one more time. I was sure Dalt was just using me, but I ached for him so hard...I let him.

I couldn't fight my need for him in the deceitful, seductive darkness, but in the disenchanting light of day I knew I had made another irresponsible mistake. Later, I didn't answer his calls or texts, like before. The next time I saw him on campus, I went right back to acting like I hated him. Meanwhile, he was out getting my name branded on his arm. Damn. He must have thought I was the biggest crazy ass bitch on the planet.

"You almost ready in there, Bud?" Dalt's knock on the door thumps my brain back to the here and now.

"Be right out." I give myself a once over in the mirror. No time for makeup. Alex would be appalled. The last time I tried to go out without makeup, he said I was 'obliterating his faith in womanhood.' Alex is *very* dramatic. But running in the sunshine earlier gave my cheeks a sun-kissed glow. I don't need makeup. What I don't tell Alex won't destroy his faith in womankind.

I shake my blown dry hair out and let it fall around my shoulders, then slip into the vintage sundress I scored at an antique shop a few months ago. It's just my style, black and white polka dots, fit and flare, with thin straps. What little shopping I do, I do at vintage clothing stores because I can get the quirky vibes I'm into without the big price tag. I step into some strappy black sandals which tie around my ankles. Could be a little much for a breakfast at the Two Seagulls Café, but it *is* springtime casual and I want to look good for Dalt.

When I open my bedroom door, I'm pretty sure I've succeeded because his languid, heated gaze sweeps from my head to my toes and back.

"Day-amn, Nik. You look good." He whistles.

"Is that supposed to be a compliment, hockey boy? You sound surprised."

"Not surprised at all," he says and pulls me into his arms and touches his forehead to mine. "It's just that as dope as this dress is, you're not going to be needing it when we get back from breakfast."

Dalt has one of those you-know-you-want-me bad boy half grins and he's using it on me right now. He's right. I *do* want him. I've never stopped wanting him, and I intend on making up for lost time.

I give him my sexy dirt-girl smirk right back. "You don't look so bad yourself. Dak's clothes fit you pretty well."

One thing about the resident hockey gods here at Bernard U, they train off ice as hard as they do on. It makes for all kinds of Michelangelo-type sculpted muscles. Dak's V-neck black t-shirt is stretched across

Dalt's broad shoulders and toned pecs to the point where I would almost consider skipping breakfast.

On second thought, I'm starving and those pancakes are calling to me. "Let's go eat, hockey boy. I'm anxious to get back for your surfing lessons." I run my hand over the roped lines of muscle stretching his shirt and down over the reenergized shaft straining his khaki shorts. "Damn, girl. You're killing me," he moans. I take his hand and lead his reluctant body out of the house.

"Ugh. I'm so full I don't think I can move."

The Two Seagulls is a small restaurant with a handful of tables. The quaint décor is the usual Maine seaside assortment of buoys, lobster traps, fishing nets, and vintage glass floats hanging from the walls. Red and white gingham cloth adorns the tables and makes up the ruffled café curtains covering the bottom half of the windows.

Yet the decor isn't what brings locals in-the-know back to the café over and over. It's the dinner plate-sized blueberry pancakes they serve; the biggest, most delicious pancakes in all of Maine. They use fresh locally picked blueberries and I become an overeating glutton whenever I'm here.

The last time I overindulged was back when Dalt and I were together. It was our Sunday morning, usually after hunger-causing sex, energy rebuilding ritual. And now here we are like all that time and heartache never passed between us. Things are different, though. At least one very important, beautiful thing.

I have to tell him about Chloe, find the right words. How do I tell him I kept his baby girl from him? I thought I was justified doing it, but after what Dalt said about my lack of trust for him, will *he* think I was justified? Will he hate me? I'm scared to death he will. It's messed up. I shouldn't be stalling. I have to tell him. He needs to know about his daughter, deserves my complete honesty, even if it's two years too late.

"You're slacking on me. I've seen you devour way more than that. You sure you can't eat another stack?" Dalt's staring at me like he's waiting for an answer, but I was too wrapped up in my own thoughts to hear what he asked.

"Huh?"

"Are you still with me, soccer girl? You look like you're a million miles away."

"I'm here. What'd ya say?"

He reaches across the table and places his hand on mine. "You don't have to worry, Nik. We're together now. We'll work it all out. I'm not going anywhere. As long as we're together and we trust each other and are honest with each other, there's nothing we can't do."

He laces his fingers through mine. His words 'honest with each other' bounce around my brain like a pinball.

This is it. This is the time for me to tell him. Yet I can't make my mouth move. What do I say? *Oh yeah, by the way, did I mention we have a beautiful baby girl? Yup. She looks exactly like you.*

"Stop looking like that, Nik. Fuck my father! He's an

egotistical, narcissistic asshole. Who cares what he thinks? I don't need him or want him in my life for one more second. All I want is you," Dalt snarls, misinterpreting my perplexed expression.

Since he mentioned it, it occurs to me his whole future is built around going to work alongside his brother at his father's production company. "You can't just push your dad out of your life, Dalt. I suppose in his own warped way he was acting out of love for you, trying to protect you. He and Garrett are your family." I'm not sure I believe my own words after his father's behavior, but I don't want to be the reason for putting a wedge between Dalt and his family.

"You're my family now," he smiles and runs his thumb across my bottom lip. "My father has never done anything out of love for anyone but himself. And I still have Garrett even if I don't work with him. He'll support me whatever I do. We always have each other's back."

"But what will you do? How will you afford to finish school? Is your hockey scholarship enough? Besides, you always planned on working for him. What will you do if you don't join his company?" My ramble of questions isn't giving him a chance to answer, but I won't be the reason he messes up his future.

He lets go of my hand and runs his fingers back through his hair like he does when he's frustrated, but this time he's still smiling. "I don't need his money, Nik. I never did. It was my mom who had the money. She came from old money, like generations of oil and steel. Shit, it was probably the reason the bastard married her. She set him up in the production company when he first started out. I don't think he ever really loved her. She wasn't even dead yet and he was out whoring around with twenty-year old wannabe starlets."

"Wow. That sucks. I'm so sorry." I reach for his hand once more, not only because I want to comfort him in some small way but also because I love how I can touch him without hesitation now.

"Yes. It does," he says, wrapping his big hand around mine. "Anyway, my mom left most of her money and investments to Garrett and me. We're pretty much set for life. My dad wasn't happy about it, but he didn't need her money anymore now that he's one of the biggest producers in Hollywood. Still, I think it's the reason he tries to do whatever he can to keep us close to him and buy our affection with expensive cars and shit. But all that's done. His conniving almost cost me my girl." His voice softens and his intense silver blue eyes are boring a path right down to my soul. "I'm never going to let anything get between us again."

"I don't want to be the reason you cut your dad out of your life. I know what it's like to live without a father."

I was twelve when my dad died trying to rescue another fireman in a house fire. A day hasn't gone by since I haven't thought about him and missed him.

"You're not the reason I'm done with him, Nik. Well, you're not the *only* reason. He was a major asshole to my mom and he wasn't even around when she was dying. We hired round the clock palliative care for her so she could stay home with us at the end. My father said he couldn't stomach seeing her like that. Instead of staying home with her, he travelled around the world for the last few months she was alive. I hated him for that, for the extra pain he caused my mom. Garrett kept smoothing it over, telling me our father loved her so much it was just too painful for him and we should cut him some slack.

"I knew it was bullshit. Garrett always sees through rose-colored glasses when it comes to our dad. Still, I wanted to hold onto what was left of our family for my mom's sake so I let it slide. A few weeks later photos came out of him and some model on his yacht in the Caribbean. My mom was dying and he was partying on his fucking yacht. I'm done. The shit he pulled with you was the last straw." His words are angry but I see the torment simmering in his eyes.

"Okay, he's not a good man. I kind of figured that out two years ago. But he's still your father, Dalt."

"Yeah. Sucks for me. He was never there for us when we were kids. My mom always made excuses for him, saying it took a lot of time to build a successful business and he was doing it all for us. I could see the sorrow in her eyes though. He was probably out cheating on her even then."

"I'm sorry, Dalt."

"Doesn't matter. It's all spilled milk under the bridge. I'm done with him."

"I think it's water under the bridge."

"What is?"

"The saying, it's water under the bridge."

"Whatever. I don't care what's under the bridge. I just know I don't want anything to do with him. And when I have kids," he reaches for my other hand, holding on to both of mine across the table, "I'll never treat my family the way that asshole treated us."

"Uh...okay...I..." My words catch in my throat. The pancakes I just ate are churning like they're going through the heavy wash cycle in my stomach. "Then, what are you going to do when you graduate?" I change the subject like the weak coward I am.

What's the alternative? *Surprise! You can prove what a great baby daddy you are right this very second.*

"I have some plans. Let's talk about all this later though. Enough serious talk for now. Let's enjoy the rest of this beautiful day just thinking about you and me. I'll get the check and then let's get out of here."

"Okay." I tighten my fingers around his. "I'm sorry, Dalt. I'm sorry for having all these messed up issues."

"You don't have any messed up—"

"Yes. I do. Ever since...even though I want to, sometimes I have a hard time trusting people, seeing the good side of people. I let it screw us up. I knew you better, or at least I *should* have."

"It's okay, Bud. You..."

I let go of one of his hands and place my hand over his mouth. "No. It's not okay. I just want you to know, despite all my hang-ups, I've never stopped loving you and I'm going to try to be different...better, in the future."

He grabs my wrist and pushes my hand away from his mouth. "No. If you try to be different I'll...nothing. I can't do anything about it if you want to be different. But I don't need or want you to be different, Nik. You're the girl I fell in love with and you're perfect just the way you are. Sure, maybe I wish you had asked me what was going on before believing my father, but I know the things you've dealt with in the past with your stepdad. It's hard to trust after something like that. We'll figure it all out. We've got each other to lean on now. It's just you and me and all the time in the world."

"Um...about that..."

It isn't just you and me.

"Let's finish this later. Like I said, no more serious talk today. We wasted enough time on the negative stuff. Let's focus on the positive for now. I was thinking we should fly out to Malibu and meet up with everyone. We could use a vacay in sunny California. What do ya think?"

"What? No!" My response comes out a little more panicked than I intended. "I mean, I can't just run off to Malibu."

"I didn't expect you to run, soccer girl. I intended for us to fly. All expenses are on me." His dimpled smirk almost makes me forget the reason I can't fly off to Malibu with him.

"It's not the money. It's not *just* the money. I have major projects to finish over the break and I have to help with the spring work at the farm and...and other things."

Tell him. Tellhimtellhimtellhim.

"You can finish your schoolwork on the beach. I hear some of the most creative artists did their best work at the seashore. I'll come to the farm and help with the shearing so it'll get done faster. We can fly out in a couple of days."

*Dammit. He's so happy and beautiful and perfect. I **don't** deserve him.*

"*No!* I mean, there's no need for you to help at the farm. My mom has a new farmhand. Well, he's not new; he's been there for over a year now. He manages everything and does most of the work. I just help out a little in the spring. Anyway, I'd rather spend the rest of our break alone together. Take the time to get to know each other again, you know?"

You're such a bullshit coward, Nikki. Just tell him you have a baby girl you can't leave.

"Anywhere you are sounds perfect to me, Bud. If you want to stay here, we stay here."

"I'll go home tomorrow and take a day to get things squared away and then I'll explain everything. Then we can spend some of the break at the farm after."

"Explain everything?" His brow furrows in confusion.

"You know. Talk more about...everything."

I need a day to talk things over with my mom and then try to explain to a twenty-month-old she has a daddy who will hopefully be a big part of her life from now on.

"Oh right. *Everything.*" Dalt waggles his brow. Apparently, his idea of 'everything' involves a bit more than talking. "We have the rest of today to get busy doing some of those things and I was thinking..." He slants his lips to one side and tilts his head.

"Yes, you were thinking?" I'm pretty sure I know exactly what he's thinking because I am too.

"It's perfect weather for sailing. You into it?"

"Sailing? Like in a *boat*?" Nope. Totally not what I was thinking.

"Exactly like in a boat. You up for it?"

"Sure, but I'm not exactly dressed for sailing." I glance down at my vintage dress.

"We can run by your house and you can change. It's still early. We have all day."

I should be finishing my course work and getting back to the farm to be with Chloe and help my mom, but I can't drag myself away from Dalt yet.

He misinterprets my hesitance. "Oh, don't worry, soccer girl. I'm still looking forward to those lessons you promised me. But like I said, we have all day *and* night." His sexy half grin causes butterflies to flit around in the tossing pancakes in my stomach.

Just one more day.

I'll tell him about Chloe first thing tomorrow morning.

Chapter Fifteen

DALT

"Wow. Whose is this?" Nikki stands on the dock gaping up at my sailboat.

"It's mine. Did you think we were hijacking a boat?" Laughing, I climb aboard my thirty-foot Oceanis.

"Yours? Are you kidding me?"

She's too damn cute standing there in those tiny gym shorts I love, black Tom and Jerry tank top, with the army surplus backpack she bought in a thrift store two years ago when we were together slung over one shoulder. Her hair is pulled up in a ponytail and the excited expression lighting up her face makes me want to skip the sailing, take her below, and shimmy her out of those shorts to show her how exciting the *interior* of this boat can be.

"Nope. Not kidding. She's all mine. Can you hand me the cooler with the food?" When I brought Nikki back to her house to change her clothes, I remembered Dak still had a set of keys to my house on his keychain on a table next to Nikki's front door. I used it to get into my house, change into swim trunks, and fill a cooler with some food for us. The refrigerator on the boat is already stocked with drinks.

"Food? Are we running away?" She hoists the cooler and her backpack up to me.

"Not exactly. I just thought we could take that camping trip out to the island we never got to take."

"Camping trip?" She shades her eyes from the sun with the palm of her hand. "I told you I have to go back to the farm tomorrow. Remember?"

"I remember. But it still gives us all night tonight. Right? Or we can just have a picnic on the island and head back before it gets dark. Whatever you want. So, you coming aboard or you afraid Captain Jack here is going to pirate you away?"

She's still standing on the dock, shielding her eyes from the sun and staring at me like I've lost my mind.

"You own a sailboat? I don't think I can be with you after all, pretty boy. First a Maserati, then I find out you're richer than Croesus, and now this." She laughs as she climbs on board.

"I'll give it all away to charity if you promise to stay in my life, soccer girl." I turn on the engine to warm it up before we cast off.

"Maybe you can just keep the boat...for now." She smiles. "When did you get this beauty?"

"Um...right after you left me. It was my refuge.

Someplace to get away and think about everything, or *not* think about everything. It's peaceful out here. It quiets the mind."

Nikki walks around and explores the boat. She takes a few steps below deck to drop her backpack.

"You sailed her alone?" she asks, coming back up on deck but keeping her eyes pinned to the cabin below. I know by the tone of her voice exactly what she's thinking when she sees the elaborate layout of the cabin, especially the plump, cushy white sofa benches. Wait till she gets a load of the bedrooms.

I know it's a dick thing to do but I can't resist stringing her along just a little. I mean, come on. As much as I love her, this girl had me strung out for two years. A minute of innocent retaliation can't hurt.

"No. Not always," I answer in a slow, taunting tone.

"Oh...right. You obviously have all the comforts of home down there. You could probably stay out here for days. Secluded, lots of privacy, no one to bother you and...whoever." She's still staring down below deck when I come up behind her and wrap my arms around her waist, causing her to jump in surprise.

"It *is* well stocked with provisions to spend days out here." I kiss the soft skin behind her ear. "And it is *very* secluded, private and..."—I trail kisses down the length of her neck—"...the beds *are* pretty comfortable."

She trembles in my arms. I love how I can make her respond like this.

"Hmmph. Your own floating lair of sin. How nice for you," she jeers and twists around to face me. "On second thought, it's probably better if I leave today to go home. I have a lot to do." She tries to push out of my arms.

"Nik, baby. Stop." I can't hold back the chuckle, which I can see is getting her even angrier.

"Let go of me and don't call me baby." She punches my shoulder.

I close my hand over her fist. "I'm sorry. I couldn't help myself. I'm just messing with you. I have never had another girl out here, just the guys."

"You haven't?"

"Nope."

"Not ever?" she asks in a relieved tone while running her hands down my chest. If they move down one more inch my cock has decreed there will be no sailing today.

"Not ever." I tilt my head to kiss her.

"You're such an asshole!" She punches me again.

"Ow." It doesn't hurt but I pretend it does and try to hold back the grin, because I can't deny I like that she's feeling territorial and jealous. "Sorry, babe." I continue to place kisses all over her face and neck. "Please forgive me. Just couldn't resist teasing you a little."

"That was mean." She pouts, but I feel her melting into my arms.

"We better get on the water or I'm going to have to give you a personal tour of my sleeping quarters and then this boat won't be leaving dock today."

"Sailing first, then *surfing*," she draws out the word and grinds her hips into my obvious erection, making my cock twitch in anticipation.

I let out a hungry growl and she giggles. I suppose I deserve her reciprocal teasing in payback for what I just did to her. Whose stupid idea was it to go sailing when I could have her underneath me right now?

"Come on. You take the helm. I'll get the bow and stern lines," she directs and pushes out of my arms.

It takes me a minute to get my thoughts back up to the head on my shoulders.

"Wait, you know how to sail?"

"Duh. I grew up in *Maine*, hockey boy," she mocks, one hand placed on her hip, her lips pursed and quirked to one side. "Learning to sail is like learning to walk." She gives me a slight grin.

Why is it every expression this girl makes is like a work of art for my eyes and a catalyst for my dick?

"Uh. Helllooo, Walker. You in there? You going to take the helm or you want me to?"

"Huh? No, I got it."

I wait for Nikki to release the lines and I move the boat forward away from the dock and out into the harbor. I keep it under engine power until we get out into open water. Nikki is sitting on the bench seat to the left of me and the whole time we're cruising out into Frenchman Bay I can't take my eyes off her. I've dreamt of this scenario so many times in the past few months, I can't wrap my head around it now. She's real and she's here.

Damn. She's beautiful. If the manufacturer of this boat could see what I see right now, they'd want to use this scene of an angel sailing on one of their boats for an advertising campaign. Watching her face beaming with happiness fills me with an inner peace I haven't felt since we were together. I'll never let anything take the joy out of her eyes or the happiness out of our lives again.

"You're staring at me, hockey boy." She tilts her head and the corners of her mouth tip up slightly.

"Just thinking how beautiful it is out here and what a perfect day it is."

She knows I'm totally bullshitting about the thoughts running through my head. She can read the longing in my eyes like a book. But besides being with the only person in the world I want to be with right now, it *is* a perfect day for sailing around the lush green islands off the coast.

It's unusually warm for this time of year. April weather in Maine can change in a blink of an eye. One minute a chilly forty degrees, and eighty the next, which is about where it is today. The cool wind coming across the ocean is keeping it a comfortable temperature.

"I thought we could sail around the bay before we dock at Stave Island. You good with that?"

"I'm more than good with that. This is amazing. I haven't been sailing since high school. One of my friends' fathers had a boat. I'm remembering how much I miss it."

"You're too good to be true, Nik. A girl who likes hockey, sailing, could probably nutmeg Ronaldo on the soccer field, *and* has an ass and tits like yours. I knew you were my soul mate the minute I saw you."

"Right. I know exactly what you mean," she says indifferently. "Remember the time you stripped out of your hockey uniform and stood in front of me naked except for your hockey pads?"

"Hey, that was on your request. I don't do a hockey strip for just anyone, you know." I laugh at the ridiculous memory. I have to admit though, it got Nikki so hot and bothered she dropped to her knees right in front of me and gave me a blow job which, on a scale of one to ten had to be about a ten thousand. Hmmm. Maybe I should get my gear out when we get back home.

"No. It was totally hot. I'm just sayin', when I saw you like that I said to myself, 'O-M-G I'm gonna marry this cock. He's totally my soul mate,'" she says in her best Valley Girl imitation and then slants her pursed lips to one side.

"Har har. Very funny, Bud."

"What? You're not the only one who can find their soul mate based upon the objectification of the person's body."

"I'm not complaining. Objectify away. If you want to stay with me based solely on the size of my cock I'm completely down with that. Just as long as you stay with me." I give her a devilish wink.

"Ugh," she groans. "You're a complete cave man."

"Yeah, but I'm *your* complete cave man." I laugh. "You ready to hoist the sails, soccer girl?"

"Aye, aye, Cap'n." Nikki salutes and moves to the halyard to pull up the main sail, cinches it with the winch, and then cleats it off. Then she does the same with the jib. The way she maneuvers the sails it's like she was born on a sailboat.

We tack around the harbor, me at the helm, Nikki at

the sails. As I take in the sight of her working the sails and the environment around us I heave a sigh of relief. The hell I've been living the past months without her is gone. Everything about her and this day is heaven.

Chapter Sixteen

NIKKI

When we get to Stave Island, we bring down and secure the sails, and Dalt anchors the boat just off the sandy beachside of the island. The island is beautiful, tranquil. It's like Dalt and I are the only two people in the world. Except I still haven't told him about the tiny human we made together and the guilt keeps jolting me out of the blissful peace the environment is providing. The most important thing to Dalt is honesty and trust. I can't think of anything that would be more of a breach in trust than this. I have to find the right words.

"You okay?" Dalt's arms wrapping around my waist from behind me startles me out of my thoughts. "Wow. Sorry. Didn't mean to scare you."

"You didn't scare me." I drop my head back onto his chest. "I was just thinking."

"Thinking about what?" He keeps his arms wrapped

around me and gently rocks us, matching the lulling movements of the anchored boat.

'How beautiful all of this is."

"The island?"

"The island, the ocean, the day, you. Everything's so beautiful, perfect."

"It is," he whispers in my ear.

"But I was also thinking about something your father said."

"Dammit, Nik!" He spins me around in his arms so we're face to face. "Forget everything that asshole said. It's not important. It was all lies."

I cup his cheek with my hand. "I know everything he said about the engagement and the money was lies but some of what he said is true."

"No!" He grabs my hand, holding it onto his cheek and squeezes, like he's trying to press the condemnation of his father into my fingers. "Everything that comes out of his mouth is bullshit lies."

"Except the part about our lives having been different."

"No, our lives—"

"Dalt." I cup his face between both of my hands to force him to look straight into my eyes. "Our lives *were* very different. You had everything, and like I said, I had nothing. There were times after my dad died I was lucky if I had a decent pair of shoes to wear to school."

"Those things mean nothing, Nik. Hear me. Feel me." He places my hand on his chest. "This is me, babe. I'm just me. We have each other now. It's all we need, all we'll ever need." If I ever had any doubt of loving this man, the beseeching expression in his eyes right now has crushed all uncertainty.

"I know." I wrap my arms around his neck and feather a kiss across his lips. "But all this has me realizing things I never thought about before. Even though we were poor, my life wasn't deprived. Except for the awful blip in our lives known as Bert, I believe we were rich in the most important sense. We lived a beautiful, clean, simple life and we loved each other. Growing up with my little family on the farm was an amazing experience."

"I get that, Nik. Except for the crap you had to go through with Bert, I never thought your life was anything but beautiful. And when I meet your mom I'm going to wrap her in a big hug and thank her for throwing that scumbag out and raising the perfect woman for me to fall desperately in love with." Dalt places a quick kiss on the tip of my nose. "Why are we talking about this? I told you, the money means nothing except for the things I can give you if you want them. Whatever you want, baby."

He's so earnest when promising me the moon and the stars. And when he gives me his lopsided grin, there's way more than butterflies taking flight inside me. It feels like a whole zoo of animals is doing acrobatics in my stomach. But even with all his heartfelt sincerity, I stop myself from being honest in return, from telling him the real reason I've been thinking about the discrepancies in our lives.

I still don't know how to tell him we have a little girl who is happy and loved and has been living a wonderful life despite the fact I kept her daddy away from her for her entire little life. How is he going to deal with that?

Especially when I think about his past, surrounded by every material desire, but devoid of love after his mom died. My heart breaks for him and the guilty weight of having kept his daughter's love from him for this long sits like a triceratops on my chest. If the tables were turned, if he had kept Chloe from me, would I be able to forgive him?

I sigh. "I'll settle for a picnic lunch and a cold bottle of water for now."

"Water? No cold beer?"

"No thanks. I'm trying to turn over a new leaf, clean up my diet a little."

I want this one perfect afternoon with him before I tell him the reason for my new leaf, before I reveal just how much of a fool I've been for the past two years and shatter his perfect illusion of me.

We pull the small raft we used to get from the boat to the beach onto the sandy shore. Dalt hoists out the cooler full of food and drinks we took out of the boat's fridge and carries it up to a shady spot under some trees. After spreading the plaid blanket I took from one of the storage benches on deck over the mossy grass, I plop down onto it.

Sitting with my knees pulled up to my chest, I wrap my arms around my legs and inhale, spending a moment to take in the beauty of the scenery all around us. Dalt lays down next to me and stretches, exposing a glimpse of chiseled abs, before tucking his arms under his head to use as a headrest. The only scenery I'm interested in now is the gorgeous manscape of humanity lying next to me.

"This is perfect, isn't it?" Dalt tilts his head up to view the ocean and the crystal blue horizon. "Just you and me, together, finally, in this beautiful world."

The hefty triceratops does a jumping jack on my chest.

I follow his gaze out over the horizon. "Um...yes...but it's..."

"Hey, Bud. Come here. What are you doing all the way over there?" Dalt stretches his arm out across the blanket. I slide down, curling up next to him. With a quick flex of his arm, he rolls me over on top of him so we're nose to nose. He holds me there for a moment, pressing my breasts into his hard chest. The intensity in his silver blue eyes makes me feel like I'm being pulled even further into him, drowning in their liquid power.

"I have a great idea," he says quietly in between brushing kisses across my lips.

"Uh huh. What's that?" I touch the whisper onto his lips and return the soft kisses.

"How about you give me those lessons you promised me?" he asks while continuing to trail kisses down my jaw and neck.

"Mmm. Right...right here? Outside...in...front of all of nature?" It's hard for my brain to remember how to make my mouth speak while he's holding me and kissing me like this.

"Yup. Right here," Dalt whispers, sliding his hands down my waist to my thighs. "In front of the birds and bees and anybody else who wants to watch us."

The way he's moving his hands in slow strokes up and down my legs has me moaning into his mouth. "Mmm...very...uh...clever...mmm...the way you referenced the birds and the bees there."

"*I* thought so." He nibbles my bottom lip and then his hands are on my ass, squeezing and kneading.

My pussy craves him, causing me to inadvertently rock into the massive shaft pushing into the fabric of my shorts. Though I consider myself a bit of a rebel, having sex outside in the middle of the afternoon where any one might happen to see us is just a little too rebellious, even for me.

"Ooo...wait, Dalt...stop." I sit up straight, my legs still straddled on either side of his hips. I have to put some distance between me and his soft, kissable lips to be able to think clearly.

"You want me to stop?" The confused expression scrunching his face makes me want to throw all sense out the window and crash my lips onto his; give him what he wants, what I want, out here in front of the birds, bees, squirrels, fish, and anyone else in the vicinity. But as a mother, I'm doing my best to be more levelheaded, trying to set better examples for Chloe. I'm pretty sure sex on a blanket on a public beach in broad daylight is not the action of a discerning mom.

"No, I don't want you to stop." His I'm-going-to-devour-you-grin is back, tipping up one side of his mouth. "But I have a better idea," I add before he has a chance to start touching me again. One more stroke of his hand and I won't be able to stop *myself* from tearing off his shorts to do some stroking of my own.

"You have a better idea than letting me push deep inside you while you're riding me until we both can't see straight?"

"Oh God," I groan and roll off him onto my back. My pussy clenches in protest, desperate for me to get right back to the splendor of being pressed against Dalt.

Dalt rolls onto his side facing me, props his arm under him, and rests his head on the palm of his hand. "I can't wait to hear this idea if it's better than that." He runs his fingers over the hint of skin peeking out from the bottom of my tank top. My skin pebbles in a needy response. When he skims over the elastic waist of my gym shorts, I place my hand on top of his to keep him from going any further. If he feels how wet and hot I am for him, there will be no stopping either one of us.

"I think we should have some lunch and then go for a swim," I suggest, pushing myself up into a seated position.

"That's it?" Dalt flops onto his back and lets out a huge breath. "That's your better idea? I think you've been away from me too long, sweetheart. You've lost all concept of the *great* things we do together."

"Oh, you think so?" I tug my tank top over my head and throw it across his face. When Dalt drags my discarded top off his face, I've already wriggled out of my nylon athletic shorts and I'm standing in front of him in my teeny black string bikini. My breasts have gotten a bit larger since having Chloe. The tiny strips of fabric making up the sliding triangles of the top are providing very little coverage and a whole lot of cleavage. The bottom is pretty much exactly what the style suggests, two strings tied on either side of my hips. Okay, I suppose this little number isn't exactly the type of example a sensible mom would wear, but this particular mom is only twenty-one and her baby daddy, who is hotter than a gamma ray burst, is drilling her with such intensity with his laser blue eyes, sensible be damned.

Dalt bolts up and reaches out for me, but I'm already running toward the water. I can almost feel the heat of his fiery glare scorching me. The shock of the cold water helps bring down the blazing rise in my body temperature.

My breath catches when I turn and see Dalt tug his t-shirt over his head and throw it across the blanket. I stop mid-giggle. *Chee-sus,* he's gorgeous. How is it possible for a man to have been put together like that? Not one damn flaw. If I hadn't already met his horribly flawed *human* father, I'd swear he was the offspring of immortal gods. The way the sun glistens off his tanned, ripped chest and abs is enough to put any woman in a mind-numbing stupor. Then there's those blessed-by-the-hockey-gods thighs. And don't even get me started on what he's got going on underneath his swim trunks between those thighs. Someone should make a plaster cast of that thing and put it in a museum as one of the wonders of the world. Seriously. How the hell is a normal, warm-blooded girl supposed to hold out when faced with all that? Lost in my distracted thought, I let out a huge sigh just as Dalt runs into the water and grabs me around the waist.

"You want to go for a swim, huh, soccer girl?" He laughs, lifting me off my feet and spinning me around.

"No! Dalt! Don't you dare!" The feel of his arms around me and his threat of dunking me into the icy water has me giggling in breathy protests. I try wiggling out of his grasp. When I realize my attempt to fight my way out of his powerful grip is a losing battle, I attempt a different, more *peaceful* tactic.

For just a moment I stop struggling, lean into him and tease my overflowing tits across his chest. I drop my head just enough to let my nose and lips brush along his neck. That's all it takes for every bit of Dalt's focus to take a nosedive straight to his cock. When it does, I take the opportunity to push myself out of his grasp and run backward away from him, laughing and splashing him with sprays of water.

"Oh, so you want to play like *that*, Bud? Game on!"

Dalt rushes toward me. I try to step from side to side to fake him out and outmaneuver him, but I can't get my footing while running in the soggy sand along the shoreline. Every time a wave crashes on shore, the squelchy sand washes out from under my feet. Dalt dives and grabs me around the legs. The next thing I know I'm sprawled on my back and Dalt's stretched out on top of me. An icy cold wave washes over us, pushing us further up onto the beach. We're both laughing in gasps, unable to catch our breath. When our eyes lock, the carnal longing in Dalt's eyes sends a jolt rippling through my body. Even in the cold water my body temperature skyrockets. The chilly water is having no effect on the thick, hard shaft straining his swim trunks. It's rubbing the perfect spot between my legs. The throbbing ache between my legs demands release with such intensity, I'm sure he must be able to feel it.

"I'm hungry," Dalt whispers, breaking the lust-filled silence.

"You're...you're *hungry*?" Not exactly what I was expecting him to say.

"Uh huh. And as soon as I get you off this damn beach I'm going to devour you. Let's have our picnic and get back to the boat."

"Good idea. I'm *famished*."

Chapter Seventeen

DALT

When we get back to the boat, I consider letting the raft and everything in it float away. I don't want to take one more minute doing anything but getting Nikki back in my arms. The way her cat eyes keep shredding me with flaming desire I'd say she has the same idea as me.

Once we have everything on deck, I waste no time pulling her into me and tugging on the string bows at her back and neck. The slick fabric of her bathing suit top slides down her body and falls to our feet. I pull her in tight. Her full tits mash into my chest. She moans in pleasure and wiggles, giving me the full effect of her pebbled nipples. Damn. Every touch of her skin on mine sets me on fire.

"Um, we're still outside and I'm half-naked," she whispers against my lips.

I take her hand and guide her to the steps leading

down into the galley. There's no way I can wait to get back to shore to be inside her. We have a lot of missed fucking to make up for.

She walks down the steps ahead of me and some kind of weird growl makes its way up my throat and into the air as I watch her sweet, barely-bikini-covered ass sway in front of me. When we get to the bottom of the steps, I pluck one of the tied bows on the side of her hip and the scrap of fabric falls down her legs. Nikki is a golden goddess standing amidst the flaxen ash wood décor of the cabin, her platinum hair and sun kissed skin glowing in the sunlight streaming through the large hull portholes.

My cock has already grown thick and hard for her, straining out the top of my swim trunks. She brushes her fingertips over the slit, wet with precum, and my cock jerks at her touch. Bringing her fingers to her lips, she moans in pleasure while licking them.

Holy fuck.

I don't think my cock has ever been as hard as it is right now. I can't even think straight. Then I remember the promise I made to her earlier about all the things I was going to do to her. I never break my promises.

Gazing down into her darkened blue eyes, I let her know how this is going to go. "I'm going to christen this boat today by making you come in every way and on every surface possible. "

She glances around the room. Her eyes go wide. It could be nervousness, or possibly excitement. "That's a lot of surfaces. We only have one day." She smirks.

I should have known. It's Nikki. No nerves, just sass.

"Baby, once I get between your legs we're going to

need to use some of those surfaces more than once." I lean in and kiss her, hard. I part her lips with my tongue and nibble her fleshy bottom lip. She doesn't protest my calling her baby this time, just moans. I capture it in my mouth. She collapses into my arms, crushing her tits into my chest once more.

There are cushioned benches on either side of the table in the middle of the galley but there are also three bedrooms on this boat: two behind and on either side of the steps and a master cabin in the front of the boat. I figure it's best to start in the master bed where we'll have more room for the variety of positions I'm going to be putting her in. Nik loves a little adventure between the sheets and I'm not exactly opposed to the idea.

"I need these off, now," she demands, and slides my trunks down to my ankles. I lift one foot at a time and step out of them, kicking them to the side. My demanding cock springs free and stretches toward her like he's telling me where he wants to go. I don't need his directions.

Palming the plump cheeks of Nikki's ass and squeezing gets me another moan. I lift her off the floor and pull her against my throbbing cock. Nikki wraps her legs around my waist, gripping me harder. I hold her in that position and walk to the front of the boat and the master bed.

Animal hunger takes over when I drop her onto the bed. I'm all raw, wild need, ready to press on top of her, claim her. But I stop, awestruck by her beauty. The contrast of her tanned perfect body, open and vulnerable, atop the crisp white bed linens is like a Botticelli painting.

"Hey. I was supposed to give you *surfing* lessons. Remember?" Uh...a dirty, shameless Botticelli painting. She pushes herself up on her elbows and purses those juicy lips into a teasing pout, offering her goddess-like body to me without restrictions.

Jesus.

This woman may kill me.

But I'm going to take it slow this time. Savor the taste of what I've been missing, make her remember what my lips feel like on her body, between her legs.

Stretching over her, I kiss those sweet, pouty lips. The gentle rocking of the boat is a helpful partner in foreplay. Her muscles and arms give up the battle and she relaxes onto her back. Taking full advantage, I kiss a path from her lips to her slender throat and down between her breasts. I linger in a slow detour, swirling my tongue around her pert, rosy nipple. It hardens even more as I savagely lick and suck it between my teeth and give it a gentle bite. Nikki moans louder this time and arches her back, thrusting her breasts up further in invitation. I accept the offer and move to her other nipple, giving it equal time and attention. Moving down her stomach to her navel, I use my teeth to give a slight tug on the double-ball silver bar piercing she got when we were dating before continuing my journey down.

When my lips reach the landing path of golden curls between her legs, Nikki wiggles and gives a prolonged "oooo" moan, pushing her hips up. Standing up, I pull her to the edge of the bed and drop down on my knees in front of her. Draping one of her legs over my shoulder, giving me better access to her wet, glistening pussy gets an, "Oh God, Dalt!"

I nuzzle the space between her thigh and pussy. Nikki moans and threads her fingers through my hair. She pushes her hips up further and tries to tug my head where she wants it. I ignore her pleading groans and move to the other leg and trail kisses along the inside of the thigh draped over my shoulder. She continues to moan like she's in pleasured agony.

Nikki's always been loud when we fuck, and her sexy begging noises succeed in making my cock beg for her pussy in return. I do everything I can to encourage those 'please fuck me sounds.' I want her desperate need to cause her to let go harder than she ever has in her life, multiple times.

When I part her lips and blow across her sweet pussy, she wriggles in urgency. I hold her in place and put my lips right at her entrance. "Get ready, sweetheart, because I'm going to eat you out so hard you're going to forget what planet you're on."

"Oh God, Dalt. Please," she begs and tugs on my hair.

I take a long, slow lick from her ass to her clit, teasing her open. Her fragrant strawberry scent and the slightly salty taste of ocean water fill my senses. Nothing has ever tasted sweeter.

Her pink clit is swollen and throbbing and when I flick my tongue over it, Nikki writhes in pleasure. I slide two fingers into her eager pussy and she pushes into my hand, gripping my fingers, lost in desire.

I keep flicking her swollen bud with my tongue and fucking her with my fingers. When I curve my fingers in a come here motion, stroking her deep and slow, Nik goes crazy. I know every G-spot on her body like the back of my hand. Her fingers twist in my hair and she groans.

"Mmm, yes, *yes,* Dalt. Right...right there. Just like *that.*"

When I add some suction, Nikki grips my hair and tugs harder, pulling my face against her while at the same time arching into me as I keep working her with my mouth. "Fuck, Nik. I've been starving for you. You taste so fucking good." My words vibrate over her clit and she trembles. I know she's right on the edge.

"That's it baby, let go. I want you to come all over my face."

And she does. Her entire body vibrates in response. She's like a wildcat, thrashing, screaming my name and tugging on my hair to hold me where she wants me. I feel her pulsing on my tongue in waves of pleasure and I keep her coming, licking and sucking and finger fucking her till she's pulling on my hair hard enough I may have a couple of bald spots. It's worth it to see her come apart in the sexy, uncontrolled way only Nikki can.

I prowl my way up the length of her body. Nikki's eyes are closed and I assume she's lightheaded, basking in sated bliss. I'm ready to push balls deep inside her, give her even more of that ecstasy and claim some of my own, but I've misjudged my energetic girl. She catches me off guard and with a push of her leg and roll of her hips, she's got me on my back. She straddles either side of my hips.

"I think it's time for those lessons now." Her hands around my wrists, she pushes my arms over my head. I could easily get free, but what kind of idiot would want to fight his way out of a naked Nikki's grasp or argue with her desire to ravage him? Not this one. That's for sure.

She slides her hands down my arms and sits straight up, positioning my cock at her entrance. "Now, *technically* for riding your *surfboard* I should be turned around with my ass facing you." She flutters her long lashes and wiggles her ass over my cock. A raspy growl mixed with tortured bliss pushes out from the back of my throat. The little hellion giggles, fully aware of the way she's driving me crazy.

"But for *this* lesson, I'm going to stay in this position so I can see you, just to make sure you're following my directions."

Christ. I don't how much more of this I can take. The warmth of her wet pussy is coating my legs. My dick is iron. "Nik, if I don't get to fuck you right now, I may die from internal pressure." I move my legs, trying to part her thighs and push my hips up to lift her onto my throbbing cock.

"You won't die." She slides down a little and clamps her strong legs around me to keep me from pushing into her. "And I promise it will be worth the wait," she purrs.

Jesus.

"I suppose if I have to die at the tender age of twenty-one I can't think of a better way to go."

"So, is it okay?" she asks in a syrupy sweet voice and bats her lashes again.

"What? Is what okay?" Fuck. What's she talking about? I can't even remember my own name.

"If I stay facing you like this?" She wiggles her ass over my thighs.

"Christ. Nik, I'm—"

"Uh, uh, uh. The sooner you answer my question the sooner we can get on with the lesson."

"Yes! Okay! Whatever! Just let me fuck you!"

"Not. Yet."

"*Nikki.*"

Damn. I'm starting to whine and beg like a horny teenager.

"First, I'm going to fuck *you,*" she chirps in an adorable little voice. It's another one of Nikki's many talents; she can say the dirtiest filthiest things in an innocent, angelic voice. I'm tellin' ya, she's my fantasy come to life.

"The first thing I have to do is get up on my *board.*" She puts the soles of her feet on either side of me, keeping her legs bent. The position puts her slick pussy in an open, more welcoming position. My cock stands erect and pulses, begging for his reward. She wraps her hand around my unruly shaft, positions it at her entrance, and drops down with such a quick movement it elicits a throaty groan from me and a gasp from her.

"Holy fuck!" I grunt like this is the first time I've ever been inside a woman. "Are you okay, babe?"

"Shhh," she whispers. "Mmm." Her brow creases and she takes a deep breath like she's trying to focus with every one of her brain cells. Although I'm in delicious agony, I can't keep from grinning. She's seriously trying to give me a sexy surfing lesson, even though what she clearly wants is to let go and fuck her brains out...mine too while she's at it.

"And then...and then I get my balance," she forces the raspy words out. She starts swerving from side to side, clenching around my cock and moving it with her. "You...you have to...unph...really f...feel the wood."

"*Fuuuck*, Nik." I close my eyes for a moment because she feels like paradise in one incredible, tight cunt. This cannot be real. Then I open my eyes, because it *is* real and I want to see her angel face as she uses me to fuck herself into euphoria. Her eyes are closed and she's licking her lips, her chest heaving deep breaths. Her breasts sway with every swerve of her body. I cup both her tits and knead them, not too rough but not gentle either. She thrusts her breasts further into my hands.

"Have I told you how much I love your tits?" Her nipples stand even further at attention in response to my words. I roll and pinch them between my fingers and her muscles tremble around my cock.

"Dalt," she moans, but goes right on with her instructions. "Wh...when you catch the wave...ahh...you have to g...grip the board."

Christ on a rip curl.

Even though I'm dying here in intensifying, rapturous torture, I have to smile. Nikki is nothing if not thorough.

"Mmmm...and ride it to...ah ah ah...to the climax!" she screeches and starts pulling up and pushing down on me hard enough I don't think she'll be able to walk when she's done. I mean, I don't want to brag, but my cock isn't exactly small. It's a lot to accommodate. But Nikki is whimpering and moaning, taking me to the hilt every time she pushes down on me.

That's it for me. I'm tapping out. I grab the cheeks of her ass and squeeze, using them to pull her up and down on my shaft and help her keep up the frenzied rhythm. At the same time, I thrust my hips up and pump, matching her pace to drive even deeper into her. The rocking of the boat isn't gentle anymore. It's joined in our feverish choreography, swaying under us. The sounds of our sweat drenched skin slapping together drowns out the sound of water lapping the side of the boat. Passionate groans and agonized curses add to the concerto of pleasure.

"Fuck, yeah. What you do to me, Nik. Ride me, baby. Ride me so fucking hard I get lost inside you."

"Oh God. Dalt! Dalt! I'm coming!" She screams loud enough the fish in the bay will be traumatized for a month.

"Fuuckk!" I answer with my own pleasured groan and I clasp her hips, pulling her hard into one final deep thrust. Everything goes white hot as I blow into her with the force of a hurricane. Nikki keeps moaning and gripping me and I keep pouring into her, flooding her with warm pulses of everything I haven't been able to give her for so long.

When my vision finally returns and Nikki stops milking my cock in spasms, she goes limp on top of me. She murmurs into the curve of my neck, "Holy...that was..."

"The best friggin' surfing lesson I've ever had," I

finish. "You're a very good instructor." Nikki giggles and the sound goes straight to my heart. "I love you so much, Nik. I'll never let you go," I whisper and place a kiss on top of her head.

"I love you so much too," she says, nestling further into my arms.

I keep my promise to never let her go, at least for another day.

Chapter Eighteen

NIKKI

Dalt is true to his word. After fucking on all three beds several times, the cushioned benches, the galley countertop and in the shower—twice, I was sure the possibility of walking for the next week was questionable. As usual, Dalt was a sex god when it came to stamina. Walking is overrated, anyway.

As I step out of the shower I hear the muffled sound of Kelly Clarkson's voice singing "Never Again." It's my cell phone ringing inside my backpack.

Hmm, going to have to change my ringtone.

I wrap a towel around me and run to get my phone as Dalt steps out of the shower behind me.

Tracey's suntanned face lights up my screen. *"Hey girl. What's up?"* she beams when I accept her FaceTime request.

"Hey! How's Malibu?"

"It's beautiful. We're missing you, though. Wish you could...Oh, did I catch you at a bad time? Looks like you just got out of the shower."

"I did, but it's fine. You a hot little surfer girl yet?" Dak was so excited about giving Tracey *actual* surfing lessons, I'm sure he wasted no time getting her out in the waves.

"Not yet, but I'm trying. Dak says I...Wait. Are you rocking back and forth or is it my camera. Where are you, Nik?"

"It's not your camera." I laugh at the way Tracey's head is tipping from side to side in sync with the swaying of the boat. "I'm on a boat. It's—"

"Hey, skater girl." Dalt walks up behind me. *"Where's your not so better half?"* Since he's drying his stark-naked body with his towel, rather than having it wrapped around his waist, I'm hoping my phone is angled in a way which isn't giving Tracey full view of his glorious package.

"He's...oh my freaking word. Dalt? Are you...did you two just shower together on a...on a boat? Oh my God! Dak! Alex! Get in here!" she yells behind her. *"Nikki and Dalt are naked on a boat. Together. I'm so happy!"* she screeches and starts jumping up and down. By the way her phone's camera is bouncing and the screen is changing from blurry tan to blurry white, I think she's clapping.

"Tracey!" I yell into my screen. "Jesus, Dalt. Could you at least put the towel around your...your..." I wave a hand up and down in front of his body, because seeing all his magnificent nakedness has my brain cells completely muddled.

"Sure. Wouldn't want to ruin Tracey's perception of Dak. You know, if she sees what a real man has goin' on." He chuckles.

"*'Sup up, asshat?*" Dak's big grin fills the screen. He apparently has taken over possession of Trace's phone. "*You flashing my girlfriend? Wait. I'll turn on the camera's magnifying lens.*"

"Oh, is that how she finds yours?" Dalt laughs.

"*Give me that.*" Trace yanks the phone out of Dak's hand. "*You two can compare the size of your love snakes when there aren't more pressing matters to discuss.*"

Love snake? She never *would* use the words cock or dick when we discussed the guys' assets. Not a bad one, though. *I'm gonna' suck the venom from your love snake.* Eh. Kinda gross.

"*I can't think of anything more pressing than this, Bambi.*" Bambi is Dak's smoopy nickname for Tracey. I can only see his shoulders behind her but by the startled grin and huge sigh coming from her, I can only guess his *love snake* may be on the move and pressing into her back.

"*Wait. What did I miss?*" I recognize Alex's voice, even though I can't see him.

"*Nikki and Dalt are naked and wet on a boat together!*" Tracey squeals.

Jesus. There are seriously no lines left to cross in friendships when it comes to social media.

"*Yeah. You missed the flashing of Dalt's insignificant*

package," Dak's taunting voice comes through the speaker.

"You're such an asshole!" Dalt yells back.

"Maybe I should call you back later after—" I try to offer the suggestion.

"What? Are you shitting me? Give me that phone." Alex's tanned bronze face comes into view. *"Hey, queen! I miss your sweet ass. Where's Dalt?"* He cranes his neck from side to side, like he's trying to see behind me.

"Nice to see you too." I shake my head. I guess a naked Dalt is more exciting than my face *or* sweet ass. Can't blame Alex, though. A naked Dalt *is* pretty thrilling.

"Right here, dude." Dalt rests his chin on my shoulder and wiggles his fingers. "How you doing, Alex?"

"Fan-fucking-tastic! How's it hanging, Adonis?"

"Long and thick, my man. Long and thick."

Alex lets out a sigh. *"Then I guess you're taking good care of our girl."*

"Okay. Nope." I shove Dalt's head off my shoulder and bring the screen right up to my face. It's close enough I'm sure Alex is getting a Blair Witch-style view of my nasal hairs. "I'll call you guys back later, when everyone has grown up, like in ten or fifteen years."

"No. Wait." Tracey grabs the phone from Alex. *"I'm so happy for you guys, Nik. Call me back when you're finished...um...making up. I want to hear all about it."*

"Yeah, call me later, Dalt." Dak snickers from somewhere behind Tracey. *"I want to hear all about it. What*

did she say? Does she really really like you? Did you give her your pin?" he teases.

"Shut up, Dak. Call me later, Nik, when the male children aren't around." Tracey rolls her eyes.

"Okay. Kiss the misbehaved children for me. Love you."

"I will." She laughs. *"Love you too. I'm beyond happy for you,"* she twitters in excitement before the screen goes black.

"Seriously? I wanted to break the news gently to our friends. Was it necessary to parade yourself in front of them?" I try to sound annoyed, but Dalt is still standing a few inches away from me in all his gorgeous nakedness and I can feel my body flushing from head to toe at the sight.

"Sorry, babe." He drapes his arms over my shoulders and tickles my nose with his.

"But now that you're back in my life I'm seriously considering *never* wearing clothes. I want to be ready to get inside you every chance I get."

"Could be hazardous when you're playing hockey."

"Mmm, could be. But I'm willing to risk it." He tugs my towel off and drops it to the floor.

"Nooo. Dalt, we have to get back to the house," I half-heartedly protest and give an almost imperceptible push to his shoulder.

"Okay. Let's get going then." He brushes his lips across the top of my shoulder and slowly trails down to my collarbone. He could be right about the permanent state of nakedness. Since this morning, we haven't been clothed for more than an hour. And even after the multiple orgasms he's had today, Gigantor is raging again. There is no way this man is human.

"Oh God," I sigh as he makes his way to one of my nipples and circles it with his tongue. "Apparently Gigantor is ready to go again."

"What?" My nipple slips out of his mouth with a pop. "What did you just say?"

Oh shit, did I say that out loud?

"Did you just call my dick Gigantaur?"

I guess I did.

"Um...no. Well...yes. *What?* It *is* unusually large."

"So you named him after a video game monster who shoots needles or some shit like that?" *His* Gigantor begins to deflate.

"No, silly"

"You think *I'm* the silly one?"

"You're ridiculous. Gigantor is a huge rocket powered robot made of iron, who has a pointy nose and is super strong."

"You mean there's another Gigantaur besides the one in Final Fantasy?"

"Ugh, *yes.* I hate that computerized crap. I'm talking about the one in the classic animated series. He fights villains and saves the world in the name of peace."

"Hmm. I'll have to check it out. You had me and my *love snake* a little worried there for a minute, making him think he was an evil villain," he laughs and brushes a kiss across my lips.

"Poor baby." I reach down between us and stroke my hand up and down his resurrecting shaft.

He whistles through clenched teeth. "If you keep

that up he may be too worn out to ever fight crime again."

"Aww, let me help him out then." I drop to my knees and stroke, lick, suck and swallow, all in the name of world peace.

Chapter Nineteen

DALT

It's been another best day of my life, and when we get back to our houses I'm not ready for it to end.

"I'll unload the car and then get changed," I tell Nikki as we haul our sex spent bodies out of the car. "Go get dressed. I'm taking you out."

"You are? I thought you were exhausted." She lets out a little yawn.

"I only have you tonight before you leave me for a couple of days. I'm going to wine and dine you in the manner in which I plan on making you accustomed."

"I don't need to be wined and dined, Dalt. Takeout and Netflix and chill sounds good to me, as long as it's with you." She drapes her arms around my neck and presses a soft kiss on my lips.

"Sounds like heaven to me too, baby. But I have a surprise you're going to love. I'll take a raincheck on the takeout and Netflix." I wrap my arms around her waist and return the kiss.

"Okay, but don't forget the chill."

"Never. The chill's the best part of staying in with you."

"What should I wear for this surprise?" She unwraps herself from me and opens the back door of the car to get her backpack.

"You can wear the sweet dress you had on earlier, but you better wear a jacket. You know how it gets colder when the sun goes down. Is an hour enough time for you to get ready?"

"More than enough." She leans in and gives me another soft kiss before heading into her house.

I watch her walk away. My smile takes over my face as I think about how fucking lucky I am.

An hour later on the dot, I'm at Nikki's door. "It's open. Come on in!" she yells from what sounds like the top of the stairs. I'm not happy she apparently left the door unlocked while she was upstairs dressing. But when I walk in and glance up the stairs I'm too captivated to let her know about my momentary unhappiness.

She's standing at the top of the stairs in the same polka dot dress she had on earlier, but with a short black leather jacket over it and royal blue cropped leggings underneath it. Instead of sandals, she has on her signature black Dr. Marten boots with thick, yellow scrunched socks peeking out the top of them. Her blue bangs match the color of her leggings and the rest of her platinum hair is hanging in waves almost to her waist. Her sun-kissed face is radiant and her gleaming smile is enough to melt my heart. I'm completely wrecked by the unique girl staring down at me. She's my quirky, gorgeous, golden angel.

"All ready." She runs down the stairs and leaps into my arms. "I missed you," she says into the curve of my neck.

"I've only been gone a few minutes." I smile into her hair and drink in her scent. I swear she smells like what sunshine would smell like on a field of strawberries...if you could smell sunshine.

"Still missed you. Mmm. I love the way you smell. And you look hot in that blazer."

What was that? Ten words? Fifteen? A handful of words and her body pressed against mine and even though I've had her multiple times in multiple orgasmic ways just a couple of hours ago, she has me on my way to another raging hard on.

"Jesus, Bud. You're making me crazy. I can't get enough of you."

"You wanna stay home? I can always order in." She plants a kiss on my cheek. There's nothing I want more than to stay in with her. I should have followed my own advice and stayed naked whenever I'm with her. But I know she's going to love the exhibit and Garrett had to call in some favors to get these tickets.

"First your surprise and dinner. Then I'm going to bring you back here and chill all night long."

"Then let's leave so we can get back." She takes my hand and practically drags me out the door.

"Where are we? What? Are you kidding me right now? No way! How did you do this? These tickets have been sold out for months."

When I pull up to the valet parking in front of the gallery, Nikki can't stop babbling in excitement. I wanted to do something special for her and I knew she would love the touring exhibit for The Original Art of Children's Book Illustrators. Proceeds from the tour are being given to several charities benefitting children. Even though the price of the tickets is for high rollers only, *getting* a ticket is about as difficult as it was to find Wonka's golden one.

Since I just found out this morning Nikki was going to be back in my life, I called Garrett when I stopped by my house to pick up the food for the picnic. Being a powerhouse in the entertainment industry provides him with connections all over the world. I knew he could hook me up. Not five minutes later Garrett called back and said my name would be on the list at the door.

I didn't tell him what I needed the tickets for, just that it was a charity event I wanted to support. I don't want him saying anything to my father about Nikki and me before I get a chance to confront the old bastard myself.

We enter the door of the gallery. I stop to give the

hostess my name and she checks me and my guest off the list. In the two minutes it took me to do it, Nikki has wandered off to the middle of the room. She's turning in slow circles, gaping at the artwork like a girl who just entered the portal to Wonderland. It's adorable how excited she is. She could almost be part of the exhibit, a sweet character in a children's book.

"What do ya think? Did I do good?" I say when I catch up to her.

"Oh my God! You did *so* good, hockey boy. Look." She tugs me across the room to stand in front of one of the drawings on the stark white wall. "Do you realize this is an *original* Theodore Geisel drawing of The Cat In The Hat?"

"No kidding? I thought Dr. Seuss did those."

"Theodore Geisel *was* Dr. Seuss, silly."

What do I know? Show me a picture of the nineteen seventy Stanley Cup Champions though, and I'll name every one of those suckers.

"And look!" Nikki screeches and pulls me to the next drawing encased in glass on the wall. "This is an original Max in his tree-covered room by Sendak. Isn't it the most beautiful thing you've ever seen?"

"No. Not exactly," I mumble, because I'm watching the most beautiful thing I've ever seen getting all excited about a drawing of a kid in a monster suit.

"Eeep! Dalt!" she screeches, moving to the next drawing. Did she just say eeep? Is that even a word? "It's Garth Williams!"

"You mean the country singer?" I tease her.

"What?" Her sweet face pinches like I just spoke Martian.

"It looks like Stuart Little to me."

"It is! Garth Williams is the artist. Oh my gosh, Dalt," she turns and throws her arms around my neck, "this is the most wonderful thing anyone has ever done for me. Thank you. Thank you."

She's squeezing me so tight I'm having a hard time breathing. I love how much she loves this and how happy she is. I'm okay with suffocating in her arms.

"I just wanted you to see what it was like," I cough out.

"See what what's like?" She loosens her grip and steps back to study my face.

"To know what it's going to be like when *your* illustrations are hung in art galleries all over the world and millions of people are admiring them."

She chuckles. "Oh right. I'm going to be the next Sendak."

"No, you're not."

She frowns in confusion. "Not quite that admired, huh?" She smirks.

"Nope. You're going to be way more famous than Sendak or this Seuss guy or whoever."

"I think you're my greatest fan. Maybe my only fan." She throws her arms over my shoulders and plants a kiss on my lips. "But it's okay, because you're the only one I want."

Man. I really love this girl.

"You're the only one I want too, Nik." I wrap my arms around her waist and pull her into me. "But I know someday I'm going to have to share your artistic talents with the rest of the world. You're good, if not better than any of these people. Let's check out the rest of the exhibits so we can get out of here."

I brush my nose across hers and I swear she purrs like a contented kitten. I know exactly how she feels.

Chapter Twenty

NIKKI

The hostess at the Reading Room leads us to a quiet candlelit table in the corner. Dalt pulls out a chair for me, taking a seat on the other side of the small table. The second he sits down he reaches across the table for my hand. I lace my fingers through his and we sit in silence for a moment. The way his crystalline eyes twinkle in the candlelight as he drinks me in says it all. Without saying a word, he has my heart thrumming in double time and every one of my nerve cells sizzling. The heat of his touch moves up my arm and travels down to the core of my body like a lit fuse racing toward dynamite.

I have to break the silence or there's no way I'll be able to make it through dinner without finding a storage closet or bathroom stall or some other equally unromantic hidden alcove to tear off his navy blazer and jeans.

"This is so beautiful. The whole day has been

amazing and one of the best days of my life. Thank you for all of it, Dalt."

"This is just the beginning of everything I'm going to give you, Nik. Anything you want. *Anything.*" His words are soft, like he's trying to maintain the serenity of the atmosphere

It's early for the Saturday night dinner crowd, leaving most of the tables in the high-end hotel restaurant empty. They won't fill until the eight or nine o'clock reservation slots. I'm not sure if it's my imagination or if the man on the grand piano across the room is playing the Nino Rota theme from *Romeo and Juliet.* The floor to ceiling window we're seated next to offers a gorgeous view of Frenchman's Bay. The full moon shimmers on the water, providing the most magical dinner theater experience Mother Nature has to offer. A gigantic cruise ship is docked several miles offshore, its lights twinkling as if signifying the merriment taking place onboard. Throughout the harbor, boats in various shapes and sizes dance in the moonlight. The soft music combined with the gentle rocking of the boats provides a soothing ballet for the senses. It's like a scene out of an enchanted story. Dalt might be wrong. Our life together just might be a fairytale.

A young man in a tuxedo interrupts the tranquil moment. "Your server will be right with you. I'm Jason, the sommelier. Can I interest you in our wine list?"

I let go of Dalt's hand as the waiter places the large leather covered binder on the table.

"Can I get you a cocktail this evening while you're deciding?"

"We'll have a bottle of Dom Perignon '66," Dalt says, handing the wine list back to the waiter without looking at it. "Uh. Wait. Is that okay, Bud? Can you break your drinking fast to have some champagne to celebrate?"

"Champagne? Sure but..." I glance at the waiter who's patiently waiting to take our drink order. "Sure. Champagne would be great."

"Very good, sir."

I wait until the waiter is far enough away from the table he can't hear me ask, "Isn't that an obscenely expensive bottle of champagne?"

"We have a lot to celebrate and two years to make up for." Dalt picks up the gold-lettered menu in front of him.

"Yes, but Dom Perignon is—"

"I don't think you're hearing me, baby." He drops the menu and reaches for my hand. "I'm grateful for everything my mom left me, but it's not what's important. I finally have something, some*one* who *is* important. And I just want to use some of the money to overindulge her. Got it?"

He's telling me I'm more important to him than anything, his money is insignificant. It's beautiful and...overwhelming.

"Got it," I concede. "As long as the *her* you're referring to is me."

"Just you, baby girl. Only you."

God. I'm falling so fast and hard for him, again.

Please don't let him walk away when he finds out what I've done.

"Nik?" his voice tugs me out of my apprehensive thought.

"Hmm?"

He runs his thumb across my bottom lip, making me aware of my nibbling on it. "You wanna' dance?"

"I...no one's dancing. I don't think there's dancing in here," I whisper, like the dancing police are on the lookout.

"There is now." Dalt stands and extends his hand to me. He leads me to an open area in the middle of the dining room, wraps his arms around my waist and I drape mine around his neck. We pull toward each other, our eyes locked.

We begin a slow sway to the piano player's melodic cover of Ed Sheeran's "Perfect." And it is. The lyrics, the moment, everything couldn't be more perfect. I'm lost in Dalt's arms, his warmth, his scent. Adrift in his vivid blue eyes, the same way I was the first time he glanced at me my freshman year—even though I tried to resist it back then. I've never felt this immersed in someone else; this consumed. He leans in to kiss me. When his tongue moves across my lip, my mouth parts in a sigh of his name.

"Dalt."

"Nikki."

Our tongues tangle in their own dance of fervent exploration. This is real. Everything I'm feeling, he's feeling, everything we're sharing, it's real. The way he's holding me, kissing me, worshiping me with his eyes, I'm not dreaming it or imagining it. Dalt loves me and I could burst into a million pieces of happiness with the love I have surging through me for him. My breathy moan of contentment gets a raspy groan in return from him.

"Let's eat and get out of here," he rasps.

I give him a dreamy nod. Words are as impossible as they are unnecessary to tell him what I'm feeling, what I want, right now.

"Better yet, I'll get us a suite here for the night and order room service. Then I don't have to wait any longer to be inside you."

God.

I love the way he uses his words. But a suite at the Bar Harbor Inn, just so he doesn't have to wait an extra hour to get me naked. It's going to take some time for me to get used to this overindulgence stuff.

"No, let's just eat here. Home, Netflix and chill, with you, sounds perfect to me."

"Like I said, let's eat and get the fuck outta here."

A dozen oysters, a shared bowl of lobster bisque, a Maine lobster pie, and a bottle of Dom Perignon later, I float— more like roll—on the after effects of champagne bubbles and the excess of food, into my house.

"Oh God. I'm so stuffed I can't even move. Wasn't I just stuffed with blueberry pancakes?" I groan my way into the living room.

Dalt walks into the kitchen with a bag. "I hope you saved room for the two pieces of gooey chocolate caramel cake we brought home." He chuckles at my groans of gluttonous pleasure.

There was no way I could think about putting another morsel of food into my mouth after the rich, delicious meal, but Dalt insisted we had to have dessert to complete dinner. I agreed, only if we could take it home to eat later. Like in a month after I digested everything else.

"Ugh. I am never going to be able to dribble a soccer ball down a field again."

"Don't worry, soccer girl," he says, coming back into the living room to help me out of my jacket. "I'm going to sweat every one of those calories off you tonight." He sweeps my hair to one side and kisses the curve of my neck. The touch of his lips on my skin sends goosebumps down to my toes, but my dress is beginning to feel like a straightjacket around my too stuffed body.

"Wait. Let me get out of these clothes and get comfortable. You pick something to watch. I'll be right back."

"I would be more than happy to help you with that." Dalt nibbles on the shell of my ear.

"Ahh...why...why don't you borrow a p...pair of Dak's sweat...sweatpants."

Jesus.

Will I ever have normal brain function when his lips are within two feet of me?

"Sounds good. I don't want to leave you to go all the way home to change." He steps away from me and moves toward the stairs.

"*All* the way home being somewhere around twenty feet." I laugh.

"Hey, you made me wait to get home. If we stayed at the inn, I'd already be buried so deep inside you everyone staying there would know my name by the way you'd be screaming it."

"God," I sigh on a huge breath. I have to rub my legs together to ease the ache already building from his sweet dirty talk.

What is it Alex calls the next-door neighbor hockey boys? Living, breathing sex on two legs. Sounds like an accurate assessment of this particular hockey boy.

"So humble." I shake my head.

"I only speak the truth, sweetheart. And you know it." He gives me his coy grin and takes the stairs two at a time.

I gaze at the way his jeans hug his delicious, round ass. Sighing at the sight of all that perfection, I slowly waddle my way up behind him to get to my room. It reminds me of what it felt like to wobble around when I was pregnant with Chloe. The sad thought washes over me. Dalt wasn't around to experience my pregnancy or the all the firsts for Chloe: her first steps, first giggles, first words. He's being so wonderful, I have to be honest with him.

He's going to hate me for keeping her from him.

No. He said nothing would ever separate us again. He loves me. He'll understand. He'll forgive me. First thing in the morning before I leave for the farm, I'll tell him.

Chapter Twenty-One

DALT

"What did you choose? What are you in the mood for?" Nikki asks as she comes bouncing into the room.

Okay. Maybe she's not actually bouncing, but in my full to the brim of happiness mind, she's bouncing. I'm stretched out on the sofa, fumbling with the remote but not thinking about television shows. My thoughts are consumed by everything Nikki. When she asks me what I'm in the mood for, my love-saturated brain thinks she's asking me what kind of sex I want: missionary, oral, doggie style. Can't help it. When I'm with her, and even when I'm not, all I can think about is the next time I can be between her legs. Fingers, tongue, cock, doesn't matter, as long as I'm there.

"What did you say?"

"What are you in the *mood* for? Comedy, action, horror?"

She's wearing leggings with pictures of Archie comic book characters on them and a cropped loose t-shirt, one side of it slipping down her arm, revealing her soccer ball tattoo. Her pebbled nipples are standing at attention, making it apparent she's not wearing a bra. Her hair is twisted into a long braid which is hanging over one shoulder, almost to the exposed skin at her waist. The way she's tilting her head has the braid swaying over her breasts, like the pendulum of a clock counting down the seconds before I'm sucking on those rosy tips and peeling Archie and Veronica down her legs.

"Oh. Right. I don't know. Whatever you want."

"I don't care as long as it's not a chick flick."

"No shit? You used to love those. How many times did you make me watch *The Notebook*?" The first time it was pretty good. Even the second time wasn't bad. But Nikki had it downloaded on her computer and I swear we watched it every weekend for months.

"It's still one of my favorites," she swoons. *Damn.* I shouldn't have mentioned it. "But Tracey and Dak are on a romance watching binge lately. And if I have to watch one more episode of *Outlander* I'm going to strangle myself with one of those Scottish kilts."

"*Outlander*? Is that a romance? I thought it was a docudrama about Scottish warriors. Isn't it the show with all the dudes in skirts cutting each other up with swords?"

"Docudrama?" She squinches her face. "Yeah, right. It's the show with all the sexy Scots wearing skirts *sans* undies, which makes their 'love snakes' easily accessible and the likelihood of all kinds of hot and heavy *love* scenes occurring in every episode. It's a chick show hiding underneath yards of plaid." Nikki plops down next to me.

"Wait. Are you kidding me right now? I walked in Dak's room the other night and he was watching it. As soon as he saw me he slammed his computer closed but I had already seen the dudes in skirts battling."

I stop to think for a second. I know he didn't say it was *romance*. I'd seen a commercial for the show a few days before and it looked pretty good. I asked him if it I should stream it. He said something about it being a dope historical docudrama all about Scotland's war with England, bloody and gruesome. But he didn't suggest I watch it. Just said he was tired and he'd finish watching it the next day.

"That sly dog. He never mentioned it was a lovey-dovey chick show. So, captain, my captain watches chick shows." I laugh at the thought of Andersen curled up and watching schmaltzy chick flicks.

"Watches it? He convinced Trace it's one of the greatest shows on television. They never miss it. *And* they even binged watched the first two seasons to 'refresh' their memories of the plot." Nikki air quotes the word refresh.

"Oh man." I fall back in a fit of laughter. "Just wait 'til I talk to that fucker. He is *so* not getting away with this."

"Don't come down on him too hard. It is kinda' cute the way they cuddle together watching a show they both love."

"Cuddling to a show they both love, huh? *Alien*!"

We shout in unison. "Sy-fy it is."

"I'll grab us a couple of waters while you find it. Or you want a beer?" Nik asks on her way to the kitchen.

"Water's good. I'm saving room for our dessert."

The one I'm going to smear all over your body and lick off.

"I could only find the second one in the series," I inform Nikki as she rejoins me on the sofa.

"Since we can practically recite the dialogue from the first one, second's good." Nik's fave romance may have been *The Notebook*, but our mutually favorite sci-fi, when we were together was *Alien*. We'd yell out lines like groupies at a *Rocky Horror Show* festival.

About twenty minutes into the movie Nikki has a revelation. "I just realized how dumb Ripley was to not know Carter was screwing her over."

"What do ya mean?"

"Think about it. He swears to annihilate the aliens but then when they find them he won't let her destroy them. Red flag much?"

"Hmm. Yeah, never thought about it."

Nikki is curled into the curve of my arm. She starts making little circles on my bare chest while pondering Ripley's dilemma. I never bother with a shirt when I'm relaxing. Sweats and no shirt, the most comfortable way to roll.

"How would a smart woman like her not have figured out she was being played by the company?" She runs her fingers over my pecs in absent-minded strokes.

"Hmm...yeah...she...she was...pretty fucking amazing." Nikki picks her head up, aware of the weird breathy way I'm answering her question. Her fingers stop stroking my chest.

Fuck. Don't stop.

She glances at my tented sweats, hops up from the sofa, and heads toward the kitchen. "Just a second. I'll be right back." I readjust my hard shaft who's begging for another Nikki fix.

"Time for dessert," Nikki announces, coming back in the room with a bowl and spoon in her hand.

"You're the only dessert I want, babe." She can't miss the confirmation of that statement inside my sweats.

"Just what I had in mind," she says, sliding the coffee table away from the sofa and dropping to her knees in front of me.

"Nik?" I'm not sure what's going on but I say a little prayer she's thinking the same thing I'm thinking.

She puts the bowl on the floor next to her knees and tugs at the elastic of my pants. "These have to come off, please." So polite. It's only right I agree to help her out by lifting my hips. She slides my sweats down my legs in a slow, drawn out movement. My hopeful cock waves in front of her face. Her eyes meet mine and she sweeps her tongue over her lips in anticipation.

Damn.

I have to stop my hips from pushing up into her face.

"Tell me if this is too hot." Oh, it's too hot alright. Explosive heat is already pulsing through my cock. She picks up the bowl and spoon and drizzles warm, gooey caramel and chocolate down my throbbing shaft.

Holy fuck!

"Mmm." She licks her lips. "Is it okay?"

I nod, unable to speak, like a happy puppy being given a treat. She wraps her slim fingers around my throbbing erection. When she flicks her tongue over the head of my dick, taking a slow lap to taste me and the warm sweetness, my head drops back against the sofa.

"*Fuck me*. Nik."

"Oh, we'll get to that." Her words flutter over my tip, causing my balls to tighten.

She flattens her tongue and licks at the sensitive spot just under my head.

"*Fuck*." I choke out and I feel her lips smile around me.

She fists her hand, sticky with syrupy sauce, around my base, and starts taking long, slow licks from my base to my tip to lap at the sugary sweetness. My thighs tremble in response. She moves her hand back and forth, pumping me into a frenzy. When she relaxes her throat to open wider for me and takes me all the way in, deep throating me, working me up and down, sucking, licking and gently nibbling, I lace my fingers through her hair to slow her movement. I want to make this last.

"Nik, baby," I groan, fighting the rush that's building inside me.

"Hmm?" The sound vibrates my shaft. When she lifts her passion filled eyes, the sight of her eating me with such fervent pleasure intensifies the sensation of the imminent orgasm getting ready to explode down her throat.

"You're too much. It's too much. I'm gonna come, babe." I tighten the fingers in her hair to keep her from moving but she ignores my warning. She sucks harder, swallowing me, taking me in deeper, eating me like she's a chocolate addict and I'm her fix.

"Oh, fuck. Nik. *Yes. Fuuuck*." I let go with a bone deep growl of pleasure and with such force, it leaves me gasping. Nik keeps making breathy moans of arousal while swallowing blasts of my warmth until my cock stops jerking in release.

After licking every last drop off my tip, she sits back on her heels. "Mmm. That was the best dessert I've ever had."

I reach down and scoop her up onto my lap. Finding her lips, I kiss her hard, tasting the mixture of chocolate caramel and me on her lips.

I can't stop kissing her and nibbling at her in between whispering her name. "Nikki."

I suck her bottom lip between my teeth. "Nikki." I let go and trail my lips down the length of her neck. She drops her head back and giggles. "Nikki," I whisper into her ear.

"Yes, hockey boy?"

"My turn for dessert."

Chapter Twenty-Two

NIKKI

I throw my arm across my face to block the intrusive sunlight shining through the window. When I move, the muscled arm curled around my waist flexes and pulls me into the warm body behind me.

Dalt.

I remember how we fit perfectly together when we cuddled in the past. Or as my mom would refer to it, spooned, a word which sounds like something right off *The Little House on the Prairie*. But it's the perfect word to describe Dalt and me, a matching set, like we were made for each other.

The warmth of contentment flows over me, wrapping me up in love and comfort. When I turn in Dalt's arms to face him, soreness flames between my legs, reminding me of the lovemaking marathon we shared last night.

I lost count of how many times Dalt brought me to

the edge and pushed me over. But it wasn't like the frenzied sex we had earlier in the day when we were frantic to ease each other's frustration.

Last night Dalt was gentle, taking things slow, whispering to me everything he was feeling as he explained in detail every dirty, lovely thing he was doing and was going to do to me.

I sigh as I take in the vision of the beautiful man sleeping next to me, his breathing soft and peaceful, his dark lashes resting on his cheeks. Watching him, I think about everything we've gone through, how far we've come in such a short period of time.

Dalt stirs and mumbles something before his lids blink a couple of times and his long lashes flutter open. I swear his crystalline eyes twinkle in the sunlight streaming through the window.

"Good morning, gorgeous," he says in a scratchy, sleep muddled voice.

"Good morning," I purr. Dalt slides one arm under me and pulls me closer. His hard shaft is already awake and ready to go.

Is he kidding?

I'm going to need a wheelchair if he keeps this up.

"I can't get enough of you, Nik. I'll never get enough of you."

Oh God. My body craves him like it's been years since I've had him rather than hours.

"I can't get enough of you either. Is this crazy? What's happening? I've never felt like this."

"Not crazy, baby. I've never felt like this either." Dalt presses the palm of my hand over his heart. The intensified rhythm matches the heightened thrumming in my own chest. "It's yours, Nik. It will always be yours."

My eyes glaze with tears and his face blurs. I'm speechless, overcome with emotion. This is everything I've waited to hear him say, everything I've wanted.

Dalt pushes me onto my back and climbs over me. When our lips meet, it's nothing like the sexually starved kisses we shared yesterday. It's tender, soft, as syrupy sweet as the dessert we licked off each other last night.

"I love you so much, Nik." His whisper a tender prayer across my lips.

"I love you so much too."

He inhales my words in a relieved sigh. "How sore are you, baby?"

"What?" I chuckle.

"How sore are you from yesterday?"

"I'm fine." I smile and try to sound convincing, while brushing a lock of hair back off his forehead.

"Sorry, babe. I just want to be inside you all the time."

When he trails his lips down my neck and then moves down to suck my hardened nipple in his mouth, teasing it with his tongue, the soreness between my legs becomes a pulsing ache telling me how much I want him too.

"I *want* you inside me all the time." His cock is thick with arousal and I push my hips up to show him how ready I am.

"God, Nik. What you do to me." His lips find mine and he kisses me with a deep, slow kiss which makes me feel treasured, worshiped. "Are you sure?"

I ravage his tongue with mine, kissing him in a way

I've never kissed him before. A passionate attempt to show him how much I adore him in return, how out of my mind in love I am with him.

"I've never been surer of anything in my life. I need you inside me." I arch into him, positioning his tip at my entrance.

With a groan Dalt slips inside me, slowly pressing into me inch by inch, stretching me. My muscles flinch around him in an initial response to the intense repeat invasion of his impossibly huge shaft. I let out a whimper. It hurts so good.

Dalt stops moving, keeping himself from pushing any further into me. "Are you okay, babe?"

In that moment the ache for him to be deep inside of me increases. My muscles relax to accommodate his size. I wrap my legs around him, desperate to keep him from pulling out of me, to pull him closer.

"More, Dalt. Please. Don't stop."

He presses his nose into the nape of my neck and pushes into me to the hilt. We both gasp at the sensation. How is it possible after having had him multiple times the night before, this feels new, intense, like the first time being with him?

"God. It feels so good," I moan.

Dalt raises his head as we move together in a slow steady rhythm. "You're so beautiful. You feel amazing. I'll never get enough of you."

I tighten my legs around his waist, digging my heels into his back. "Will it always be like this, Dalt?"

"Always, baby. Always," he groans. He pushes up on his elbows, pulls out almost all the way, then plunges deep and begins driving into me faster harder. "I'm crazy in love with you, Nik."

I want to watch his beautiful face as he loses control but the hunger to find my own release is overwhelming. I can't speak, can't think. My eyes close. I'm lost in sensation, chasing my own wild need. I grip his ass with my hands to drive him deeper. My legs begin to quiver as my hips push up to match his pace.

"Come for me, baby. I can't get enough of the feeling of you coming around my cock."

Mindless ecstasy grips me as the orgasm surges through me. My body is crippled with pleasure, intense and insane. When I open my eyes and Dalt's eyes meet mine, I watch him falling apart. Sweat glistens over the taut muscles of his face and neck. His lips are parted, groaning guttural sounds. His heavy-lidded eyes roll back and close as his body jerks hard, every muscle tense. He explodes into me with a final savage grunt, filling me with his warmth.

This is everything. He's everything. If he hates me after what I have to tell him this morning, how am I going to live without him?

Chapter Twenty-Three

DALT

"As much as I want to stay inside you all day long if we don't get out of this bed we may never be able to walk again." I smile at how good this is: how good she makes me feel, how beautiful she is, how perfect the world is now that she's back in mine.

"What would you like to do today?"

"You mean besides continuing to ride your surf-board?" She laughs, her head dropping to the side to face me. We're lying on our backs, both of us trying to regain normal breathing patterns and slow down our racing hearts.

"Yeah. Besides that." I roll onto my side to face her, brush my nose across her shoulder and place my palm on her flat stomach. Her skin pebbles in goosebumps.

"I hate leaving you but I told you I have to go to the farm."

"Damn. I almost forgot. Let me go with you. I want

to help, and besides, I think it's time I meet your mom." Her stomach muscles tense under my hand.

Doesn't she want me to meet her mom? Maybe she's still worried about the differences in our lifestyles.

"I love llamas. Can't wait to meet them too." I try to reassure her I'm not about big city life. I can be all about small farm life or outer space life, for that matter, if it means being with her.

"Alpacas."

"What?"

"We raise alpacas, not llamas"

"Oh, right. I knew that."

Is there a difference?

"Dalt, listen," she says rolling on her side to face me. "I have to—"

"Okay. Got it. You have to go do some things at the farm. At least let me make you breakfast before you go. I'm giving you one day. Just one." I hold up a finger. "I can't live without you any longer than that." She stares at me without saying a word. Her eyes, which appear more azure in the light of day, become liquid with tears, bringing back the memory of the time she laid next to me in bed and told me about the loss of her father.

"What is it, sweetheart. You okay?"

"It's...nothing. I...I'm just so happy." She cups my face with her hand and I reach up to hold it there.

"Me too, baby. Me too. After tomorrow it's you and me together, forever. There's something I want to talk to you about over breakfast." She blinks a couple of times and a lone tear escapes out of the corner of her eye. I catch it and brush it away with my thumb.

"Why don't you go jump in the shower while I whip us up something to eat. I know my girl. It's been way too many hours since you've had food." I wait for her usual snarky comeback when I comment on her favorite pastime.

Nikki can eat more than some of the guys on the team which, by the way, is another thing I love about her. She eats what she wants, giving zero fucks who's watching her, not having to pretend she has to eat like a bird because she's a girl. But the sarcasm doesn't come. She slips out of bed and heads into the bathroom with a quiet, "Okay."

Something doesn't feel right. Food first. Then conversation.

Nikki walks in the kitchen and drops her backpack by the door. "Smells good." Her wet hair is woven into two long braids on either side of her head. She's wearing overalls covered with embroidered multicolored flowers. The legs are rolled up at the hem to accommodate her black Dr. Martin boots. Underneath she's wearing a striped rainbow-colored tank top, which no doubt has some classic cartoon character sprawled across the front I'm unable to see.

She's a beautiful burst of sunshine on a cloudy day. A nineteen seventies burst of sunshine, because Nik is all about vintage clothing. She says it reminds her of a time when people were kinder to each other. I fuckin' love everything about this girl.

"Hey, sunshine. I could hear your stomach growling all the way from the bathroom," I tease her.

"That wasn't my stomach. I was singing," she laughs. There she is. My sassy, funny girl is back. "Mmm. I'll do a lap dance for some of that bacon." She comes up behind me and wraps her arms around my waist as I push the scrambled eggs around in the frying pan.

"I was going to share it with you for free but forget it now. I'll take the lap dance." I tilt my head back to kiss her cheek.

"Ha. I was totally going to give you the lap dance for free. But forget it now. You'll have to supply me with lots of bacon if you want it."

"What do I get for bacon *and* eggs?" I smile, handing her a filled plate.

"Everything. Anything." She says in a soft voice and gives me the Nikki look which could bring a monk to his knees, and not in prayer. My cock twitches.

"Ohh coffee. Yes. Please." She pulls a mug from the cabinet and pours herself a cup. Just like that the mood changes and she's back to focusing on her food. "You want some?"

"No thanks." I chuckle. "Already have some. It's not too good. I tried my best to make fresh brewed but all coffeemakers hate me. They only love Batt."

"You mean coffeemakers are into the strong, silent type? Huh. Never knew that." She teases and takes a sip of the motor oil disguised as coffee I managed to brew. Her flinch confirms what I already know about the taste.

"Pfft. Strong silent type. You mean brick wall who doesn't want to waste any time using his mouth to talk to the ladies because he has more important things to do to them with his mouth?" Batt's the smoothest non-talking ladies' man I've ever known. Whatever he's got, the puck bunnies hop over each other to get to him.

"Strong silent type sounds nicer." Another sip of coffee elicits another cringe. She shovels a forkful of eggs into her mouth to chase the bitter taste.

"Sorry. I'm not the best in the kitchen." I join her at the table with my coffee and plate of food.

"No. It's good. The eggs are delicious. Besides, hockey boy, you have other talents to make up for your lack of homemaking abilities." She winks.

"Hey. Didn't we already discuss this? You're not allowed to sexually objectify your person like that anymore." I wave my fork at her.

"Oh, okay. I'll never think of you in a sexual way again in the name of political correctness," she says in a serious tone and continues eating.

"Fuck that noise. As I said yesterday, objectify away. Consider me your plaything, inept at everything except the use of my tongue, fingers, and cock to keep you coming all day, every day." I wink right back at her and she chokes on the mouthful of coffee swill she just sipped.

She fans her hand in front of her face. "It's this coffee. It's super hot."

"Uh huh. The coffee made you hot." I grin into my cup and take a sip.

Gah. How is she drinking this shit?

We glance up at each other every few seconds while continuing to eat our breakfast in silence.

"We need to talk," we blurt out at the same time, breaking the silence.

"Sorry. You go," she says.

"No. You go ahead."

"No, really. You go." She takes another sip of coffee. Now I know she definitely loves me if she's willing to drink this toxic waste to not hurt my feelings.

"Okay. Here's the thing. I obviously have no intention of ever working with my father or for the studio and production company as long as he has anything to do with it. Right?"

"Uh. Right. I guess...if it's what you want or...*don't* want. What about Garrett?"

"Garrett's fine. He's practically king of the movie industry already and he has an entourage of people who work for him. He doesn't need me."

"Okaaay?" She crosses her legs underneath her Indian style and stops her fork mid-scoop to listen.

"I'm going to accept the offer to play for the Winds."

"Excuse me?" she coughs.

"The Santa Ana Winds. I'm going to accept their offer to play hockey for them. The contract they're offering is phenomenal. It's a dream come true, Nik."

"In...in California?" Her fork slips from her hand and clatters on the dish. She keeps swallowing even though I don't think there's any food in her mouth.

"Last time I checked that's where they were located."

I know this must be a shock coming out of the blue like this. But I didn't know until yesterday the whirlwind path our lives were going to take. It's coming out of the blue for me too.

"I know everything's happening kind of fast but they want me out there right away. I've been holding off giving them an answer because...well...because I wanted to stay near you. But timing is perfect now. I'm pretty much done with my course work. I talked it over with Coach De Luca. He says I can work everything out with my professors and finish whatever I need to online. What do ya think?"

"You're...you're leaving?" *Jesus.* Her eyes are tearing up again.

"Not *me*, baby, *we*." I take her hand in mine and stroke the back of it with my thumb. She's shaking like a leaf.

"I'm not going anywhere without you. I told you I'm never leaving you. I want you to go with me. It's perfect. We can get a house on the beach. You can put your toes in the sand and draw all day in the California sun."

"I...I can't move to California, Dalt." Her voice quivers.

"I can't move without you, Nik." If she thinks I'm moving three miles away from her let alone three-thousand, the multiple orgasms I gave her last night must have fried some brain cells.

"Listen. You can finish your degree out there. Some of the best art schools in the country are there. And if you want, Garrett can find you a job working for a studio on kid's movies or something. Not at ours, of course. I don't want my fucking father anywhere near you. I don't know. Whatever you want. We can figure it out."

"But the farm. I can't leave my mom and the farm." Her voice is soft and she's trembling.

"I thought you said your mom has some new superman in her life who's taking care of the farm now."

"She does but—"

"Nik, honey. Even if you didn't want to move to Cali, you'd have to move somewhere to do the kind of work you want to do, at least until you're as famous as Seuss." I sweep one braid back behind her shoulder. "Where are you going to show your work in Winter Harbor? The five and dime?"

Even though I know this is a major decision, not something to take lightly, I offer the glib comment to make her smile and relax. But truthfully, the comment isn't too far off the mark. Winter Harbor is the size of a postage stamp. Nikki's talents are way too special to be hidden away in a remote corner of the country.

"I know but...wait...how did you know the farm was in Winter Harbor?" Her sparkling eyes narrow and drill into me.

"Um...pretty sure you mentioned it."

"No. Pretty sure I didn't."

Shit. What's the big deal if I know her farm's in Winter Harbor?

"What? I had Wolfe do a little cyberstalking for me. No big deal." Her inquisitorial stare becomes wide-eyed and shocked. At least she doesn't look like she's going to bust out crying anymore.

"Nik, baby. You can't blame me. I missed your sweet face. I wanted to know how far away you were."

"The whole time I was out of school you knew where I was?" She's bouncing one knee up and down in agitation now.

"Why are we even talking about this? What differ-ence does it make now? Let's get back to the moving out to L.A. topic."

"You knew where I was but you never came there to find me, right?" Her leg is still bouncing and now she's chewing on her lips. Uh oh. She's pissed because I knew where she was but didn't go there to try to get her back. She's right. I was a complete asshole for not going to find her.

"Well...no. But it wasn't because I didn't want to see you. I—"

"Okay. Good." She blows out a big breath of air and stops fidgeting.

Okay, good? What the hell does that mean? Forget it. Get back to the important topic of conversation here.

"Right. Good."

What the fuck?

It's going to take me a lifetime to figure out what goes on inside her beautiful head.

"So, uh, what do you think about me signing with the Winds and us moving to Cali?"

"My family, school, the team, my scholarship. It's not that simple, Dalt."

"I realize it's asking a lot from you, Nik. But...well... dammit, I love you and we both know what it's like to be apart. I can't go through that again, babe. Can you?" She gives a slight shake of her head, keeps chewing on her lips and letting out shallow sighs. But doesn't say anything.

"You can play for another school out there. I'm sure any school would go crazy to have a striker like you. They'd be happy to offer you a scholarship. Or play for the college of your choice without a scholarship. I told you, money isn't a problem. Anything you want, Nik."

Still not a word.

"Nik, baby? This is one of those times you're going to have to say something. I need to know what you're thinking."

"This is a lot to take in, Dalt. A couple of days ago I was trying to figure out how to live my life without you. Today? Let's see. You made me come, what was it, about twenty times? Told me you're a gazillionaire. Professed your love for me and said you want to be with me forever. And now you want me to drop everything here: school, team, family, and run away with you to California to lay on the sand while you play professional hockey. Is that about it? Do I have it all straight?"

"Everything but the coming thing. I think it was more like thirty times."

"Real funny, hockey boy. Can you be serious, please?"

"I'm totally serious. You forgot to count the multiple times I used my tongue and fingers to get you screaming my name." Teasing required to get her to relax. But I'm not wrong about her count being off.

"Dalt..." I love her cute admonishing whine.

"Okay. You want serious, soccer girl? Here goes. There's only two things in this world I've ever really wanted. To play hockey was one of them. The other most important thing is sitting here right now giving me her best super-annoyed glare. You tell me what you want, baby girl. If you want to stay here to finish our degrees and take the next step when we get to it, I'm here with you. No pressure, no regrets. Because if I've learned anything in the last couple of years it's that nothing means anything if you're not in my life. I'm all in wherever or whenever you want. It's your call, Nik."

This may be the first time in our relationship I can't read her expression or body language. She looks distantly contented by my words but I'm also sensing an edge... nervousness or a tinge of melancholy.

"I...can I think about it? I need a little time to...just think."

"Sure, babe. Like I said, no pressure. But as I also said, I'm not going anywhere without you. If you say no, I'll move to Winter Harbor and get a job at the five and dime." I lean over and kiss her. The coffee tastes a lot better on her lips.

"I don't think they'd hire you, hockey boy. You're too much of a pain in the ass." She smirks and picks up her cup of sludge.

"Nice." Always the little smartass even when she's conflicted. "Now what did you want to tell me?"

Am I disappointed she didn't behave like the usual impulsive Nikki and throw herself into my arms saying of course I'll move to California with you? Sure. But realistically, it's a major decision and understandable why she needs some time.

"Tell you?" She pushes her eggs around her plate and she hasn't touched her bacon. If Nikki isn't gobbling down available bacon, you know something is weighing heavy on her mind. Could be my asking her to uproot her life and move with me at the drop of a hat, but I think there's more to it than that. Something was bothering her even before she went to take a shower.

"Nik?" I've never seen her this reticent. She normally has no problem telling me what's on her mind, giving me her opinion, telling me I'm a dumb fuck when I am one.

"Okay." She blows out a breath. "Well...um...I have something..."

My cell phone begins vibrating on the countertop. Nikki stops mid-sentence and glances at it. I ignore it until it stops buzzing.

"Sorry. Go ahead."

"Um...so...after you went..."

My fucking cell phone starts rattling on the counter-top, interrupting her again.

"You better get that," she says. "It could be important."

"Sorry. Let me see who it is. I'll get rid of them." I hop up and scoop my phone off the counter to see Garrett's number across the screen. I swipe the accept button.

"Hey, bro. 'Sup?" I hold a give-me-a-second finger up to Nikki. "I'll tell him I'll call him back later." I half mouth half whisper to her.

"*What?* Say that again." I put a finger over the micro-phone while my brother keeps ranting things I can't understand into my ear. "Sorry, babe. I have to take this. It might take a while. Can you hold that thought?"

"It's fine. I'm going to head back to the farm. I'll give you a call later." She rinses her plate and cup in the sink. "Oh and hockey boy?' She turns and places a kiss on my cheek. "I dammit love you too." She repeats the fucked expression of love I gave her earlier.

"Hang on, Garrett. I can't understand what you're saying." I drop the phone to my thigh and press it into my shorts to muffle the sound. "Wait, Nik. Don't go. Give me a few—"

"It's fine. It can wait a little longer. Talk to your brother. I'll call you when I get to the farm. Just lock up before you leave."

Garrett's yelling is frantic and loud enough, I can feel the sound vibrating my thigh.

"Hey. I dammit love you too," I call to her as she picks up her backpack and walks out the door. That gets me a sweet wave of her fingers and a forced smile. The melancholy semblance is back and it has me worried.

Chapter Twenty-Four

NIKKI

Yep. I chickened out. Hopeless chicken shit. When Dalt's phone rang I almost sighed in relief.

I climb behind the wheel of my rusty pickup and speed out of the driveway before Dalt has a chance to finish his phone call. The bald tires, which needed to be replaced about a hundred miles ago, spew gravel everywhere.

I'm a horrible, awful person taking off like this, running from the opportunity to tell him about Chloe, I know. But everything is moving at lightning speed. Now he's making plans to move to California to play hockey. It's getting more and more complicated.

It's not that I think Dalt will reject Chloe or be upset about her. Before my encounter with his meddling father, I pictured Dalt as someone who would be great with kids, a wonderful, loving father. When I found out I was pregnant, I didn't stress about telling him. I was certain he would be happy because I was sure we would be together forever. Starting a family a little earlier in our relationship would be tricky but we'd work it out.

The only reason I didn't tell him the minute I found out was because I wanted it to be romantic. I wanted to tell him when we were camping alone under the moonlight and stars. *Poetic mush,* as Dalt would say. Of course, now I know it was a monumental mistake. Because what frightens me the most about telling him, is that he may reject *me* when he finds out how I've deceived him. I want to believe he'll understand. But the more time I spend with him and remember what an amazing man he was and is, the more I can't even convince myself I was justified in keeping him out of Chloe's life.

When I get back to the farm, I'll talk it over with my mom. She'll be able to give me some advice on the best way to give Dalt the news which will change his life and the things he believes about me, forever. And when he hears it, will he want to move to L.A. and start his new life without me? How will this whole mess affect Chloe? Ugh. My head is swimming.

As I pull up to the driveway, the first thing I see is the wood sign my dad put up fifteen years ago. I remember him letting me 'help' him paint the big black letters on it, even though I didn't know how to spell yet. The rustic plague couldn't convey my dad's personality better if it was a complete biography.

WARNING!!
Alpacas can cause
An overwhelming
Loving sensation
to your soul.
Anyone with a
weak heart enter
at your own
risk.

Walking in the front door, I drop my pack under the coat hooks. I take in a huge breath. It's home: warm, comforting. Mom's baking. My stomach rumbles at the recognizable delectable smell of her homemade chocolate chips coming from the kitchen. She's the rock star of the biggest, gooiest chocolate chip cookies in Hancock County.

When I walk in the kitchen, she's bending over the stove taking a fresh batch of cookies out of the oven. Chloe is playing with cookie dough at the child-size table Matt built for her out of leftover pieces of lumber he found in the barn.

Matt is my mom's new farmhand. I keep saying new but he's been here for a little over a year. In the past year, I've seen him and my mom grow close. I was hesitant at first after what she'd been through with Bert. But Matt is the polar opposite of Bert. Matt's a good guy. He fawns over my mom like she's a queen. And she deserves that kind of love and attention because she's been taking care of everyone and everything else for so long, it's about time someone takes care of her.

"Mama! Mama!" Chloe screeches when she sees me standing in the doorway watching the heartening scene in front of me. She's a female mini-Dalt and if it's possible, his black hair and those stunning blue eyes are even more gorgeous on a girl. She's wearing her favorite outfit, pink leotards and tights, with a little tutu over them. I bought it for her after a weekend class trip to an art museum in Portland. It was a splurge, but I've haven't been able to give her very much. I figured if I cut out a few lunches, I could budget it in. I don't think she's taken it off since. My poor mom has to wash it almost every night when Chloe is in bed. She'll only take it off to get into her Cat in the Hat pajamas. Maybe there's a little of me in her after all.

"There's my little munchkin! How's my sweet baby?" I hold my arms out and Chloe runs toward me. I scoop her up and squeeze her tight. She smells like cookie dough and sweet baby girl.

"Nikki!" My mom's face lights up when she sees me.

I remember the day I told her about the mess with Dalt and had to add to the wreckage that I was pregnant. I was afraid I would never see the pride in her eyes again. But I couldn't have been more wrong. Her pride for me and the love she gives me has never wavered one iota. Not then, not now.

"Hey, honey. I didn't expect you until dinner time."

"I got an early start." I move across the room to her, while still holding Chloe in my arms, and kiss her on the cheek. She wipes her hands down her apron and wraps one arm around my shoulder to give me a mama bear hug.

"Smells like heaven in here." I take another big whiff.

"Chloe and I are making your favorite cookies. Aren't we, baby girl?" She places a kiss on my cheek and then one on Chloe's.

Chloe nods her head up and down in glee. "Tookie, Mama. Eat tookie." She wiggles in my arms, reaching down toward the butcher block island in front of the sink. Evidence of a morning's worth of baking is spread across it, racks of cooling cookies at one end. I check to make sure they're cool enough and lean Chloe down to grab one. The giant five-inch cookie is almost too big for her tiny hand.

"Bite. Num." She holds it to my mouth and repeats the words she's heard my mom and I say when spoon feeding her.

I take a big chomp of the gooey deliciousness and do a cookie monster imitation. "Num, num, num. Cookie good." Chloe giggles. I hug her tight in my arms, nearly crushing the rest of the cookie.

My eyes well with tears. For someone who hates crying, I've done more than my fair share lately. Squeezing my eyes closed, I attempt to push the tears back where they came from. When I open my eyes, the smile is gone from my mom's face, replaced by a worried expression.

"Nikki? Is everything okay?" I know what she's thinking. The last time she saw an expression like this on my face was when I was struggling to get over Dalt.

"Everything's fine. I just...can we talk when you have a minute?"

"Of course, sweetheart." She places one of my braids behind my shoulder.

"Hey! My three favorite girls, all in one room." Matt walks in and makes a beeline to my mom. He plants a kiss on her lips and I note the way she blushes but leans into him.

I can't deny I'm still a bit uncomfortable about their relationship. It's not Matt. He couldn't be more wonderful. Like I said, he dotes on my mom and couldn't be sweeter to Chloe and me. He's taken on the role of a grandfather to Chloe. She even calls him Papa, which is kind of why it's a bit weird.

My mom was only nineteen when she had me, which means she's only forty now and is still an incredibly beautiful woman. In fact, despite some of the tiny lines she acquired around the corners of her eyes from her years of worry and stress after Dad died, she could pass for my older sister rather than my mom. Matt is only thirty-three, hardly old enough to be anyone's grandfather. And despite the fact he behaves fatherly to me and grandfatherly to Chloe, I don't feel like he's much older than me. Could be because he doesn't appear to be much older than some of the guys I go to school with.

Mom met him when she was doing volunteer work for the firehouse my dad used to work out of. Matt is a volunteer fireman, which is the reason he's built like a Redwood tree. He's a little taller than Dalt and a bit wider across the shoulders. Where Dalt has the lean muscles of an athlete, Matt has solid but beefier muscles. He towers over my petite five-foot two mom and it's still kind of weird to see her with him. I mean, my dad was a big burly fireman too but he looked like a dad, not like Mr. July on one of the infamous firefighter calendars.

But when I see Matt and Mom together, I couldn't be happier for her. Matt gazes at her like she's the moon, stars, and all the planets in one little package. And I haven't seen Mom's eyes twinkle like that since my dad was alive.

"I hear we have our girl home for a few days." Matt smiles and drapes his arm around my mom's shoulders, tucking her into the safety of his huge frame. His lips tighten. A concerned demeanor sweeps across his face when he sees my expression.

"How's everything going, Nik. You okay? Anybody causing you any trouble at school?"

Since he has become such a big part of our lives, Mom asked me if it would be okay to share our story with Matt. When I was certain he only had our best interests at heart, I agreed. When he found out what Dalt had done, Matt threatened to come to Bernard and I quote, "ram that hockey stick up that pretty boy's ass." Thank goodness Mom was able to talk him off the ledge of fatherly retaliation. But she can't do anything about the way he hates Dalt, even though he's never met him. If he even hears his name mentioned, Matt growls. It might take him some time to get used to the new developments in my love-hate-love saga.

"I'm good, Matt. Everything's great." My forced smile may belie my words but I'm not ready to tell him what's going on with Dalt. I need to talk to my mom first.

"Papa! Papa!" Chloe wriggles in my arms and stretches her arms out to Matt.

Matt unhooks his arm from around my mom, takes Chloe out of my arms, and lifts her in the air. "There's my little ballerina. What are you up to today?" He spins her around a couple times and Chloe giggles.

"Tookies," she hiccoughs in between giggles.

"Cookies? Did you make one for your old papa?" He bounces her.

Her old papa? You mean her fitness model papa?

Anyway, the scene couldn't be cuter. I realize Matt is the only male figure Chloe has ever known and I love how much they love each other. Nevertheless, as I said, our little extended family is slightly peculiar.

"Matt, why don't you take Chloe out to visit Belle for a few minutes?" Mom suggests as she puts the teakettle on the stove. "Nikki and I need to have a cup of tea and some girl time."

"No problem, hon. Would you like to go see Belle, sweet pea?" Matt continues to bounce Chloe on his hip.

"Belle!" Chloe is more than happy to take him up on his offer. Belle is the newest addition to our livestock. Chloe was present at her birth and has decided Belle is her new baby.

"Belle want tookie." Chloe holds up the remainder of the melting cookie she's been clutching in her hand.

"Belle only likes her mama's milk right now, sweetheart. But maybe her mama wouldn't mind if you fed Belle a bottle of that. What do ya think?" Matt leans Chloe over the sink and washes the remnants of cookie and gooey chocolate off her hands. "Take your time, ladies. Chloe and I will be out in the yard having some fun." He bends down to give Mom another kiss, this time on the cheek.

"Thanks so much, Matt. I'll be out in a minute to give you a hand with the shearing."

"No need, Nikki girl. Your mom and I make a good team." He winks at my mom and a flush of pink colors her face. "We've almost made it through the whole herd."

"Already? The vacuuming and shearing both? Wow. You guys *are* a good team." Mom's eyes sparkle as she gazes up at Matt and he stares at her like she's his 'tookie.'

"Okay. Out of here you two. Lunch will be ready soon." Mom gives Matt a pat on his backside and there may have been a little squeeze added. More than I need to see, *ever*.

"See you in a few minutes, munchkin." I wave to Chloe as Matt carries her out the door.

The kettle whistles on cue. Tea is Mom's cure for anything ailing you, emotionally or physically. She decides what type based on your mood or illness. As a kid I drank my weight in Echinacea tea anytime Mom heard the slightest sniffle. Today I'm betting it will be her special blend of chamomile and rose petals for calming and stress relief.

"I have a wonderful new blend of chamomile. How does that sound?" My mom, the tea whisperer. Wait. She doesn't whisper to the tea. Whatever.

"Sounds perfect." I take two of her treasured cups and saucers out of the glass-doored cabinet in one corner of the kitchen and set them on the long trestle farmhouse table in the middle of the room.

My dad gave her the tea set with the delicate rosebud pattern on their second wedding anniversary. She takes such attentive care of it you would think it was china from the Ming Dynasty. It's the same way she cares for anything that provides a memory of my dad.

I take a seat while Mom pours the tea and then places a plate full of warm cookies on the table.

"Is everything okay at school?" she asks, taking the seat next to me.

"Everything is wonderful." I smile into my teacup before taking a sip of the comforting warm liquid.

"But...?"

"But it's a little complicated." I shrug.

"Complicated how, sweetheart?" She peers at me over the rim of her cup.

"Well...I'm...I'm back with Dalt," I blurt out and hold my breath, my eyes clenched closed. Silence, except for the sound of her cup sliding across the saucer.

I peek one eye open to see if she's fainted and managed to put her cup down first to keep it from getting broken. She hasn't. She's staring at me like I have two heads and one of them is spinning Exorcist-style.

"Oh, Nikki. No. I know he's Chloe's father and you miss him, but after what he did to you, honey. I don't think you—"

"No, Mom. He didn't do anything. Turns out his father lied about everything. Dalt wasn't engaged to anyone else and he didn't send his father to offer me the money. Dalt didn't know anything about it."

My explanation comes out in a bit of an angry tone. Not directed at my mom, of course, but at the man who nearly destroyed the life Dalt and I had together and kept Dalt and Chloe out of each other's lives for almost two years. I suppose, technically, I was the one who kept them apart, but Mr. Walker was definitely the noxious facilitator.

"But why? Why would his father do such an awful thing?" She shakes her head like she can't believe what I'm telling her.

"Apparently he tries to control everything Dalt does. He didn't want him to be involved with someone of my... my status, or lack of it. He wants Dalt to marry someone wealthy. There's some girl in California he wants him to marry. He made up the whole engagement and money thing to get me out of Dalt's life. And I was foolish enough to believe him and not trust in Dalt."

"I don't understand. He met with you without Dalt knowing about it, lied to you, and offered you money like you were some kind of...of...Why? Why would a father ever want to do something so horrible not only to you but to his own son?" Her hands are trembling around her tea cup as she contemplates the ramifications of Harrison Walker's actions. She swipes away the tears spilling from her eyes.

How do I explain something I don't understand myself? How could a woman who would have run through fire to keep me happy and loved ever understand why a father would do everything in his power to manipulate his son's life in the name of wealth and status, indifferent to any kind of love?

"I don't know." I let out a big sigh. "But Dalt has been nothing but wonderful to me now that we both know the truth. And he wants us to be together. We both want to be together."

"That's wonderful, sweetheart. I'm very happy for you." She places her hand atop mine. "But how does his father feel about it?"

"Dalt hasn't spoken to him yet. He wants to confront him in person." Mom nods in understanding. She's regained her composure enough to pick up her cup.

"The thing is...well, Dalt wants us to move to California. He's been offered a contract to play for an NHL team out there."

Uh oh. The cup is trembling in her hand again.

"California?" The word catches in her throat. "You and Chloe will be moving to California?" Her eyes are glazed over with tears but I can tell she's trying to hold them back. As usual she won't say a word to influence me one way or the other until she knows what I want.

"That's the other thing. Um...I haven't told him about Chloe yet." I'm not even sure I said the words aloud until I hear Mom's cup crash into its saucer. Thank goodness it didn't break or I'd have to heap my guilt over its loss on top of everything else.

"Oh, Nikki. Why? You know I was reluctant when you decided to keep her birth a secret from Dalt. But when you told me the circumstances and I thought about how horrible the Walkers were, I understood why you wanted to protect Chloe from them. But you can't keep his baby girl away from him one second more now that you know the truth. If he finds out before you tell him yourself, he's going to feel as betrayed by you as he was by his father."

She hasn't said anything I haven't said to myself a thousand times in the past two days.

"I know I have to tell him. I've been trying but I... I'm..."

"You're afraid you'll lose him again. I understand." She brushes a wayward strand of hair off my face. "When I got pregnant with you, I was scared to death to tell your dad. I thought he'd dump me and run from the responsibility, even though in my heart I knew he was a better man than that. He was all the wonderful things put together I had fallen in love with. When I told him, he took me in his arms, told me he loved me more than life itself, and said I'd made him the happiest man on Earth. We got married the next week."

Wait. What? They got pregnant with me before they were married?

Definitely a conversation we're going to have to have on another day.

"Tell him, Nikki. He'll understand your conflict after what his father put you both through. If he's half the man you believed he was when you fell in love with him, he's going to adore Chloe *and* you for giving her to him."

Our conversation is interrupted by the sound of a car coming up our graveled driveway.

"Who could that be? We're not expecting anyone else today."

Almost as if I could read it in the tea leaves, a feeling of dread sweeps over me.

Chapter Twenty-Five

NIKKI

My stomach drops when I see Dalt's shiny black Levante coming down the driveway. The panicked validation thumps in my head. Everything I've been fearing for the past two days is about to come true. I glance around to see where Matt and Chloe are, but they're nowhere in sight, probably still in back by the pen. I just need some time to talk to Dalt before he sees Chloe. Another scene in a Shakespearean tragedy about to take place. I run out to greet him.

"Hey, hockey boy!" I give an attempt at an excited welcome, but it sounds strained even to my ears. "Couldn't live without me even for one day, huh?" With a nervous laugh I throw my arms around his neck and he wraps his around my waist.

"Sorry, babe. I didn't mean to stalk you. I know you wanted the day to get things squared away but all hell's broken loose back home and Garrett's about to lose it. I couldn't leave without seeing you first and telling you face to face. I'd ask you to come with me but I know you said you need to help out here." He brushes a kiss across my lips and I find myself wishing I had some kind of magic powers to blink and whisk us both away. "Unless you'll change your mind and take a trip with me to Cali?"

"What happened? Is Garrett okay?" I glance around to see if the proverbial nerve-wracking coast is still clear.

"He's fine. But apparently my fucking father has gotten himself into a well-deserved pickle." He smirks.

"A...a pickle?" I'm trying to focus on what Dalt is saying but my mind is screaming at me to find somewhere to take him where we can talk before it's too late.

"Evidently the old bastard has gotten himself arrested for sexual abuse of a minor. He claims he didn't know the girl was only sixteen. The dumb fucker was wearing his big fake smile and nothing else when he let her take pictures of the two of them in his hot tub."

"Oh my God. He's just awful." The more I hear about his father the more I wish I hadn't stopped myself from throwing up on his shoes.

"Tell me about it. Now there are all kinds of women coming forward with sexual harassment charges against him. It was only a matter of time. I told Garrett it was bound to happen. The man is disgusting." Dalt runs a hand through his hair.

And then it happens. I hear Chloe's giggles and laughs coming toward us. She runs right past me and wraps her little arms around Dalt's legs like she's known him for years.

"Who's dis?" She cranes her neck back to look up at him.

I take a step back. Did the thought cross my mind to run away? Um...maybe, for just a second.

"Well hello there, sweetheart." Dalt squats down bringing his face level with Chloe's. She immediately reaches her arms out for him to lift her up. When Dalt scoops her into his arms and stands up, my breath catches in equal amounts of joy and terror.

"What's your name, gorgeous?" He bounces her like an expert at toddler bouncing.

"Toey," she answers and runs her tiny hand down her daddy's cheek. "Mama, who's dis?" she turns to me and asks. And there it is, the wide-eyed shock I've been dreading to see on Dalt's face.

"Mama?" His brow pinches in confusion. "Nikki, what..."

He stops midsentence and refocuses on Chloe. I know the second the dawn breaks and Dalt sees his own eyes staring back at him.

"She...she's mine." His voice breaks. "How? When? I don't—"

"It was Jägermeister night, in your car. Chloe's twenty months old," I answer in a quiet voice. "Chloe, this is...this is Dalt," I add, since my baby girl is looking between her muddle-headed mom and the stranger holding her, wondering what the heck is going on.

Dalt stares at me for a moment his head tilted, his brows squished together in utter confusion. In that moment everything he's thinking passes between us. How could I do this? Why did I do this? How could I have kept this from him even after everything we shared the past two days?

"Please, Dalt. Let me explain."

He shakes his head as the realization of all his unanswered questions fill his eyes with unshed tears. He holds his hand out to stop me from speaking. I clutch my arms around my waist not only to keep myself from falling apart but also to keep myself from reaching out to him. I'm afraid if I try to touch him he'll push me away.

"Dote." Chloe giggles and taps his face.

Dalt looks at her. "That's right, sweetheart. I'm Dalt. I'm your...I'm Dalt." He crushes her to his chest, burying his nose in her hair. I can't see them but I know the tears he's been holding back must be falling into Chloe's hair because his body is trembling with the strained attempt to keep Chloe from hearing him cry.

"Dalt, please. I...I was going to tell you." My voice cracks. My entire body is trembling. "I found out right before you left for the Boston game. I planned on telling you after you came back when we were alone on our camping trip. Then your father showed up and I was confused and scared." He's still clutching Chloe in his arms in a tight hug. He doesn't look at me. I don't even know if he's listening to me.

"Mama," Chloe whines and wiggles in his arms. I can see how tightly he's clutching her. She begins whimpering. Dalt becomes aware of her discomfort and when he loosens his grip, she reaches out to me. I take half a step toward them and Dalt hands her to me without looking into my eyes.

Oh God. This can't be happening.

I can't be losing him again. Not after everything we've said to each other.

"Nikki, honey. Is everything okay?" my mom calls out as she and Matt approach us. I don't know how long they've been there, how much they've seen.

"Mom, this is Dalt." I swipe a finger under both eyes. "Dalt, this is my mom, Rose, and Matt."

Dalt doesn't say a word, just swipes his palm across his cheeks to wipe away his tears and tips his head toward them. This is a scene right out of my absolute worst-case scenario nightmare.

"It's very nice to meet you, Dalt. I wish it was under better circumstances. You and Nikki need to talk, especially for Chloe's sake." Mom takes Chloe out of my arms. "Come on, baby girl. Nana's got lunch all ready for you."

"'Tay. Bye, Dote." Chloe waves, apparently having forgiven Dalt for the too tight squeeze.

"Bye, Chloe," Dalt whispers.

My heart is breaking. I want to hold him, comfort him. But I can't, because I did this to him. Not his father, me. I put that anguish in his eyes for the second time in two days. But this time it's worse. He won't even look at me.

"I hope you'll join us for lunch, Dalt. We'd love to have you." My mom looks up at Matt and blows out a big breath.

"Listen, kid," Matt growls. "You oughta give Nikki a chance to explain. You and your fuc...freakin' father put her through hell for two years."

Mom grabs Matt's arm and shakes her head in disapproval.

"Yeah, well, I understand you didn't have anything to do with it. But Nikki didn't know that," Matt says. "She was only trying to protect herself and her baby. What your dad did was fu...was messed up." Matt glances at Chloe.

Dalt takes a deep, pained breath and closes his eyes.

"Matt, I think we should give them some space. Give them time to talk, alone." Mom gives me a smile of encouragement and the three of them head back into the house.

When Dalt opens his eyes and glares at me for the first time in several minutes, I know this is every bit as bad as I had imagined it would be. This time his beautiful blue eyes aren't filled with torment, they're cold and as hard as flinty steel. He stumbles backward toward his car.

"Wait. Please listen." My brain is useless, filled with sludge I'm trying to wade through to find the right words to explain why I did what I did. "Try to understand. When your father came to the dorm the night you were away and told me all those lies and then offered me the money, I was so frightened. I was devastated by what I thought was your betrayal. But when I ran out of the dorm, away from him, all I could think about was my baby, *our* baby. It occurred to me how rich and powerful he must be to offer someone that kind of money on a whim. I thought if he found out I was pregnant he would try to make me either get rid of her or take her away from me. I couldn't let that happen. I loved the part of you growing inside me."

"So you lied to me. You lied to me because you thought I was as big of a monster as my father." His voice is flat, monotone.

"I was confused. I—"

"How about for the past two days while you were whispering words of love in my ears and we were fucking each other's brains out. Were you *confused* then?"

"No. I was scared...scared I was going to lose you when you found out what I had done." I drop my chin to my chest.

"What you had done? You mean lying to me about my child? You mean not telling me we had a baby girl? Keeping her away from me for almost two years? What? You were angry with me because you thought I had some other girl in California so you decided to take your ball home and not play with me anymore? She's not a fucking toy, Nik. She's a child who needed her daddy." His arms flail through the air as he snaps off the list of contemptible things I've done to him.

"No. I wasn't angry...I was..." I reach out to him and take a step toward him.

Dalt throws his hands up to block my touch. "Oh. No. That's right. You were scared. So scared, that last night when I was buried inside you or this morning when we were discussing our future, you still couldn't bring yourself to tell me I had a kid."

"Dalt, please." I reach for him again. My eyes are liquid with tears. His face has become a hazy blur.

"No, Nik." He backs away from me, this time grabbing the handle of his car door. "I love you. I do," his voice softens and my heart makes a hopeful leap. "But ," and with one word it crashes down to my toes, "you lied to me. Not just lied. This is the biggest, most hurtful deception I could ever imagine. And not only hurtful to me, you also hurt Chloe by keeping me out of her life. Christ. I thought this kind of shit only happens in some bad movie or cheesy novel." He pulls his car door open and it feels like the air is being sucked out of my lungs.

"I'm sorry. I'm so sorry. Stay. Please."

"I can't. I need some time to figure things out. I have to go to California for a few days to help Garrett work this shit out with my father. I'll...I'll call you." He slides in behind the steering wheel.

"But...but Chloe."

"I'll be here for Chloe. No matter what." He slams the door closed.

Wake up, Nikki. Just wake up. This isn't happening. This can't be happening.

Dalt's tear-filled eyes stay locked with mine for a moment. He places the palm of his hand flat against the window glass and mouths the words, "Bye, baby." His car circles in the driveway around me.

Raindrops begin to fall. I drop my head back to let them splash on the heat of my swollen face. When I lift my head and see the back of Dalt's car disappear out the gate at the end of our driveway, my legs give out from under me.

"You promised you would never leave me again," I whisper from my kneeling position before collapsing onto the gravel.

Chapter Twenty-Six

DALT

"I don't give a fuck if the motherfucker rots in jail. Do you know what he did? He deserves to rot in hell. Jail's too good for him."

I was supposed to be the one calming Garrett down after the shit hit the fan with my father, but now that I know exactly how thoroughly he managed to fuck up Nikki's, Chloe's and my life, I can't do anything but think about how much I want to punch my father's fucking face in.

I spent five hours on the private jet Garrett sent for me going over it and over it in my head. At one point I was so upset, Cindy, our flight attendant asked if she could get me a Xanax. I didn't take it because I don't want to feel calm. I want to face the bastard with every ounce of wrath I've been holding inside for him for all these years. If they hadn't already carted his sorry ass off to jail, they'd be picking up the pieces of him to arrest.

"I know," Garrett says apologetically from the leather executive office chair behind my father's massive hand carved mahogany desk. The pretentious prick had it shipped from overseas, claiming it would impress his business partners.

"What do you mean you know? You know what he did to Nikki?"

I can't believe what I'm hearing. I thought Garrett had my back. Why didn't he tell me?

He shrugs. "He told me she was a gold digger. Just some skank trying to get into your pockets."

"Just some skank? I told you I was in love with her. I poured my heart out to you. How could you let him do this?"

"Dad said she—"

"Nikki! Her name is Nikki."

"Yes. Nikki."

"She was pregnant for fuck's sake. If he knew she was pregnant, he wouldn't—"

"He knew."

"What did you say?" My eyes narrow as I try to glare a hole right through my brother's head.

"He knew she was pregnant. He'd been having her followed for weeks. He knew when she visited the ObGyn. His guy paid off one of the secretaries to get her records."

I come around the desk to stand next to him. "You sonovabitch! How could you go along with your mother-fucking father on this?" I grab him by his two-hundred-dollar shirt collar and pull him out of the chair. "You knew she was pregnant and you let him do that to her?"

He hooks his hands around my arms to try to get me to stop shaking him.

"He's your father too," he chokes out.

"He's never been a father to anyone. He doesn't know the meaning of the word father. He's just a sperm donor." I jerk him like there's a chance I can rattle some sense into his stupid head. "And you! You didn't even have the decency to tell me she had my kid?" I throw him back down into the chair.

"Dalt, for chrissakes calm the hell down."

"Calm down? I should punch every one of those fucking veneers out of your backstabbing fucking mouth." I run my hands through my hair to keep me from using them to bloody my own brother's face.

"He said the baby wasn't yours!" He yells over my rant. "Dad said she was spreading her legs for every jock in the school."

That's when I do it. For the first time in our lives I punch my brother in the face with every ounce of hatred I ever held for my father.

"Jesus Christ, Dalt. I think you broke my damn nose," he cries in a muffled whine, pinching his nose to try to stop the bleeding.

"I was in love with her, shithead. We were in love with each other. She never cheated on me and Chloe looks exactly like me. It's like staring into a mirror!"

"Chloe?" he squeaks through his hand which is still covering his bloody face.

"Chloe. My baby girl, you asshole! I gotta get outta here."

I'll call Dak. I need to vent or I'm going to explode.

But when I pull my phone from my pocket and push the button the screen doesn't light up. Shit. My phone's dead. I forgot to recharge it on the plane.

"I don't care what you do about the scumbag or the business," I inform my Judas brother as I head toward the door.

I'm crushed by his betrayal. I've lost my best friend in the world—my two best friends, all in one day.

"Hire one of his million-dollar lawyers to take the case. But I hope you, him, and your whole fucking empire go up in flames."

"You mean she kept the baby?" He grimaces when he moves his hand off his face.

Yep. By the looks of it I broke his fucking nose. He's lucky I don't keep going and break the rest of his traitorous bones.

"He told me she took the money and got rid of the baby."

"Tell me something, Garrett. How can you be such a complete dumbass when it comes to our father and yet be such a successful businessman?"

"Fuck. I didn't know. Dalt, I didn't know. I swear. I'm so sorry, bro," I hear him say to the back of the door as I slam it behind me.

Chapter Twenty-Seven

NIKKI

The sound of rain pummeling the roof jolts me out of my sleep. My head is throbbing. I blink at the ceiling a few times and remember I'm home at the farmhouse, but I don't remember getting in bed. The bedcovers are tucked around me. I breathe a sigh of relief. It was a dream, more like a nightmare. Either way, everything is okay now. I'm awake. I'll go back to Dalt's house and tell him about Chloe. He'll understand.

When I roll onto my side, I'm startled to see my mom sitting in the rocking chair in the corner of the room. Her head is tilted to one side and she's making gentle snoring noises. She hasn't fallen asleep sitting in my room since I was a child sick with the flu and she insisted on staying there all night in case I woke up and needed anything. Or...wait...no, the last time she slept here was when I came home from school after my encounter with Dalt's father and I was a basket case. I couldn't eat, couldn't sleep, almost couldn't breathe. She'd stayed in my room every night for a week.

I glance around the room once more and realize it's not morning. It's dark except for the soccer ball night-light plugged into one of the outlets. Throwing back the covers, I find I'm still in the same clothes I was in when I came to the farm; the same clothes I was wearing in my nightmare. Mom is still in the same clothes she was wearing. I touch my eyes. They're burning and my head throbs harder now that I'm sitting up. Oh God. It wasn't a dream. I gasp and the sound jolts my mom out of her uncomfortable slumber.

"Nikki? What are you doing, honey? Do you need something? How about some water? Let me get you some water." She pushes herself up from the rocker.

"No. I'm...how did I get up here?" I whisper because even the soft sound of my words pound inside of my head like a hammer.

"Matt carried you up. He found you sobbing on the ground in the middle of the driveway. You cried yourself to sleep." She sits on the edge of the bed next to me and strokes my hair. Her touch is soothing. I close my eyes and revel in her comfort. "Give him some time, sweetheart. With everything you told me about Dalt when you were dating, I'm sure he's a good man and he loves you. He'll come back to you and Chloe."

My eyes pop open when I hear his name. "What time is it? I have to go." I jump off my bed, run out my bedroom door, and down the stairs, taking two steps at a time.

"Go? Go where? Nikki it's the middle of the night

and it's pouring out." Mom races down the stairs behind me.

I grab a rain jacket off of one of the hooks and pick up my backpack and keys from the spot where I dropped them when I came in.

"Can you watch Chloe for me, Mom? I know I was supposed to be here over break but I have to go. I have to see him before he leaves for California."

"How do you know he hasn't left already? It's been hours since he was here."

"I'll call him on the way to check, ask him to wait for me." I lean in and kiss her on the cheek. "I have to try, Mom. I said all the things today except the most important one. I didn't tell him how much I love him."

"Wait. Let me get Matt to go with you. The weather is miserable."

"It's okay, Mom. I'll be fine. I'll call you when I get to Dalt's. Kiss Chloe for me." I hesitate before running out the door. "And thanks, Mom for always being there for me."

"Be careful, sweetheart, and call me as soon as you get there. I don't care what time it is." She wraps me in one of her big warm hugs and I hug her in return. I don't want to worry her, but I can't wait another second. I have to get to Dalt before he leaves.

I don't know what came over me. I'm stronger than this. Instead of simpering like a little girl, I should have simply stood my ground. Yes, I may have kept the significant knowledge of his having a daughter from him. A horrible, terrible mistake, I admit. But I was a pregnant woman on a mission to protect her child from his monster father, and as far as I knew at the time, from him too. Yes, I may have wasted two years of our lives together being a doubting fool, but does it mean we should throw away the rest of our lives together? Waste even more time? We have a beautiful little girl who needs us. He's just going to have to get past his hurt and anger and whatever other unconstructive emotions is getting in our way because dammit, we love each other and—to use his own words—we belong together. That's what I should have said long before now and what I'm going to say when I see him tonight.

I start up the engine. Before shifting into drive, I pull up Dalt's number and press the call button. The call goes straight to his voicemail. Either his phone is turned off or he's blocking my calls. I press end call but hit redial just to be sure. Straight to voicemail. I'm hesitant to leave a message, but since I have an hour drive back to Bar Harbor I decide to leave one to let him know I'm coming. Hopefully he hasn't blocked me and he'll get it. He might delay his trip to California if he knows I'm on my way.

"Dalt, it's me...Nikki."

Stupid. Of course he knows it's you.

"Um, anyway. I hope you haven't left yet. If you haven't...um...please don't leave yet. Please wait. I'm on my way back to your house. I...I love you...so much. Please, just wait for me."

I hit end call, shift into drive, and skid out of the wet driveway.

The things I want to say to him repeat inside my head as I push down on the gas pedal. The rain is coming down even harder now. I blink rapidly a few times and squint like it will help to improve my visibility. Cranking the speed of the windshield wipers to high, I try not to dwell on any negative thoughts like: Dalt hasn't tried to call me in hours, he hasn't returned my call, even though I only left the message a few minutes ago. Or he's turned off his phone, or blocked my number because he doesn't want to get any calls from me.

Sunlight is just beginning to glow over the horizon when the curve in the road looms in front of me. The thought flashes across my mind, *you're going too fast to take this curve.* I hear the screech of my tires right before the world turns upside down and everything goes black.

Chapter Twenty-Eight

DALT

"Stop. Just stop talking." Dak holds up a hand to stop the verbal vomit I'm spewing all over Tracey, Alex, and him as I pace. They're sitting on lounge chairs around Dak's pool at his parents' Malibu beach house. Up until now no one had said a word, too dumbstruck by my story. Batt and Wolfe are missing my tirade. Batt met some chick on the beach today and they're somewhere giving each other '*surfing*' lessons and Wolfe is getting an actual surfing lesson from Heaven, Dak's little sister.

"Are you telling us you have a kid?" Dak asks.

"Oh my God." Tracey beams. "I'm an auntie."

"Oh, my fucking word. You and Nikki have a baby girl? She must be a little goddess," Alex swoons.

"Congratulations, dude!" Dak walks over and lifts my hand to shake it.

"What the hell are you guys talking about? You're

missing the whole point here. Yes, I have a baby girl. But my father *and* my brother cooked up this whole scheme to break me and Nikki up, even though they knew she was pregnant. And *Nikki* lied to me for two years and didn't tell me about Chloe all that time. I've had a daughter for two years and she didn't tell me!"

"Aww, Chloe. Gorg name." Alex nods his approval.

"You're father's a fucked-up mess," Dak says. "Sorry, dude. But it's not like you haven't known that since you were a kid. Now, Garret's another story. I'm not sure how he falls for your father's evildoings time after time. You know he's always had blinders on when it comes to dear old dickhead dad. Who cares about them now? Where's Nikki and Chloe? You guys can stay here while you're dealing with the rest of the shit with your father."

That's it? Congratulations? I'm an auntie? 'Gorg' name? That's their words of wisdom and sympathy at how horrific my family and Nikki have treated me?

"Yeah. Where is the sneaky little thing? I knew I recognized the little girl in her drawings. I just didn't put two and two hundred together on how she's the spitting image of you, Dalt. Nik is so going to hear about keeping my beautiful little niece from me," Tracey laughs and waggles a finger. "Where is she hiding to keep me from giving her a piece of my mind?"

"Uh...um...Nik's not here."

"What do you mean she's not here? Where is she?" Alex blinks a couple of times, waiting for my clever answer as to why the love of my life, the mother of my child, and said child, aren't here with me.

"She's...they're in Winter Harbor at her farm. I...I

kind of left them there." As I stutter through my answer the reality of what I've done occurs to me: I left Nikki—the woman I professed unending love for just the day before—crying as I drove away from her. And I let someone take my baby girl, whose first two years of life I was absent for, out of my arms and walk away.

"What do you mean you *kind of* left them there?" Tracey stands up and gives me a narrow-eyed glare.

"I...I was hurt, pissed off." I run a hand down the back of my neck. "She lied to me for fuck's sake about my kid! What was I supposed to do, say no biggie? Not a problem. I had a kid for two years and you kept her a secret."

"You fucking asshat. *You* were hurt? *You* were pissed off?" Dak mimics me in a whiny voice. "What are you, a thirteen-year-old girl?" He shoves me in the shoulder. "You're an even bigger pussy than I thought you were when you wouldn't kiss Susie Akers at her tenth birthday party when the bottle pointed to you." He shoves me again.

"What the fuck, man?"

"I'll tell you what the fuck, man. Nikki is a one in a million lady," Alex chimes in. "If I was playing for her team I would have stepped in and stolen her away from your tight, fine ass a long time ago." He snaps his fingers.

"Dalt, she's crazy in love with you." Tracey's voice softens. "And what about Chloe?"

"I'll tell you what the fuck else," Dak snarls his two cents. "*You've* been madly in love with *Nikki* ever since the first day you laid eyes on her. All the guys knew it. We watched you fuck around with bunnies just to try to get over her and saw the way you got all irate and miserable every time you saw her with another guy. Are you going to let your douchebag father get in the way of everything you've wanted since you met her, you big dumbass? Are you going to be complicit in his scheme to keep you separated from the love of your life and your kid?"

I let out a big stream of air and drop my chin to my chest. The weight of my stupid, empty head is too much to hold up for one more second. They're right, of course. I told Nikki yesterday I couldn't live without her and I meant it. I already knew my father had messed with her head big time, but even then, I didn't realize how evil he could be. Why the fuck am I taking it out on her and Chloe?

"I have to go make a call. And a plane reservation back to Maine."

"Yeah you do." Trace embraces me and plants a kiss on my cheek.

"Okay. That'll be enough of that," Dak laughs and pulls us apart. "Go get your own lady back." He hooks my head in a lock and this time the fucker gives me a noogie, but I don't elbow him in the gut because I owe him big. My bro's wisdom may have just saved me from losing the woman of my dreams.

I head out to my rented Rubicon, parked in Dak's driveway. I left my phone plugged into the charger. When I pull up the screen I see I have a missed voice message from Nikki from last night. Shit. She probably thinks I'm ignoring her. I push play on the message screen and when I hear Nik's sweet voice plead with me to wait for her and then tell me she loves me, I get a stab of pain in my heart. I don't know how I'm going to wait five hours to get back to her, but when I do I'm going to drop to my knees and beg her for forgiveness.

I push Nikki's number to return the call. After several rings a woman answers. For a second I think I called the wrong number, but when I pull the phone away from my ear and the screen lights up, Nikki's number is displayed across it.

"Hello? Is Nikki there?"

"I'm sorry, Dalt. Nikki can't come to the phone right now." The woman's voice on the other end of the line is quiet. I don't recognize it and can barely hear what she's saying. *"This is Rose. She's—"*

"Oh, Mrs. Dixon. Rose. Please. I know Nikki probably doesn't want to speak to me. I shouldn't have left. It was a stupid kneejerk reaction to finding out about Chloe. But please, I need to speak to her. I want to tell her how sorry I am. I—"

"Nikki's been in an accident. She's...she's in a coma."

I don't know if the call disconnects before or after I drop my phone. I can't have heard her right. I try to call back several times on my way to the airport but Nikki's phone keeps going straight to voicemail and I don't have any other number to contact her mom.

Fuck. Fuck. Fuck.

I slam the steering wheel as I drive about a hundred miles an hour to the airport. The next few hours are the longest hours of my life.

Chapter Twenty-Nine

DALT

I drive straight to the farm from the airport, praying someone will be there to tell me where Nikki is and what the hell is going on. It's nine o'clock by the time I get there and already dark. I can see lights on in some of the downstairs windows of the farmhouse. They're home. Maybe I misunderstood what Rose said on the phone.

Please God. Let it be a misunderstanding.

After I pound on the door like a wild man, Matt answers. He's clearly distraught. It's unnerving to see a guy his size with a swollen face and red eyes. His hair is disheveled and his face is covered with unshaven scruff. It's like seeing a cement wall crumble right before my eyes.

"You. What do you want?" he spits the question at me and swipes his palm across his face.

"I...I'm looking for Nikki. Is she here?"

"No." He starts to close the door in my face but I slam my hand onto the peeling paint to stop him.

"Is she...is she okay?" I want to scream 'please stop wasting time. I have to get to her.' But I'm afraid if I don't remain calm, he won't give me any information.

"No. She's not okay. She's at the hospital. She flipped the truck chasing down your sorry ass. She's unconscious. Her mom is with her. I have Chloe. Not that you give a rat's ass."

Thank God. Chloe is okay.

"Hospital. What hospital?"

"What do you care, pretty boy? Leave her the fuck alone. Haven't you hurt her enough?" *Jesus Christ.* This guy is bigger than me and might crush me but if I have to I'm going to beat the information out of him to get to Nikki.

"No. I mean, yes. Please. I know you must hate me right now and I don't blame you. I hate myself, but I have to go to her. Please. She needs me. I know she would want me there. Please."

Does he want me to beg? If I have to get down on my knees and grovel, I will.

He doesn't say a word.

"Just tell me where the fuck she is!" I swear I see fire flash in his eyes when I yell. "Please, sir," I lower my voice. "I'm a big, dumb jackass and all the rotten things you're thinking about me are probably true, but I'm in love with Nikki and I think she loves me. I have to be with her."

He rubs a hand down the back of his neck. "She's at Maine Coast Memorial." He relents and puffs out with a shrug. "They wanted to Medevac her but it would have taken longer to get the chopper here than if I had the first responder medics from the fire station get her there."

Christ. Medevac. It's bad.

"Thank you." I start to leave but hesitate for a second. "And thank you for taking such good care of Chloe." I take the porch steps two at a time to get to my car.

"Hey, pretty boy!" Matt yells as I open my car door. "If Nikki pulls through this and you ever hurt her again, you're going to need your own bed in the hospital. You got it?"

I nod because I know he just asked me a question, but I don't comprehend one word he says after, 'if she pulls through this.'

The woman at the receptionist desk glances up at me from over the top of her glasses.

"Sorry. Visiting hours are over. They're from nine to seven." She continues tapping at her keyboard.

"They brought a young woman here earlier. She was in a car accident. Nikki Dixon. I have to see her." I sputter out into between gasps of much needed air after sprinting from the parking garage up four flights because the elevator was taking too long.

"I'm sorry. Visiting hours are—"

I stop myself from jumping over the top of the counter to push her out of the way to check the computer myself. Time to use the honey instead of the vinegar approach.

"I'm sorry to be such a pest...uh..." I take a quick glance at her nametag, "Grace, but I've travelled about nine hours and three-thousand miles to get here to see my fiancé. I hopped right on a plane the second I heard about her accident. I have to see her. We never go to bed without saying goodnight and giving each other a kiss."

I lean over the counter to give her a good view of the ridiculous puppy eyes I'm throwing her way. "Even if we're on different sides of the country we make sure to FaceTime and uh...do whatever we need to do to be sure we take care of each other before we go to sleep. You know what I mean?" I run my tongue over my lips in the flirtatious way that drives the ladies crazy. Grace's gaze drops to my mouth and she takes off her glasses and starts using them to fan herself. They can't be giving her much of a breeze.

I know. I'm an asshole. But since it's become my MO these days I may as well use it to my advantage. It's fucked up I have to be doing this crap at a time like this but I am not waiting until tomorrow morning to see Nikki.

"I just have to see her." I suck in my bottom lip and I swear to God Grace licks *her* lips and sighs. Her fingers return to clicking away at the keyboard. She pulls her gaze away from mine for a quick glance down at her computer screen.

"Ms. Dixon is in the intensive care unit on the fifth floor," she purrs. "They brought her..."

I don't hear the rest of her sentence because I'm

already on the elevator before she finishes. In the few minutes it takes to get to the fifth floor, I dial Garrett. He picks up on the first ring.

"Dalt, listen, man. I thought I was doing what was best for you, bro. I swear."

I'm not interested in listening to his apologies or reasons right now. We can deal with all of it later. *"Garrett, I need you to contact some of your connections from Mom's hospital."* Technically it's not my mom's hospital but it is the hospital Garrett and I had built in her memory, the Cynthia Walker Memorial Hospital.

"I need you to find out who the best traumatic brain injury doctor on the East Coast is and send the private jet to get him or her here."

"Send him there? Where? Where are you?"

"I'm in Maine. I need you to do it ASAP." The elevator dings and the doors take an eternity to open. Okay. It may have only been seconds but it doesn't stop me from wanting to rip them open with my bare hands.

"What are you talking about? Are you okay? What the hell are you doing in Maine? Weren't you just here this morning?"

His understandable confusion is grating on my nerves more than the elevator doors. I don't have time for this.

I step from the elevator and search in both directions to determine which way to go. I get the answer when I see Rose pacing back in forth in front of the nurses' station down the hall.

"What do you mean send a doctor to—"

"Garrett, I need you to shut the fuck up and listen to

me. As I see it, you owe me big time for believing every fucked-up thing our father has ever told you and doing your best to ruin my life." He doesn't ask any more questions. I can almost hear him nodding.

"I need you to find the best TBI doctor and get his ass on our jet to Bangor International ASAP. I'll have a chopper waiting to bring him to Maine Coast Memorial. Do you understand me?"

"Yes. I understand you," he says in a slow and distinct tone, as if to assure me he's not an idiot. Since yesterday, however, I question his genius level I.Q.

"Good."

"But why do you need a TBI doc and how am I supposed to find out who that is and get him out there at this short notice? I'm not a magician for chrissakes."

"I don't fuckin' care if you have to pull him off his yacht, or out of his woman, just get his ass out here. Nikki's been in an accident. She's unconscious. I don't know if she's…just get him out here."

My throat tightens at the thought of using words like *coma* or *survive*. I have to hold it together. Nikki needs me to be strong.

"Jesus Christ. I'm so sorry, bro. I'll get him out there. What else can I do?"

"Call me back with the info as soon as you've contacted him. I want to know when to expect him."

"Got it. What else?"

"Have your lawyer contact the administrator of this hospital and get me clearance to stay with Nikki. I don't want to deal with their bullshit rules. I don't care if we have to build them a wing in Mom's name. Give them

whatever it takes because I am not leaving her side. Also, Dak is out there on break. Can you give him a call and let him know what happened? He'll want to know."

"Will do. Dalt, man, I'm so sorr—"

"I gotta go."

The thought of my vibrant Nikki lying helpless in a hospital bed because of me flashes across my mind. I can't deal with my dysfunctional family issues right now.

"Do this for me, Garrett. Please." My voice cracks. *"I can't lose her."*

"It's done. Hang in there. She needs you."

Chapter Thirty

DALT

It's easy to see where Nikki gets her amazing piercing blue eyes. Her mom's are the same stunning color. Although, even from twenty feet away, I can see Rose Dixon's are red and swollen right now. As she watches me approaching, her tired weary eyes are doing the pulverizing laser-beam glare thing Nikki has thrown me more than once in the past few months. Needless to say, Rose isn't happy to see me. Every bone in her small frame stiffens as I walk toward her.

Her stature is different than Nikki's. Where Nik has the strong, solid frame of an athlete, her mom is petite and fragile in appearance, though from everything Nikki has told me about her, Rose is as resilient as they come in tough situations. Her delicate appearance but irrepressible character reminds me of the way *my* mom described the Verbena daisies she had in the flower garden she spent hours in before she died, delicate in appearance but resistant to harsh conditions.

Rose's shoulders pull back and her stance widens like she's about to block the fire breathing dragon from getting to her daughter.

I surge ahead. "How is she? Can I see her?"

I should be begging for her forgiveness for what I've done to Nikki, but there will be time for apologies later. Right now, being by Nikki's side is the most important thing. When I get within five feet of Rose, I discover the entire wall across the hall from the nurses' station is glass.

I'm unable to breathe while at the same time my heartbeat kicks up and pounds against my ribs when I see Nikki lying in a bed on the other side of the glass. Aside from the tubes and lines protruding from everywhere on her body and the full leg cast covering her right leg, she looks like Sleeping Beauty. Her platinum hair is spread out on the pillow propped under her head, her blue bangs are brushed to one side, and there's not one scratch or mark on her beautiful face to indicate she was in a horrific accident.

I press my hand onto the cold glass trying to will Nikki to open her eyes.

"What have they told you? What's her diagnosis?"

Rose walks up beside me and stares through the window at her broken daughter. Fresh tears follow trails down her already stained face.

"They're not sure," she whispers. "They won't know anything for a day or two unless she wakes up before that. They can't get an accurate evaluation because of the tracheal tube and residual effects of surgery."

"Surgery? She had surgery?"

"Her leg. She had multiple fractures. I...I don't know if..." Rose breaks down and begins sobbing.

I drape my arms around her in an awkward hug. She may push me away, but the only thing I have to offer in compensation for what I've done is a small amount of comfort and support. She doesn't push me away, and instead collapses into me, sobbing uncontrollably.

"She's going to be okay. Nikki's strong. She's a fighter. She'll be okay."

I'm not sure who I'm trying to convince, Rose or me. But her shoulders stop convulsing, her sobs quiet, and she steps back.

"Do you love her?" she asks. "Because if you do you should be by her side. But if you don't, I don't want you here to hurt her any more than you already have."

"She's my life and I'm not going anywhere," I answer without hesitation.

Rose nods and pushes open the door to the intensive care unit, gesturing for me to go in. As she stands there holding the door for me, I note her exhausted appearance.

"Excuse me? Is there somewhere Mrs. Dixon could lie down for a few minutes to get some rest?" I ask the nurse sitting at the station desk.

"Yes. I have a bed down the hall we use for family members in these circumstances," the nurse replies. "I suggested several times Mrs. Dixon should try to get some rest." She comes from around the desk and puts her arm around Rose's shoulder. "You can't let yourself get run down and sick. Your daughter's going to need your strength when she wakes up."

The nurse's encouragement works and Rose nods in agreement.

"I won't leave Nikki's side," I tell her, then let her know about the specialist I have coming to evaluate Nikki.

She doesn't ask any questions. Her exhausted mind and body are probably too drained to ask for any information. Still, the tension drops from her shoulders a bit and she breathes out, "Thank you," and walks down the hall with the nurse.

When I'm about to enter Nikki's room, my phone vibrates with an incoming text message.

GARRETT

> Dr. Daniel Hensley. Top in the field. He's coming in from Johns Hopkins. I chartered a jet in Maryland for him. It's faster than sending ours cross country. Four hours, tops. Hang in there.

> Thank you

Standing next to Nikki's bed, I feather my fingers down her cheek. Her skin is soft and warm. I lean down and replace my fingers with my lips, brushing a kiss on her cheek and then one on her forehead. "I'm here, baby. Please open your eyes, sweetheart. Wake up for me, Nik. Chloe and I need you to stay with us."

I pull up a chair next to her bed and continue to plead with her for the next few hours to come back to me.

I'm not sure how much time has passed when I feel a hand on my shoulder jarring me awake.

"Dr. Hensley is here, Mr. Walker."

I must have drifted off to sleep while whispering in Nikki's ear. I'm slumped over in the chair, my head resting on her pillow. The first thing I see when I blink open my eyes is her beautiful profile. My nose is pressed against her face.

"Dr. Hensley is here, Mr. Walker," the person shaking my shoulder repeats. I sit up. The stiffness in my back and neck sends a painful reminder not to fall asleep hunched over in a chair.

"What time is it?" I try to get my bearings.

Nikki. Accident. Hospital.

The terrifying realities come flooding back.

A gray-haired man in a tan button-down sweater vest and olive-green corduroy pants is standing over me next to Rose and a different nurse from the one at the desk last night.

"Not the best sleeping position for your spine, son." The man, who I assume is Dr. Hensley, points out the obvious. "This young lady must be Ms. Dixon." He leans in to take a closer look at Nikki. His appearance is more that of Mark Twain than Charles Mayo. If we weren't in an intensive care unit I'd expect him to pull out his corn cob pipe.

I glance at Nikki. She's in the exact same position she was last night. Her eyes are closed, her hands still strapped to the bed to keep her from pulling out any of her lines if she should move in a sudden spasm. The dim spark of optimism I held hoping she would be awake today fizzles.

"I'm Dalton Walker, and you must be Dr. Hensley." I pop up from my chair-bed and extend a hand in greeting.

"Yup." Dr. Hensley acknowledges my introduction but doesn't take his assessing eyes off Nikki to take my hand.

"Thank you for coming, Dr. Hensley. I appreciate you traveling all this way."

"With the generous donation your brother gave my research foundation, Mr. Walker, there's no need to thank me." He runs his hand down Nikki's left leg through the covers.

"Whatever it takes. Money is no object. Just bring Nikki back to me."

"How long has Ms. Dixon been out of surgery?" He turns to the nurse without commenting on my offer.

"Fifteen hours, doctor."

He glances over to me. "Give me a chance to evaluate Ms. Dixon, then I can give you my prognosis."

"Yes. Thank you, sir." Something about his no-nonsense demeanor tells me if anyone can help Nikki, this is the man to do it. My optimism rekindles.

Dr. Hensley turns to me for the first time since entering the room. "But I have to be honest with you. Money isn't the issue here, son. There's no amount of money that will bring Nikki back to who she was before if there's too much brain trauma."

I had almost forgotten Rose was standing there until she lets out a little gasp. Dr. Hensley's words succeed in extinguishing my hope.

He must read the despair on my face and hear the sound of Rose's distress because he adds, "But let's not put the cart before the horse here. Give me some time and I can give you a better idea as to what we're dealing with."

"How long before you have some idea, doctor?" Rose asks in a weak voice.

"I've already read Nikki's charts and I've spoken to the attending physician. If you can give me some time to do my own evaluation, I can better answer some of your questions. Ms. Blanchard, will you stay and assist me, please?"

"Of course, doctor," the nurse replies. "Mr. Walker, if you and Mrs. Dixon will have a seat in the guest area, I'll call you in when Dr. Hensley is finished with his evaluation."

I don't want to leave Nikki even for a minute but I brought Hensley here because he's one of the best in the country. I have to follow his instructions and let him do whatever it is he needs to do to help her.

Chapter Thirty-One

DALT

I pace the floor of the lounge area outside the intensive care unit for traumatic injury. Glancing up at the clock on the wall, I note the seconds ticking by in slow, methodical clicks. It's only six a.m. It feels like it's been a lifetime since I heard the news about Nikki's accident.

I wonder what it feels like to Nik, cocooned all alone inside her own head. Does she remember what happened, where she is? Is she scared? I want to be in the room with her, holding her, telling her everything will be okay. Will she even know I'm here and how much I love her? Does she hear me when I tell her I'll never leave her? Ha. Yeah right. Will she ever believe me again when I make the bullshit promise I reneged on after one day?

"Can I get you a cup of coffee?" Rose's voice pulls me out of my restless thoughts.

"Uh...thanks, no. Can I get you something?" I should be the one trying to comfort her. She looks like she's on the verge of needing to climb into a hospital bed herself.

"No. Thank you. Matt will be here soon. He said he packed some food. Even though I told him I wasn't hungry, he insisted." A slight smile tips the corner of her lips but disappears almost as fast.

"Is he bringing Chloe with him?"

I can't wait to hold my baby girl. But I'm not sure she should see Nikki like this. All the tubes, lines, and machines hooked to her mama might frighten her too much.

"No. I want to wait until Nikki wakes up in the next day or two for Chloe to see her." She says it with such conviction, like there's no doubt in her mind Nikki will be awake by tomorrow or the next day. "My friend Ellen is coming to stay with her. Chloe knows her. We've been friends since we were girls and Chloe thinks of her as another grandma." She stares at the wall in front of her as she speaks. Her voice sounds hollow as she distractedly answers my question. "Do you need Matt to pick anything up for you?" She glances at me for the first time.

"Well...yes, actually." The thought occurs to me it may be the only way I have to get these items without having to leave the hospital. "I've been trying to figure out how to get these." I pull a pen from my pocket and click it open. Looking around the room for something to write on, I spot a roll of paper towels hanging on the wall. I tear one off to use as makeshift notepaper. After scribbling my list, I hand it to Rose.

"Can you ask him to find somewhere to pick these up?"

Rose reads over the list, giving me a puzzled look. "Nikki has most of these at home in her room."

"Perfect. Can you ask him to bring them, please?"

"Yes. I...I'll give him a call right now before he leaves."

While waiting for an excruciating hour and a half for Dr. Hensley to finish his evaluation, I use my phone to do a search for his credentials. The guy may appear eccentric but he's a rock star when it comes to brain injury, neurosurgery research, and acute care. The list of studies he's participated in is as long as my arm. Which is the reason why when Nurse Blanchard comes into the lounge to tell us Dr. Hensley is ready for us, I stop breathing for a moment. I know whatever he tells us about Nik's condition and prognosis, good or bad, is the most accurate information we're going to get.

Rose's apprehensive expression is mirroring my own. Matt, who arrived about an hour ago, has his arm around Rose's shoulder and has somewhat pulled himself together since I saw him at the farm. It's obvious he's trying his best to remain stoic for Rose's sake. But when he glowers back at me, the stoicism is replaced by pure hatred. He can't be thinking anything worse about me I haven't already thought myself.

As we follow Ms. Blanchard down the corridor to Nikki's room, Rose reaches out and takes my hand, interlacing her fingers in mine. Matt grunts behind us but I'm grateful for Rose's support, even though I don't deserve it.

Dr. Hensley wastes no time taking us aside, away from Nikki's bed, and firing off his findings. He tells us after consulting with Nik's physician they agreed the tracheal tube could be removed since it had been long enough for the surgical sedative to wear off and Nikki was breathing on her own. Without the hindrance of the tube and effects of the sedative, he was able to get a more accurate assessment of Nikki's condition.

"Her Glasgow score is borderline. She's ranging somewhere around a ten, which means there is some motor withdrawal response to pain stimulation and some incoherent verbal response. However, she hasn't opened her eyes. I reviewed her CT scan and MRI. There doesn't appear to be any intracranial pressure or severe injury, although there is some slight bruising on the cerebellum. It appears to be minimal, which is good. But it may cause some problems with balance and coordination in the future. It's hard to say at this time."

"But she's a soccer player," I blurt out like a mindless ass. The man is telling us whether or not Nikki will live or die or have permanent disabilities and I'm worried about soccer.

"Soccer is very important to Nikki. Her father taught her to play when she was only three and she's been playing ever since," Rose interjects and squeezes my hand to assure me my concern for soccer would be a priority to Nikki as well.

"It's too soon to know anything regarding coordina-tion issues, but with the severity of the leg injury, soccer may not be in her future, regardless of the cerebellar issue," he whispers.

"Can she hear us?" I glance over at Nik. How would I feel if I opened my eyes one morning and someone told me I'd never be able to play hockey again?

"Yes. In all likelihood she can. Most moderately comatose patients I've treated in the past have said they could hear voices in the room though they couldn't always discern what was being said."

"But you're saying she *will* wake up?" Matt asks, the most important question of all. "Matt Grisham. Nikki's stepfather," Matt declares his recent promotion to fatherly status and extends his hand to Dr. Hensley. Rose looks up at him in wide-eyed astonishment then smiles when Matt gives her a return once-over which seems to say 'that's right, you heard me.'

"When it comes to brain injury and healing, it is as diversified as there are people with brains. We can never be one hundred percent certain of anything. Since Nikki is still unconscious and not completely responsive, a prognosis at this time can be difficult." Dr. Hensley takes a deep breath. "At this point I'm cautiously optimistic about Nikki's prognosis. I will report it as fair to her physician."

"How long before she wakes up?" I ask.

"I understand you want a definitive timeline. But with head trauma and coma patients, it's impossible to give a decisive answer. As I said, Ms. Dixon's score is borderline. It's not low enough to be considered severe but it's not high enough to be considered mild. Perhaps in a few days she can be reevaluated to get a more positive answer, but for right now I've given you the best information I can."

That's it? She's not too bad but she's not too good either? What does that even mean? There must be something more we can do.

"What should we do for her in the meantime? To help her, I mean."

"The doctors and nurses here are giving Nikki the best care possible. Ms. Blanchard will keep a watchful eye on her to assess any changes. The best all of you can do is take turns staying with her. Talk to her. Touch her. Reassure her. Provide stimulus. She'll know you're here. It can help to pull her out of the darkness."

Darkness.

I hate this. It's like we're trapped in a bad episode of *Stranger Things* and Nikki has been sucked into the other world.

Then I remember the bag Matt brought in with him. I run back to the lounge to get it.

When I get back to Nikki's room, Dr. Hensley is in front of the nurses' station with Rose and Matt. They're shaking hands and thanking him for coming.

"Yes. Thank you again for coming all this way on such short notice." I offer my hand. This time he accepts it.

"Well, I'm not sure I told you anything more than her doctors here could have told you, but I'm very grateful for the generous donation. I assure you we'll put it to good use. There's so much more we need to learn about brain injury and treatment." His voice takes on a note of sadness.

I'd fund his research for the next twenty years if he would stay here and take care of Nikki until she opens her eyes, but he already explained he has critical patients he has to get back to. As I make arrangements for his return flight back to the airport and then to Maryland, he asks me to keep him informed of any changes and says if we need him to come back he will.

Meanwhile, as I take the seat next to Nikki's bed and pull one of her books from the bag Matt brought, I pray she'll wake up before Dr. Hensley has a chance to even board his return flight.

Chapter Thirty-Two

NIKKI

Lovely memories float through my mind. The Bernard Arena is packed. Dalt receives the perfect short outside pass from Dak right out of the faceoff. The crowd goes wild when Dalt hits a scorcher and the puck sails to the back of the net. The vision of Dalt and I at the quad having a one on one soccer game fades into view. It's a blustery autumn day, and the weather is crisp and clear. Fallen leaves crunch under our feet as we crisscross the field. I giggle at Dalt's amused frustration when I manage to use some fast scissor cuts to tease him with the ball, fake the direction I'm going, and then sail the ball into the goal. I want to smile now, remembering how he tackled me to the ground, laughing at how he was going to punish me when we got home for tricking him. I can't make myself smile. I'm stuck in this tunnel of thick darkness, unable to move. My mind sweeps toward another memory of Dalt and I swaying in each other's arms to the lilting warmth of *Perfect*. Dalt's whispering in my ear. I can almost feel the warmth of his breath on my face.

I hear his voice somewhere in the distance. It sounds methodical, like he's reciting something. What? Poetry? I can't make it out. I can't move toward his voice to hear him better. Instead I float away. Dalt calls to me. I understand his words this time.

"Nik, baby. Open your eyes. Come back to me, please."

I try to move toward him. I have to tell him what I set out to tell him before he leaves for California. He can't leave me. I won't let him leave. We love each other. We belong together.

I can't move. The darkness is too thick and heavy.

I feel the soothing stroke of a hand moving down my arm. My skin tingles in response. It's Dalt. I know it's Dalt. I force my fingers to move to catch his hand as it moves down.

"Nikki! Can you hear me?" He sounds panicked.

I can hear you! I want to scream, but my lips won't move. A twinge of pain shoots down my leg and I jerk in response.

"Just wiggle your finger again if you can hear me, sweetheart."

Wiggle my finger. How hard can that be? I can do that.

"That's it, baby. You're doing it. Rachel, I think she's waking up!" Dalt's voice gets louder. Who the hell is Rachel? And why is she waking up here? I struggle to force my eyes open. I need to see Dalt, talk to him. I get my eyes open.

"Nik, open your eyes. You can do it," Dalt pleads with me. I hear his words clearly now. I feel the warmth of his fingers on my face. I want to turn my face into his hand, touch my lips to his fingertips, but my head throbs when I try to move it.

Dalt's soft breath tickles my ear. "Do it again, baby. Open those beautiful blue eyes for me."

I have to do this. Dalt is begging me and he sounds so concerned. I blink and slowly push my eyelids open. There's not much light. I can see the blurred silhouette of someone. I can't focus. It's too difficult. I close my eyes again.

"No, baby. Don't close your eyes. Please look at me, Nik. I need you to open your eyes."

Dalt needs me to open my eyes. I can do this. I push my lids open and force my vision to adapt to the blurry dim light. I see his beautiful face. I try to reach for him but I can't move my arms.

"Where..." I want to ask where we are but my throat is too dry. It hurts to talk or even swallow.

"We're at Maine Coast Memorial," Dalt says. "You were in an accident. Your truck skidded on the wet road."

I remember. "I was coming to you." My words are raspy. I don't recognize my own voice.

"Yes. You were coming to me because I was stupid enough to leave you. I'm so sorry, Nik."

"I won't let you leave. You can't leave." I close my eyes. It's exhausting trying to express what I need to say to him.

"Nik, please keep your eyes open. Listen to me. I'm not leaving you. I promise I'll never leave you again.

Never. And you have to promise to stay with me. I love you with all my heart. You're my reason for living. Chloe and I need you."

Chloe.

I try to sit up. My head pounds and a sharp pain shoots down my leg.

"Wait, Nik. You can't get up."

"Chloe?" I ask, dropping my head back onto the pillow.

"She's fine. She's been at home with Matt or your mom's friend Ellen for the ten days you've been here."

"Ten...ten days?"

I've been in the hospital for ten days? How is that possible?

"Yeah. You had us all pretty scared there, crazy girl. What were you doing racing around in the middle of the night during a storm? Don't you know I can't survive without my air to breathe, without my sunshine, without my reason for living?"

For the first time I can see well enough in the dimly lit room to notice Dalt's disheveled appearance. His clothes are rumpled like he's been sleeping in them, his face is covered with the scruff of several days of not shaving, and there are dark circles under his eyes.

"Me either. It's why I had to tell you..." I can manage to push out through my dry throat.

"I know. Everything you had to tell me is exactly what I was going to tell you as soon as I confronted my father. It just took me a little longer to figure it out. I'm a guy, after all. Our brains aren't always firing on all cylinders." His coy smile is as heart melting as ever.

"I'm going to get Rachel. Don't close those beautiful blues. Okay?"

My puzzled expression prompts Dalt to answer my unspoken question. "Rachel is the nurse. I'm going to get her. I'll be right back."

I try to reach for his hand. He bends down and whispers in my ear, "I'll be right back. I'll never leave you, Nik. How many guys are lucky enough to be blessed with a hat trick of chances at the most amazing girl in the world? My prayers have been answered today, and I'm going to spend the rest of my life showing you how grateful I am."

A young nurse with a short black bob haircut walks into the room, Dalt following close behind. She appears to be a little older than me.

"Welcome back. I'm Rachel, the attending night nurse. How are you feeling?"

"My throat." I try to gesture toward my neck but my wrists are restrained.

"Feeling a little scratchy? It's from the trach tube. How about some water?" She pushes a button to raise the upper portion of my bed.

When I nod, she holds a plastic cup to my lips and I take a few slow sips from the straw. I relish the coolness of the water as it washes down and soothes some of the parched scratchiness in my throat.

"I don't think you'll be needing these anymore.

They're just a precaution to make sure you didn't pull out any tubes," she explains, undoing the restraints around my wrists. She hands me the cup to hold. "Small sips, please." She glances at Dalt. "Okay, dreamboat. You did good with all your reading. Now you're going to have to leave her to us for a little while and let us take care of her."

"Is she going to be okay?"

"I'm okay." I assure him. I don't want him to leave but he looks like he needs about a week's worth of rest himself.

"She'll be fine," the nurse says. "Her doctor is on his way. Why don't you give a call to her family and let them know she's awake? It's the middle of the night but they'll want to know. And then you might want to try to get some rest yourself before we have to start taking care of you as well."

"I don't need rest. I'm not leav—"

"You'll have a few hours to rest up before you can see her again." Nurse Rachel must be a strong little thing because when she pushes Dalt toward the door, the wall of hockey muscle actually moves. "She's in good hands and she'll be right here when you get back. Go take care of yourself."

"I'll call your mom and Matt and I'll be back soon," Dalt says to me over his shoulder as the nurse closes the door behind him.

"He's relentless, isn't he? I think if he read *Cat In The Hat* one more time something was going to go bump and make us all jump when he passed out in complete exhaustion and fell off his chair right here in this room." Rachel chuckles. "But all his reading must have worked its magic because here you are."

"Reading?"

"That boy must have sat here and read every classic children's book ever written three times over. Did you see the stack of books he brought in?" She points to a pile of books in the corner of the room. "He told us you're going to be a famous writer of children's books yourself one day."

I smile at Dalt's confidence in my writing abilities. Now I realize it was his voice I heard reading to me, pulling me out of the murky darkness.

"It was sweet, really. You're a lucky girl to have a guy love you so much he didn't want to leave your side for a minute." Rachel removes an IV tube from my arm.

"Yes. I am." Every muscle in my body unwinds in simultaneous relief. This time when I close my eyes it's to relax into a comforted slumber.

Chapter Thirty-Three

NIKKI

Two Months Later

"You are the most gorgeous bride I've ever seen." Her eyes glistening, Trace wraps me in a tight hug. "You're like a nineteen forties Hollywood goddess."

"Thanks." We exchange cheek kisses. "You're next, skater girl."

"We'll see." The mischievous gleam in her eyes tells me this isn't the first time the subject of her and Dak getting married has come up. "I'm beyond happy for you guys, Nik. And Chloe is so perfect and beautiful. By the way, I totally knew she was Dalt's when I saw your drawings. She's like his Mini Me."

"Is that so? And yet you didn't say one word. It's not like the Tracey I know to keep her opinions to herself, especially when she knows she's right." I smirk at my sweet best friend.

"Okay, I didn't know." She shrugs and flips a piece of my waved hair behind my shoulder. "But my little Godbaby is still the most beautiful baby on the planet."

When Dalt and I asked Dak and Tracey to be Chloe's Godparents, I don't think Tracey stopped squealing in glee for a full week.

Trace walks behind me and bends to straighten the train of my fitted Vera Wang wedding dress. Standing, she primps the draped silk piece which wraps around my hips and gathers at the bottom of the deep cut out opening at the base of my spine.

She sighs. "You're perfect."

I had no intention of buying the ridiculously expensive vintage gown when I found it online. I was merely trying to find someone who could match the style in a knockoff version of the V-neck trumpet silhouette silk dress. I knew the antique beaded straps were going to be impossible to copy but I figured I could find something to make it work.

I made the mistake of letting Dalt come with me to the dressmaker. When he realized what I was trying to do, he insisted the only dress I should have was the original. He made some panty melting remark like, "You're my one of a kind, totally original, beautiful girl and you should have a one of a kind original dress." When I pointed out the absurd price, he reiterated the money is no object speech. Two days later the dress showed up on my doorstep, Fed Ex delivery. Seriously. Is he the perfect man or what? Now here I am, all Vera Wanged out in my figure hugging white silk gown.

There's barely any limp to my gait as I walk holding

onto Matt's arm toward the gazebo set on the banks of our lake. Chloe, Tracey, and Alex are in front of us. Chloe looks like a living doll in her A-line, tea length, mini Vera Wang, peach color dress. It has a satin scoop neck top with a matching sash tied around the waist into a large bow, and of course several layers of full tulle on the bottom. Tracey has to bend down every few steps and remind Chloe to keep throwing rose petals from her basket because Chloe is too busy spinning in her new ballerina dress to remember.

Tracey is exquisite in her peach Vera Wang strapless, chiffon column dress; not vintage but every bit as stunning. My mom made me promise I wouldn't pick any "atrocious Goth color like purple or black for a maid of honor dress." Her exact words. I had no intention of picking a so-called Goth color for the dress, but I love her like crazy so I let her believe the peach chiffon was her idea.

The day couldn't be more picture-perfect. The sky is the color blue an artist would use to paint a crystal-clear horizon on a June day. In fact, as I gaze across the setting in front of me, I'd say the whole scene might have been the inspiration for a Monet painting if he lived in Maine: pink water lilies floating on the lake, purple and yellow irises along the bank, and summer wildflowers popping up throughout the fields. The warm breeze blowing across the grassy fields is a comfortable seventy-five degrees. The cooing of the white winged doves in the trees is a hymn added to the romantic harp and violin version of "Perfect" being played as we walk toward the gazebo on the edge of the lake. It's the same song Dalt and I danced to the night we knew we belonged together. Even the swans in the pond, swimming in pairs in and out of the water cascading from the newly added center fountain, are demonstrating their lifelong commitment to one partner. It's their contribution to complete the picturesque setting of a day filled with promises of forever, a day of giving our hearts surrounded by a setting which truly speaks to our hearts.

I'm exceedingly grateful for everything Dalt has done to make this day a beautiful beginning to the rest of our lives. I still don't know how he managed to get a crew of men to spend mere weeks to renovate the thirty by forty-foot barn on our farm and transform it into something right off the pages of *Architectural Digest*. The barn hadn't been used for decades. But since I was still going through rehab and wasn't able to travel, Dalt saw the antique structure and somehow envisioned it into what it is now.

After talking it over with my mom and Matt, the construction began. Dalt filmed the progression of steps it required to take the barn apart, clean the antique white oak wood, and put the mortise and tenons back together in an elegant configuration perfect for weddings or parties. The architect Dalt hired succeeded in keeping the rustic quality of a classic New England barn, complete with hand hewn timbers and rustic railings running the length of the balconies on either side of the thirty-foot-high building. The old wood plank floors were refinished to a high gloss shine. Hanging down the center of the expanse are four three-foot wide crystal chandeliers. On each vertical timber lining either side of the room, electrified double candle sconces glow. Overhead, tiny twin-kling white lights covering the exposed beams give the ambience of a wedding space fit for a fairy woodland prince and princess.

When construction was complete, Dalt made me close my eyes as he walked me through the doors of the barn for the first time. When I opened my eyes, I gasped at the breathtaking transformation. I could feel the history of the building, but even more than that I could feel the passion and artistry Dalt and the crew working on the building had put into it.

Later, when they were ready to set up for the wedding, Dalt left the interior decorating of table settings and flowers up to Tracey and Alex. The long tables with crisp white linens mixed with touches of peach and the giant arrangements of wildflowers down the centers of the tables completes the perfect backdrop for a perfect wedding.

Needless to say, when Dalt posted pictures of the completed project on social media, inquiries came flooding in for people wanting to rent the venue for their event. Apparently, Dalt, Matt, and my mom have embarked on a new business together. Matt and Dalt have excitedly been planning the other additions they want to make to create the complete wedding venue package. I'm happy to say this new venture with Dalt eventually being an absent but financial backer has brought him and Matt closer. Matt doesn't growl anymore when he sees Dalt, which is a good thing.

Gazing around at the picturesque setting in front of me, seeing our family and friends beaming with love and happiness for us, the whole day is like a beautiful dream. But it's not. It's real. I'm here.

I walk toward the flower-covered gazebo where Dalt is waiting for me. Garrett and Dak are next to him. Although they're all handsome in their black tail coat three-piece morning suits with peach color vests and ties, Dalt is easily the most gorgeous man I've ever seen in his perfectly tailored suit. Garrett leans in and whispers something to Dalt. When he looks up and sees me, his ear to ear smile lights up his face. And when his beautiful blue eyes lock with mine, my heart beats in double-time. I can't believe he's mine. I can't believe I get to marry him.

My heart feels like it's going to explode. I return his smile and think about how much our connection to each other has changed in the few years we've been together. Prior to his father's meddling our relationship had been lighthearted and youthful, everything young love should be. Enjoying each other without a care in the world other than studying together for our next big test, wrapped in each other's arms. Or training together to be in shape for our respective teams. Things are different now. We aren't much older, but in those few years we've matured, and our relationship has done the same, ripened into some-thing...more. We're in love. Truly, deeply in love.

My smile widens when I think about Dalt getting down on one knee during one of my physical therapy sessions to ask me to marry him. Only Dalt could make the sterile setting the most romantic place in the world for a proposal.

He looked up at me from his kneeling position and said:

"Nik, I knew you were my soulmate the first day I laid eyes on you covered in mud, running up and down the soccer field. I knew it the night you jumped off a table into my arms and sang out of tune to me in the car. I knew it every time you managed to trick me into moving in the wrong direction to dive for the soccer ball. I knew it every time I heard you yell at me from the stands for doing something stupid on the ice or cheer louder than anyone else in the arena when I did good. Every time you used one of your crazy nicknames for a certain one of my body parts, I knew you were the only woman who could keep me smiling for the rest of my life. And when I found out you gave me Chloe, the greatest gift of my life, I may not have told you right away but I knew the only thing I wanted was for all of us to be together, forever. I know I've been a dumbass more times than I can count and I know I don't deserve you, but please marry me, Nik. You're the only one I want to spend the rest of my life with. You're the love of my life."

It couldn't have been more romantic than if we were sailing in a gondola down the canals of Venice or standing in a flower garden in Paris. When he reached up to offer me the open velvet box holding a ring with a diamond the size ·of a mini soccer ball, I managed to slowly bend my leg to drop to my knees, kiss him with every ounce of love I had in me, and tell him, "*You had me at 'soulmate.'*"

Now, as I stand next to him, in front of Father Morley, Dalt leans in and whispers, "I'm the luckiest man alive. You look like an angel. But as beautiful as that dress is, I can't wait to see it on the floor around your ankles." He waggles his brow. My face warms to the color of Dalt's vest when I glance up and see Father Morley flipping through pages of his bible, trying his best to pretend he didn't hear what Dalt said.

Before I can respond Dalt scoops Chloe up in his arms and tells her how much he loves her.

She strokes his face and says, "Butterfy tis, Dada."

When Dalt tickles her cheek with butterfly kisses and she giggles, I know the truth. I'm the lucky one.

Epilogue

DALT

Three Months Later

I look around the locker room and can't believe I'm actually here, ready to play my first pre-season game with the Winds. My agent—yes I have an agent now—worked it out with management and they graciously allowed me some extra time to get out here. Enough time for me to stay with Nikki while she recovered and went through the initial stages of physical therapy.

While she's not completely rehabbed, she's doing better than the doctors had expected at this point. Great news is she doesn't have any residual balance or coordination problems from the brain trauma, although they say it's too early to tell if her leg will ever be fully recovered enough to be able to play soccer. It's tough to shun my overwhelming guilt about that, but Nik keeps telling me to get over it. She says I can't take credit for all the stupid mistakes we've made in our past. She claims it's a moot point anyway since she'll be on the field hip faking me in no time. I believe her. My girl is one tough cookie.

She and Chloe moved out here with me after the wedding. We got our little house on the water in Newport Beach. Okay, not so little at around six thousand square feet, six bedrooms, and a guest bungalow. But my girls are worth it and it gives us plenty of space for our friends and Matt and Rose to visit whenever they want.

Rose claims as soon as the wedding season slows down they're going to come out and stay for two weeks because they miss Nikki and Chloe, and me too they added just to be polite. The new business has taken off like wildfire. Rose and Matt only took off one weekend to make time to have their own private wedding. I hope they do get to come out. Nikki and Chloe are missing them.

Nikki is taking online courses to complete her degree. Turns out she doesn't completely hate doing her work with her toes buried in the sand while Chloe builds sandcastles next to her. She says I'm going to turn her into a fat, spoiled, married lady. I'm doing my best to prove her right about the spoiled part, but the way she runs a little farther every day up and down the beach and then spends at least an hour doing soccer drills in the sand, there's no way she'll ever accomplish the fat part.

As we take to the ice and the fans go wild, am I nervous to play my first pro game? Not really. I'd say it's more of an adrenaline rush knowing I'm going to be paid to do the thing I would have done for free if given the opportunity. My new teammates made me feel welcome from my first day here. Having Wolfe on the bench for support from a familiar face is an added bonus.

One of the goalies is injured and out for the season. They brought Wolfe up from the farm team last month. I'm sure it won't be long before he gets his turn at the pipes. It's awesome we'll both be playing for the same team again. When Dak called to tell me he, Tracey, and Batt were going to be in the stands for my first game, I was beyond stoked to have my posse here to cheer me on.

Garrett showed up too. He says he'll be at every one of my games, at least the home ones. We worked things out about the crap my father pulled. The old bastard isn't going to be seeing anything but the four walls of a jail cell for a while. Karma's a bitch.

Garrett and I changed the name of the company to Walker Brothers Productions, distanced ourselves from our dad, and cut him out of everything to keep the company from going down with him. While Garrett is CEO now and running the show, he says my place is ready and waiting for me whenever I get tired of gliding on razor blades up and down the ice. I'm grateful for his support and I know Mom is looking down, happy and proud of the men we've become.

The thing I'm most grateful for, the thing I say a little prayer of thanks for every day, is having Nikki and Chloe in my life and in the stands right now to root for me. I offered to get them seats in the executive suite box where most family members sit, but they all wanted to sit in the seats next to the Winds' bench.

"Nah, man," Dak scoffed. "We came to watch the game, not eat hors d'ouevres."

Nikki added with a coy grin, "I won't be able to watch your sexy bubble butt move up and down the ice from up there."

When I skate past the bench, I see Nikki pointing me out to Chloe. When she spots me, she starts jumping up and down on Nik's lap and clapping. It's the most beautiful thing I've ever seen. My chest swells with pride as I take my seat on the bench.

It takes some time to get used to a new line of guys but when we make the switch a few minutes into the first period, everything falls into place like I've been playing with them my whole life.

Gifford, our right winger, and I fly down the ice. He's driving the puck. The opposing team's D-man drops back toward the goal and cheats toward Gifford. I'm moving into the perfect receiving angle when Gifford slaps the puck right onto my tape without looking at me, like he knows where I'm going to be. I laser a snap shot right into the hole over the goalie's shoulder. When the horn blows, it's the sweetest sound I've ever heard, next to Nik's moans of ecstasy, that is.

When the game ends, we have our first win of the pre-season and I have the first pro game win of my career. After celebrating on the ice with the guys, I skate to the boards and place my palms on the Plexiglas in front of my girls. Both Nik and Chloe touch their hands on the glass where my hands are.

I was wrong when I said life couldn't get any better the night Nik and I unknowingly made Chloe. Life can get better. Every day with Nikki is even better than the day before and this, this right here, is one of the best days so far.

Epilogue

EPILOGUE II

NIKKI

I'm glad we didn't sit in the executive suite the wives and families of most of the players sit in. I love being this close to the ice when Dalt skates out with his new teammates for the first time. I have a huge goofy ear to ear smile covering my face. I'm so proud of him and his decision to free himself from his father's shackles and do what he's wanted to do since he was a little boy. When I point him out to Chloe as he skates by and glances over during their warm up, she nearly bounces off my lap laughing and clapping and yelling for her "Dada." And when Dalt scores his first two goals of his professional career, I'm cheering so loud I'm grateful for the sparkly pink noise reduction headphones Trace bought for Chloe.

As I watch him move up and down the ice, my heart races in pride and love. And lust. I'm fangirling hard for my guy. When he skates up to the boards after the game and places his hands on the Plexiglas for Chloe and me, I fall madly in love with him all over. I'm ready to climb over the boards and start peeling off his uniform on the spot.

"Hurry up," I mouth through the glass and lick my lips. His eyes go all dark and smoldering, telling me he gets the message. He pushes his way through the other guys already heading down the tunnel into the locker room.

"We're going to stop for food and a few beers at the Flying Puck before heading back to your house," Dak says to me. "You want us to wait until Dalt's done showering or you want to meet us there?"

Everyone is staying at our house for the weekend. It's one of the reasons I'm glad Dalt convinced me we needed the monstrosity of a house. It's big enough for everyone to stay before they have to go back to school or work. At the moment, I'm even happier Dalt and I will have an hour or two before they get back to the house. What can I say? We never got to have an official honeymoon, and besides, I'm a sucker for a man in hockey pads.

"No. We're going to head home to get Chloe to bed. I'll have a bottle of wine open and waiting for you guys and hopefully a sleeping two-year-old *not* waiting."

"Okay. See you in a few." Dak gives me a hug.

"We'll take our time," Tracey whispers in my ear when it's her turn to hug me. She gives me a sly wink before bending and kissing Chloe on the cheek. What'd I tell ya? Us girls gotta stick together in this whole love thing.

Even though Dalt takes what could be considered a

record breaking quick shower, Chloe is already asleep in my arms when I meet him outside the locker room door. Dalt slips her into her car seat as gently as possible and hurries to get behind the steering wheel. I'm already buckled in and bouncing my knees with nervous anticipation.

When we get to the house, I unlock the door and Dalt gingerly carries Chloe upstairs to lay her down in her crib. I don't even bother to change her clothes because I had changed her diaper before we left the arena and she's wearing a comfy fleece one-piece outfit. No need to risk waking her up. I turn on the baby monitor and we tiptoe down the hallway to our bedroom like two kids trying to be quiet enough to catch Santa leaving presents.

"Get your pads," I urge Dalt, tearing my clothes off. He needs no instruction from me, He's already half naked, rummaging through the closet for his hockey pads.

Just as we're about to get into the roleplay we discussed on the way home, the sound of a darling little girl blasts through the baby monitor on our nightstand. If she could verbalize her thoughts I'm sure they would go something like, "Not so fast, you guys."

Dalt blows out a big breath. "I got it." He takes a step toward the bedroom door.

"Uh, babe...maybe you better..." I gesture toward my favorite part of his body which was just beginning to say hello to me. He's standing there with nothing on but his hockey pads and I have to rub my legs together to keep myself from dropping him to the floor and having my way with him right this second. Told ya, I'm a sucker for a hockey player, but a hockey player in nothing but his shoulder pads, especially the one I happen to be insanely in love with…well, stick a fork in me and consider me done. My ovaries are jumping up and down like a cheerleader at a pep rally.

"Oh, right." He grabs his robe from the hook on the closet door and hurries to Chloe's room.

While he's out of the room, I change into the new lacy bra and thong panties I was saving for a special occasion. Do we need to roleplay to keep things exciting? Hell to the no squared! Just the sound of his keys in the door gets my lady engine running. And if Dalt hears me make the slightest breathy sound he perceives to be a sigh or a moan, he's on me like white on rice.

I was on the patio the other day setting the table for lunch and I sneezed. I'm not sure where Dalt was at the time, but he came flying out of the house, threw me down on one of the lounge chairs and…let's just say he had an appetizer before lunch.

The role play was something we came up with in the car on the drive home tonight, when Dalt saw how hard I was crushing on my very own pro hockey player.

"Hey, sweetheart. Shh, shh, Daddy's here. I thought you and I had a deal?" I can hear Dalt with Chloe through the monitor speaker. Every few seconds I hear a soft kissing sound and quiet soothing words. Chloe's no longer crying. She's cooing, I assume in her daddy's arms. Dalt has that effect on women of all ages.

"I told you if you were a very good girl and stayed

asleep me and Mommy would make you a baby brother or sister, remember?"

Say what, now?

Not that I'm opposed to the idea. Having tons of Dalt's beautiful babies is fine by me. Well, not tons. Some, some of Dalt's beautiful babies is fine by me. But I didn't even know he was thinking about having another baby right now. I'm not sure I'm ready for another tiny human.

Then when Dalt starts singing "Hush Little Baby" in a soft voice and I hear the creaking of the rocking chair as he serenades his baby girl, my heart melts and does its pitter patter skip a beat thing all at the same time. Bring on every one of those baby-making sperm. I'm telling you, Prince Charming has nothing on this man.

A few minutes later Dalt comes rushing back into the room and closes the door behind him

"That kid of yours is real cute, but she's quite a little cock blocker. She's finally sleeping."

"Eeew, Dalt. It's just wrong to talk about cock blocking in the same sentence as your baby girl."

"Sorry. Just trying to stay in character. Now, where were we?" he asks, stalking toward me. He's not usually in this much of a hurry, but between the possibility of Chloe waking up and our friends coming back from the bar, Dalt's on a mission to get back to our game.

"You found me waiting outside the locker room and when I asked you to sign my boobs you scooped me up into your arms, threw me in your car, and brought me back to your place to fuck my brains out."

"Right," Dalt says, dropping his robe to the floor.

Oh God. The sight of his muscled chest and thighs wrapped up like a sweet gift for me in hockey pads has my legs quivering.

"Wow! Mr. Hockey Man. Do you think your big, hard, hockey stick can come out to play?" I purr in what I imagine is a sexy fangirl voice.

"Mr. Hockey Man?" Dalt chuckles. "No puck bunny would ever say that, Nik. I love you, but you're a terrible puck bunny."

"Oh, is that so?" I drop the robe I had slipped on while he was out of the room, revealing the lacy strings of fabric underneath.

"Holy shit, Nik!" Dalt takes another step toward me.

"Uh, uh, uh. There's no Nik here, hockey boy."

"What? I've been demoted from hockey man to hockey boy, now?"

"Yup. You said I was a terrible puck bunny."

"You are, but you're my gorgeous, sexy, delicious, favorite wife in the whole world." He closes the space between us and wraps his arms around my waist.

"Very sweet, but you're ruining the whole thing." I pretend to pout because I'm already aching so hard for him I'm about to push him against the wall and use his pads as leverage for climbing assistance.

"Okay. Let's see. I want you so bad...uh...what's your name? Cathy? Kelly?"

"Candy."

"Right. Candy. I'm so hard for you, Candy. Get down on your knees and suck me off," he commands in faux Christian Grey style.

There's nothing faux about his cock being as hard as

iron for me. It's throbbing against my stomach hard enough to cause a bruise.

"Oh, look whose big, hard, hockey stick is up off the ice and ready to take a slapshot." I run my hand down his thick shaft.

"Fuck, Nik...uh...Candy. You're killing me here. Forget the game. I need *you*, so bad."

"Aww. Let Candy help you out with your *big* problem." I gaze up at my perfect husband from my kneeling position and proceed to do just that. I assist his big, strong, hockey stick in shooting and scoring. In fact, Dalt has no problem in keeping it scoring over and over for the next two hours.

As Dalt gazes into my eyes after sliding out of me for the third time he says, "I don't need you to be Candy or Cathy or any other puck bunny. I just need you to be my one and only fan girl, Nik, because dammit, I love you." He places a soft kiss on my lips.

I glance at the infinity tattoo on his forearm, where the word 'Chloe' has been added to one of the curves. I kiss him back. "I dammit love you too."

"I mean it, Nik. I love you with all my heart. Thank you for being mine."

Did I mention how lucky I am? Have I changed my mind about there being no such things as happily ever afters and fairytale love stories? Absolutely. Because it may have taken us a few detours along the way, but Dalt and I have found our happy ever after. And we're living a better fairytale love story than I could have ever even imagined.

Before You Go...

If you enjoyed my book please take a second to leave a short review. These reviews help me as an author be found by other amazing readers like you.

Thank you so much! :)

Keep reading for a ***sneak peek*** at the third book in the On the Edge Series, Cross Crease.

Sneak Peek

ON THE EDGE BOOK #3

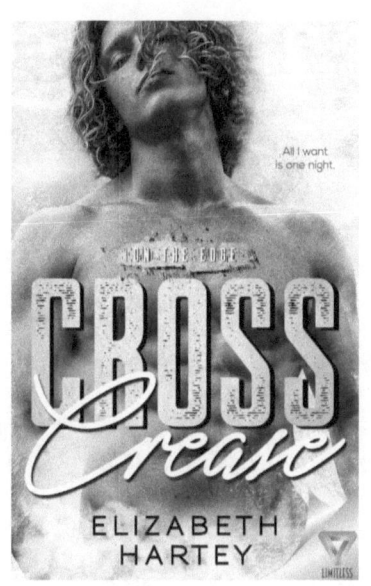

Cross Crease

ON THE EDGE BOOK #3

PROLOGUE

HEAVEN

"Hey, brat. What's up?" The screen on my laptop fills with my brother's taunting face.

"Hey, doofus. Not much. Same old same old. School, studying, school. One exciting thing after the other. How 'bout you?"

"Same. Except throw in some hockey in the middle of these crazy ass courses I'm taking." The close-up on his face is unforgiving. He looks tired.

"No infamous Friday night house parties this semester?"

"Not so much during hockey season. But occasionally, if we have a free weekend. I try to steer clear though if I can. I need as much quiet study time as possible."

"Wow. Who are you and what have you done with my pain in the neck brother?" I laugh. Dak not wanting to party with his hockey bros? His classes must be harder than usual. "Tough classes this semester?" I close the anatomy book I was reading, happy to have the reprieve from my own studying.

"Yeah. This graduate course I convinced the Dean to let me take may have been a mistake. It's really..." Dak's voice fades when he drops his head to adjust the noise canceling headphones covering his ears.

The living room behind him comes into view. It's apparent he's sitting at his kitchen table with his back to the living room. But the room isn't the thing distracting my attention from Dak. My eyes snap to the vision on the sofa: *Damon Wolfe*.

My Karmic punishment for having spent the past ten years telling my brother how much I hate hockey players. My fantasized-about-to-the-point-of-distraction bad boy who can turn my otherwise adequate brain into stupefied goo with one glance and a sly grin.

Dak lifts his head, blocking the view behind him. "Thankfully the professor paired me up with a genius girl. She's agreed to tutor..." He drops the pen he's been tapping on the table and bends over to pick it up, giving me another Wolfe-filled bird's eye view.

His head is tipped back, his long hair spread out around his face along the sofa back. He must be sleeping.

Dak sits up. "...in exchange for me doing a skating routine with her in the Winter Fest." His face fills my screen, bringing my attention back to his conversation.

"Wait. What did you say?"

"I said, she agreed to tutor me in exchange for me skating..."

"That's what I thought you said. What do you mean? Like *figure skating* skating?"

"No. Like we're going to do a hockey skating routine." Dak shakes his head and purses his lips to one side. "Of course, I mean figure skating, dummy. It's the Winter Fest."

"But you haven't figure skated in years. Not since you got into hockey full time. What makes you think you can still do it? And a pairs routine, no less. You're crazy. This girl must be something special to get you to agree to figure skate." I quirk my brows up and down. "You're going to break your pretty face just for her pretty face."

"You're the crazy one. You just watch me, brat. I've..." A loud moan coming from behind Dak pulls my attention away from his absurd protestation concerning his ability to do a pairs routine in a show. Dak can't hear the curious groaning coming from the living room because his headphones only allow him to hear me, nothing else around him.

Maybe Wolfe is having a nightmare. I strain my head from side to side, as if it will allow me to see around Dak's giant head—the head which is growing larger by the second as he touts his imagined ability to figure skate. I'll admit he was good when he was twelve, almost a decade ago. Now the only skating he excels in is hockey.

"You know it's true. Right?" Oops. I have no idea what he just asked me.

"Huh?" My brilliant response.

"You're not even listening to me. What the hell are you looking at?" When Dak turns around to see what

I'm craning my neck to get a look at, we simultaneously see the tableau occurring on the sofa.

"What the fuck?" He rips his headphones off his ears. "What the fuck are you doing, dipshit?"

Wolfe isn't sleeping. Without Dak obstructing my view, I can see the blonde head bobbing up and down at a frantic pace between Wolfe's legs.

Holy smokes! Wolfe is getting a BJ right out in the open in the living room where everyone and anyone can see. The way his eyes are clamped shut in a frown and the muscles in his neck are taut and straining it almost looks like he's in pain. But I'm reasonably certain he isn't moaning in agony, at least not *painful* agony.

Meanwhile, I can't pull my pervy, voyeuristic eyes away from Wolfe's not-so-private porno show. I'm definitely going to need a panty change and a very cold shower.

"My sister is here, asshole. She can see you!" But Dak's anxiety-ridden announcement concerning my digital presence doesn't deter Wolfe from his mission. In fact, I'd say it encourages him.

"Heaven?" He moans my name as if it's my mouth wrapped around him. He turns his head, and forces his eyes open just enough to stare directly at the computer. *At me?* I'm sure he's looking at *me* with his lust-filled eyes and pulling me into their vortex.

He threads his fingers through blondie's hair and directs her movements without taking his eyes off the computer. "Heaven," he groans again. *Oh my God.* I'm two seconds away from slipping my hand into my sleep shorts when Dak yells out, reminding me it's not my mouth pleasuring Wolfe and we're not alone.

"Seriously, dude? I cannot fucking believe..." My screen goes black when Dak apparently comes to his senses and slams his computer closed.

But Wolfe's heated gaze is still burning inside my head. There will be no more studying this evening. Placing my computer on the night table next to me and reaching into the drawer, I retrieve the black silk bag nestled in the back—where my mom is least likely to find it. Flicking off the light and kicking my books off the bed, I snuggle down under the covers. It's going to be another night with my battery-operated friend substituting for the goalie who has been my obsession since I was four-teen years old.

CROSS DROP PLAYLIST

Pink - Julia Michaels
We Could Be Heroes – Alesso
Let's Marvin Gaye and Get It On – Charlie Puth
I'll Make Love to you – Boys II Men
Why – Bazzi
Havana – Camila Cabello
Drunk in Love – Beyonce
Never Again – Kelly Clarkson
Romeo and Juliet – Nino Rota
Perfect – Ed Sheeran

Acknowledgments

First, I have to thank the team at Limitless Publishing. You guys rock. Working with you on this series is a dream come true. But the level of efficiency from the team at Limitless makes the difficult job of writing an easier dream to achieve and I'm so grateful.

To my editor, Felicia. Thank you once again for your feedback and attention to detail. You make me fall in love with my characters even more.

To the team at Deranged Doctor Design, thank you so much for the beautiful covers. You capture the essence of my heroes perfectly.

Thank you to all the bloggers who work so hard to help get the info about my books out there to readers. Your tireless efforts to help spread the word are amazing and I love you for everything you do.

To my family, thank you for putting up with the hours I spend locked in my office creating my stories and characters. I wouldn't be able to do any of this without your support and input.

Finally, to my readers, I can't say thank you enough for reading my stories and helping me fulfill a lifelong dream of sending the characters in my head out into the world. I appreciate each and every one of you and the time you take to talk about and review my books. Your support is inspiration for me to keep working diligently to make my writing stimulating and fun (and of course, swoony.) Stay tuned for bad boy Wolfe and sweet innocent, Heaven's story.

See you between the 'covers'.

Love,

Elizabeth Hartey

About the Author

As a lover of the northeast United States, Elizabeth moved with her husband to the Poconos several years ago to open a Chiropractic Clinic. Four children and a menagerie of animals later, she has finally found time to fulfill her lifelong dream of writing novels. A dreamer at heart, romance is the genre she spends most of her time writing and reading into the wee hours of the morning. When not juggling work responsibilities and writing, she enjoys hiking the beautiful hills and woods around her home, swimming, knitting, travelling, and spending time with her family. She is an avid hockey fan, which means she has to compromise with her husband, one night of hockey for her, in exchange for one night of football for him.

Website:
https://www.elizabethhartey.com
Newsletter:
http://eepurl.com/cZCEuL

www.ingramcontent.com/pod-product-compliance
Lightning Source LLC
Chambersburg PA
CBHW051955240626
47153CB00005B/1772